Praise for *USA* Crane's psy

"Her writing is dark, intriguing and she is a master of the unexpected twist. Ms. Crane cleverly blends a series of plots and subplots together to produce a satisfactory ending. Not all questions are answered and I'm looking forward to the next book in the series." – Peter Ralph, white-collar crime fiction writer, author of *Blood Gold in the Congo,* #1 Amazon best-selling author

"Pamela Crane introduces a mind-twist that takes everything you love about thrillers, pushes it outside the box, and electrifies you with clever prose and a plot that will terrify you. A must-read thriller...an instant best seller!" – Southern Editor Reviews

"A captivating mystery with prose that fans will devour." – Literary Lover Reviews

"If *Dexter* and *Gone Girl* had a love child, this would be it!" – reader review

"An author to watch, Pamela Crane packs a punch to her prose and will keep you on your toes with her twisted plots. Let your mind be blown—I guarantee you'll savor every moment. Psychological thriller fiction at its best." – Thriller Fan Reviews

"I'm a die-hard thriller fan. But Crane duped me! Just when I thought I had figured it out I was thrown for another loop...and loved it. Kudos to mastering the mystery genre!" – reader review

THE ADMIRER'S SECRET

THE ADMIRER'S SECRET

PAMELA CRANE

Tabella House
Raleigh, North Carolina

Thank you for supporting authors and literacy by purchasing this book. Want to add more gripping reads to your library? As the author of more than a dozen award-winning and best-selling books, you can find all of Pamela Crane's works on her website at www.pamelacrane.com.

For the broken-hearted, the lonely, the outcasts, the dreamers whose dreams always feel out of grasp, this story is for you. Never give up on yourself.

I loathe the day I met you,
the day you tried to destroy me.
Yet I love the day I met you,
the day you set me free.

He who is devoid of the power to forgive is devoid of the power to love.

– Rev. Dr. Martin Luther King, Jr.

Prologue

The stain of guilt is a bitch to wash out. It took me almost three decades to realize this.

One cut. One swift movement across pink flesh. In a moment of desperation it sounded so easy, so quick. A slow seeping death would await me at the end, like being submerged under a wave, the world blurry and sloshing above me, until the cloud of darkness descended.

I held the knife in a white-knuckled grip, but still my hand shook. The veins under my translucent skin stood out like aqua blue tributaries on a map. I'd always been able to see the radial pulse in my wrist. It thumped steadily now, a lot faster than normal. I pressed the knife experimentally against my wrist and felt its serrated teeth biting into my flesh. What was I waiting for? Just rake it across. Get it over with.

I can't. Not yet.

I withdrew the blade, staring in fascination as the horizontal white stripe it made faded before my eyes.

"The coward's way out," I heard my mother clucking her tongue in a distant memory. "Suicide leaves nothing but pain for those left to pick up the pieces."

So what if I was a coward? I was already much worse.

With sobering clarity, I winced, imagining the jagged teeth tearing through my skin. It would hurt, wouldn't it? I regretted being so hasty in picking up the first knife I saw.

1

A smoother blade would hurt less, but I couldn't chicken out now.

Stay strong.

Remember why.

The memory startled me with its ferocity. The body crumpled on the floor in a blossoming pool of blood. Thick red swipes across his t-shirt where he cradled the body, checking for a pulse. When he looked up at me with dark, empty eyes, I knew what was unspoken. Dead. I was next. So I ran. And ran until my legs burned and my lungs screamed in pain and panic squeezed my heart.

I knew he was coming for me. Unless I beat him to it.

No doubts, no hesitating. One slice and this part would be over soon enough. Then I wouldn't have to remember anymore. I wanted to forget it all. The slap of limp limbs on hardwood, the squish beneath my shoes as I slipped across the bloody floor, dead eyes gazing into nothingness.

Please forget, please forget, please forget.

Tightening my clammy grip on the knife handle, I steadied my hand. Press it down. *Harder.* There, that wasn't so hard.

I never felt the blade pinch and then slide into my skin, catching on the thin tendon about halfway across. My mind blocked out the pain, focusing my thoughts on one face—the only face that mattered to me now.

Empty eyes pleading for help beyond the grave. Mouth agape in an everlasting scream. Hair matted with gore, skull crushed open on the floor.

With a little gasp I pulled the blade out, leaving a livid red streak, then leaned into the cushions of the sofa. Blood oozed from the cut, trickling down my palm like rivulets of rain on a windowpane. The droplets puddled in the crazy quilt afghan beneath me, the red chaotically joining the kaleidoscope of colors. Ridiculously, I wanted to blot the stain, though I wouldn't be here tomorrow to see it.

I needed to make the phone call while I still had the strength and ability to dial. Feeling lightheaded, I fumbled to open my cell phone, then concentrated on pressing each of the memorized numbers. The line rang. Voice mail picked up, just as I'd hoped.

"I kept my promise," I said, then hung up. There'd be no more pain after this, no more nightmares, no more fear.

This was the only way to make everything better. Life had become all pain and suffering. I was tired of suffering. And I was tired of watching others suffer. If only there was hope out there to make it all worthwhile ... but there was none. None that I knew of, at least.

I closed my eyes, feeling my life force ebb. My body relaxed but my thoughts cruelly rumbled on.

The body, sprawled out on the hardwood, blood seeping into the cracks like a tiny snake working its way into the floor. Him standing over it, eyes empty and coal black. Evil—that's what I saw in those eyes at that moment. Eyes that had once upon a time looked adoringly at me, now filled with hatred.

Some people say you see your whole life flash before you when you die. Others claim you're irresistibly drawn toward a white light. I saw neither. I envisioned a single image. His smiling face, the man who tore my heart open and my life apart—then trampled all over it.

Chapter 1

February 1992
New York Regional Hospital

I couldn't stand the touch of Daddy's hand a moment longer. The way his gnarled fingers knotted around mine.

I'd always loved his hands, tracing the deep crevices, rubbing the coarse patches where farming had hardened them. Rough yet tender, my father's hands. Not anymore. Now they were like the hands of a mummy, dry and papery. They repulsed me, and I was ashamed.

"Are you afraid to die?" My question drifted off into the Lysol-scented hospital room as Daddy rebuffed me with a turned head. Only his beeping heart monitor answered. It was the day before my twelfth birthday and somehow I sensed Daddy wouldn't live to see it.

I squeezed his hand before his loose grip released my fingers. I didn't want to hold it anyway. If I squeezed them too tightly, I was afraid they'd crumble to dust. The water in his eyes caught the gleam of the harsh lighting.

It isn't fair...

It never was. Mommy reminded me of that all the time—when I wanted to stay up late to watch a movie, when I didn't want to do chores, when all the kids in my class were invited to a party except for me.

"Haley, don't ask things like that."

I turned to Mommy, whose voice sounded colder than the chill of the room seeping through my sweater. She'd found the teal-and-brown-striped monstrosity at a

4

secondhand store, proclaiming it a "rare find," mainly because it was my size—never mind that it looked like a clown's hand-me-down. I wore it at least once a week, sometimes twice when I didn't care if my classmates picked on me. They always picked on me anyway.

"Please sit with your sister, Hale. And let your father rest," Mommy scolded me from the doorway where she waited for the doctor.

Hadn't he rested enough? Daddy hadn't moved from the bed in weeks.

"But I wanna know."

"That's not something you should be asking him."

"Why not? I want to know how Daddy's feeling. Don't I have a right to know?" We shared everything, after all. When I was little I had planned to marry him, until I found out I wasn't allowed to marry my Daddy. So I had decided to marry my best friend Jake instead.

Mommy sighed, shook her head like she was disappointed in me. I felt her exhaustion, I knew she was burned out, but I needed her to at least give me this. Give me one last moment with my dad—the hopeless final words, hard questions, and all.

"Haley, I just don't think your father wants to talk about ... that ... right now. Please ..."

That. Why not just say death? It was lurking behind him like a grim shadow and yet it was an unspeakable curse word.

"Why not? It's happening, Mom." She'd gone from Mommy to Mom now, because damn it, I was twelve and practically grown up. "You know it, I know it, Daddy knows it. I just want to know if he's ... okay with it. At peace, y'know?"

"No, Haley! How could he possibly be okay with it, leaving behind a widow, two kids, a farm, a mountain of medical debt? What do you expect to hear? That everything is fine and dandy? And why do you think he'd want to talk about dying with a child? You're too young ... you probably shouldn't even be here."

"Mom, I'm his daughter, not a stranger. And I'm practically a teenager. You let doctors you don't even know into your lives more than you let Courtney and me in—your own family. Don't you think I can handle it?"

She leaned against the doorjamb, her shoulders sagging under the weight of the fear we all felt. Her chin dropped, and I knew I had broken her.

"No, honey, it's not that you can't handle it. It's that you shouldn't have to. Your father was supposed to see you graduate high school, size up your first boyfriend to make sure he's good enough for his little girl, walk you down the aisle one day, be there when you gave birth to your first baby, wrestle with his grandkids ... all the corny stuff a dad does with his daughter. You—we—shouldn't be losing him so soon. It's too soon ..." Her words faded into a soft whimper. I saw a tear fall to the floor, then another and another, making a tiny puddle at her feet.

"Mommy—" I wanted to patch her ripped heart, but I didn't know how, "it's okay. I understand." I rose and went to her—a child comforting her mother. What did I know about the dreams my parents had for me? I hadn't realized it was never about Daddy, or Mommy, or debts, or the farm ... it was about me and Courtney—always the kids. It was about the life we'd miss out on because of the gaping black hole threatening to swallow up.

How would we recover from Daddy's death? Would we lose the farm? Where would we go?

So many questions, so many worries ... none of which I could voice. Mom didn't understand that she wasn't the only one facing this dark tunnel, fearing what awaited on the other side.

I felt the fear wrapping its fingers around my neck,

choking me. I wondered if Daddy felt that same fear about what he would face on the other side. Daddy was a big old teddy bear, but he could be distant about some things. We went to church dutifully, but he'd never spoken openly of his religious beliefs. I wondered if he envisioned a biblical heaven, with all its splendid and rapturous trappings; perhaps he preferred the peace of nothingness.

Anger burned like coals in my gut. Why my father? Why our family? Hatred churned in my stomach. I wanted to hate my dad for getting sick. I could never say so, but I felt it—an unspoken fury that he was leaving us all behind to suffer.

In the seclusion of my bedroom last night, I had prayed for God to punish Daddy for not fighting harder. I didn't know why I prayed that. It made no sense, but in my twelve-year-old mind the anger evoked a dark side of me, of rage and injustice and fear. So I retaliated. And for the first time, God answered. Daddy was being punished now, wasn't he? But why did God choose that prayer to answer? What about all of the other prayers I'd wept over the past several months for Him to heal my daddy? In the shadows of my room I had hated my own dying father, and I hated God too. The fact that he was dying was just as much God's fault as it was Daddy's for giving up.

With no words left to be said between Mommy and me, I turned to Daddy, tugged on his pale blue sleeve until the scratchy cotton fabric slipped from my fingers and my arm lay rigid on the bed. I shuffled to the window, glancing at the people battling against the winter wind in the parking lot two stories below. Propping my hands under my chin, I swiped at a stray tear and stared into space, fixing watery eyes on the gray sky.

Click, clack, click, clack.

I flinched at the sound of irritatingly upbeat footsteps as the doctor entered the room, gesturing to Mom to follow her into the hallway. Even over the beeping machines and Daddy's wheezy snoring I could hear everything. Why don't they close the door? They spoke in hushed tones, so I listened harder.

"The cancer is spreading too fast, Mrs. Montgomery."

Cancer—arguably the most dreaded word in the English language. My arm hairs prickled, even though this was old news.

"Gabrielle, please," I heard Mom correct her. "What are our options now?"

"I'm sorry, Gabrielle, but there's nothing more we can do for him. We just need to make him as comfortable as possible, and I'd suggest saying your goodbyes."

Goodbyes. I wasn't ready for those yet. I never would be.

My heart thumped a little harder.

And then the matter-of-fact final words of the doctor: "I'm afraid he's not going to make it through the night."

Something clawed at my heart just then, a monster out of a nightmare, because I felt its nails rip through me. The words repeated like Dad's scratched Prince record that always skipped during "When Doves Cry." While the rest of the world in 1992 had embraced CDs, Daddy stubbornly stuck to vinyl records.

The doctor's footsteps click-clacked away, fading into the din of nurse chatter and rushing gurneys with squeaky wheels. Mom's sobbing followed her down the hallway. I buried my tears inside.

This can't be happening. Make it stop.

I dealt with it the only way I knew how—by pretending it away. I envied my younger sister, Courtney, blissfully dangling chubby legs over the seat of the visitor chair in the corner. The smaller version of me twisted the blond curls of the baby doll in her lap around her pinkie, babbling cluelessly. I wished to be her. I didn't want this memory. It wasn't fair.

Courtney must have heard my sniffling and sensed my sadness. Suddenly she was standing beside me, dolly tucked under her arm.

"Watch!" she commanded, tugging on my sleeve. She pressed her face against the windowpane, making a pig nose and giggling. "Now you, Haywy!" I was so taken with her innocence that for a few miraculous seconds I forgot Daddy was dying. It felt like there was no one else in the world except Big Sister and Little Sister, and there was nothing more important to do than making smudges on the glass, like we'd done a thousand times at home.

And then Daddy gave vent to a low, rattling moan.

"Daddy sick," said Courtney somberly, pooching out her lower lip.

I hugged her with all my might. "Yes, honey. Daddy sick."

Death was now a palpable presence in the room. Though Mom tried to protect me from the truth, she would never know how deep this wound would be for me. I could never, would never, tell her.

Mom's tennis shoes squeaked across the tiles. I turned to meet her puffy eyes and tear-stained cheeks.

She knelt down and grabbed my shoulders so hard it hurt as she pulled me to her chest. I closed my eyes, retrieving a distant memory of Mommy's happy face. Back before Daddy got sick, back when we ate dinner together, read books in front of the fire, sipped hot cocoa and watched movies and laughed together. But that mom was gone. A haggard version took her place, with creases around her mouth and lines crawling out from the corners of her eyes. Soft fingertips brushed stray hairs away from my brow, and I felt Mom caressing my cheek like when I was a little girl. The lavender scent of her skin was a small comfort.

"You look so much like your daddy ..." she said so seriously that it scared me. "Go say goodnight to Daddy now. We have to leave."

"I don't want to. I'm not leaving him." I needed to stay until the end. I had to. If only I could keep him awake, maybe, just maybe ...

"C'mon, sweetie. It's time to go. We really don't have time to argue about this. I have to take you and Courtney home."

What Mom wasn't telling me what that she was dropping us off so she could come back alone to watch my daddy, her husband of fifteen years, slip from life. As Mom reached out to grab my hand, I pulled away.

"Mom, I'm staying here with you. I want to be with Daddy."

"I'm sorry, sweetie."

"No. You're not protecting me—you're making it worse by making me leave. Dad needs me here."

Mom slowly shook her head. "I know this is difficult for you, but I don't want you to see this, honey."

"He won't die as long as I keep him awake. If we just keep talking to him, he won't leave us. Please let me try." I was begging now, crying the words out, every part of me hoping I could save Daddy, save our family.

"You can't stop this, Haley."

"Yes I can!" Immaturely, I stamped my foot for emphasis, like a little girl. Tittering, Courtney imitated me.

"No, honey, you can't. We'll get through this. I promise it'll be okay ..." As Mom's voice trailed off, I heard the truth in the empty promise, saw it in her bloodshot eyes. Mom didn't believe it either.

"How will we ever be okay?" I choked on the words, barely able to push them out.

Mom's lips twitched as she tried and failed to bravely smile. "Your dad raised you to be tough, honey. You, me,

Courtney—we all have to be tough ... for each other ... for him."

"No, no, no!" I screamed. "This isn't fair! I shouldn't have to be this tough!"

As if watching from across the room, I saw Mom fall back as a blunt force slammed into her shoulder. Then another. When I looked down, I saw my own balled fists uncontrollably pounding the only object within reach, my mom, again and again. If I just kept punching, maybe I could numb the pain.

"Honey, stop! You're hurting me!"

But I couldn't stop. I couldn't hear her over the screaming inside my head.

This one's for Dad leaving us.

This one's for God killing him.

This one's for the doctors who couldn't save him.

Tumbling backward, Mom managed to catch both wrists. "Stop it! Now."

A feeble cough from the corner of the room drew our attention.

"Haley," a scratchy voice mumbled.

Daddy weakly raised a hand and motioned for me to come closer. I hesitated, then crept toward him, the journey from the window to the bed endless.

I sucked back my tears and rested my head next to his pillow. I had never seen him like this... so fragile with tubes snaking out of his nose and needles stabbing his wrists. This ghostly man wasn't my daddy. I missed the sun-kissed complexion he once had; this stranger looked nothing like him. So weak, so small. The man that once towered over me, cuddling me with superhero arms and shoulders big enough I could sit on, was gone, replaced by this frail counterfeit. It couldn't be him... but it was.

I felt the cool thinness of his skin as he leaned his forehead against mine. It was just the two of us.

Everything around us vanished into space; the walls and people faded as the moment froze in time. Our eyes locked as he held my chin between his finger and thumb. I refused to blink, even as my eyes stung, as if one misstep would send him off of this planet and out of my life. As long as I maintained eye contact, he couldn't leave me. I stared so hard that my eyes burned. His fingertips gently brushed against my cheek and absorbed a stray tear.

"I'm sorry you have to go through this, honey." His husky voice sounded like it always did. A welcome sound.

"Daddy—"

"No, let me say this. I know this isn't easy for you, pumpkin, and I wish I could make all of this better for you girls. But Haley, you're strong." He paused to catch a shallow breath.

My reply got stuck in my throat somewhere. My brain rumbled through all the things I wanted to tell him, but they seemed so pointless now.

"You know I love you, don't you?"

I nodded. "Yes, Daddy. I know. I love you too."

Our palms found each other, and I timidly squeezed, still afraid I'd hurt him. I felt all our years together in that hand; miraculously, it had the same reassuring strength that I recognized. He squeezed three beats: I love you. I returned the covert message with four: I love you too. It had been our private, wordless language since before I could remember. Somehow we always knew what the other was trying to say with each squeeze.

That message was his last secret communication to me.

"Promise me something." He wheezed before finishing the thought. I dreaded hearing it; it sounded too much like last words. I didn't want last words. "I want you to follow your dreams no matter what."

"Yes, Daddy, I will."

"One more thing. Promise me that you'll let go of the pain."

Let go of the pain? The words cruelly smacked me with the realization that he knew what he was doing to me—leaving me, forcing me to get over it before it had even begun.

A dying man's last wish. Not just any dying man, but Daddy. I didn't understand the weight of his request just then—how it would shape my entire future—and I wouldn't understand it for years to come. It was a promise I couldn't keep, wouldn't keep. But I didn't know that then.

So I uttered the vow anyway: "I promise, Daddy."

But the words were too late. His bony chest sunk down, suddenly still. Life had disappeared from his eyes. He was gone ... and he took my happiness with him.

Chapter 2

The point of the shovel hit the wet earth, each slice thick and heavy with the weight of exhaustion. A hole big enough for a body was dirty, hard work that I hadn't prepared myself for. Blood soaked the front of my shirt in a blot of rusty red, and my jeans felt sticky against my thighs. I welcomed the patter of light rain tapping the leaves above, if only to wash away the guilt that stuck to my skin like tar.

Wiping the drizzle of raindrops mixed with sweat from my forehead, I rested a moment, caught my breath, leaning against the shovel handle with blistered palms. I hadn't thought to bring work gloves; after all, I hadn't expected to be burying a body.

I jerked around at the sound of rustling branches. Blackness engulfed the shrubbery where something watched me from within its new spring growth. I could feel its presence—its curious eyes, its held breath, its twitching muscles.

I had no time to lose waiting for it to either show itself or run off, so I hefted the shovel and sunk its blade into the earth. Another, then another, moving earth bit by bit, shovelful by shovelful. I might as well have been hauling cement at the rate I was going, but it had to be done. Tonight.

Fear drove my limp arms, my achy wrists, my blistered

hands to keep digging, digging, digging. This deep black hole would bury the nightmare once and for all. One unmarked grave—that's all I needed in order to put the past behind me.

But was it ever really behind me? Because even as I dug, I felt my choices wrap their murderous fingers around my neck, squeezing me, choking me. Sucking in a patch of air, I could barely breathe. As much as I wanted this to be the end of the suffering, a cold reality chilled me to the bone: it was only the beginning. The nightmare had just begun. First with his manipulations and empty promises, and now murder. I was covering up a dead body for him—to protect him. And who'd be the one to go to jail if the secrets unraveled? Me.

Hours passed as the cresting moon turned the dewdrops dotting the sprouts of spring grass into a glistening carpet. In any other moment I would have savored the pearly sparkles a little longer as I bundled myself tighter in my sweater, but right now I just wanted to run. Anywhere but here.

Dawn had almost arrived. I glanced at the body that lay in exactly the same position as it had been tossed hours earlier. Something inside me had hoped it had wrestled with death, won, and moved. If only it was a bad injury and nothing more. But the wide, empty eyes and mouth, frozen in an astonished rictus, spoke the macabre truth.

Standing in the hole, it appeared deep and wide enough, even if I had to bend the body to fit. I embedded the shovel in the mound of dirt and heaved myself up out of the hole, the ache of hours of digging shocking my muscles with sudden weakness. And I was only halfway done—I still had to bury the body.

I straddled the corpse. Those cloudy dead eyes had been watching me dig for hours now. I could no longer abide their judgment. I was afraid to touch it, but more afraid not to. Knees knocking, I leaned over and, with the index and middle fingers of my right hand, gently lowered the eyelids.

I exhaled. That was easy enough. I was feeling well pleased with myself when the lids rolled back and those damnable eyes snapped open. Yelping, I reeled backward and would have stumbled into the grave had I not grabbed the shovel handle. My stomach roiled; I dry heaved into the empty hole. When I finally felt the urge pass, I inhaled to clear my mind.

Focus. I needed to get this done before daybreak.

Adrenaline and panic fueled me, but even they were running dry. Grabbing the arms, I dragged the body to the makeshift grave and dropped it in with a dull thud. The arms twisted in a mangled heap, and the legs fell askew like broken limbs. After pushing body parts around with the toe of my boot, it rested—almost peaceful looking, except for the gray now tinging its flesh—in the pit.

I gave it one last gaze and said a silent prayer. Prayer not so much for forgiveness, but for peace. Peace for me, peace for the one whose life shouldn't have been cut short, and peace for the one who caused it all.

Then I grabbed the shovel and buried my very last secret.

Chapter 3

February 2009
Westfield, New York

It's the chill that shocks the tiny hairs on your neck, the creeping paranoia that makes your heart patter a little faster—this was how I knew he was watching me.

Always watching me.

I'd first felt the eerie sensation I couldn't shake a couple of weeks ago. At first I was afraid, a natural reaction. Strange things had been happening. Little things, like my mail going missing, a flower pot on my porch being moved, a heart drawn into the grime caking my car window. Random fears began flipping through my mind: Who was watching me? Where did he hide? What secrets did he know about me? Was he planning to hurt or kill me?

That last one was the breaking point for me—when I scrutinized every movement, every sound.

As the days passed without incident, I began to relax a little. Maybe the shifting shadows and bumps in the night were all in my head. Maybe there was no threat. Maybe there was no watcher.

I was soon proven wrong.

That's when the letters began. The first one innocent enough—the sweet, earnest declaration of a secret admirer's infatuation. Flattering, really. All too silly to take to the cops: *Hi, officer. I'd like to report this anonymous person who sent me a nice letter.* I couldn't do it. So I kept it to myself.

But now here we were. It wasn't so innocent anymore.

The letters had kept coming, each one a little more confident and explicit than the last. The paper crinkled between my fingers as my eyes trailed every word, absorbing the inky swirls, wondering what hand reached over from the other side to send me this latest one:

I know. I know your darkest secrets, your dull existence. The loneliness that haunts you at night, when you turn your head to find the other side of the bed empty ... again. How can a stranger possibly know you better than you know yourself, you ask? I've been watching. Watching as you shiver at my vast understanding, tremble from the sheer thrill as I probe you so deeply. Like you, I feel so contradictory, yet compelled to clear my head on paper, which is why I write you. Unfortunately, it's not working today. My mind is still plagued with thoughts of you. I breathe for you. I bleed for you.

I want to help you. You need me, like I need you. I can make all your burdens lighter—free you from the debt that you carry. Let me prove myself to you. Only one thing I ask in return: your heart.

I believe it was E. L. Doctorow who said, "Writing is a socially acceptable form of schizophrenia." Should I be awestruck or afraid at my crazed feelings for you?

Love,

Crazy for You

Another day, another letter. Chillingly beautiful.

And spattered with blood.

This letter should have sent me running to the cops.

Yes, it was crazy of me to keep it to myself, but over several weeks I'd grown accustomed to the writer's eccentricities. While bloodstains were a far cry from quixotic cologne-scented notes or tear-stained letters, the sender's passion and pain resonated with me. Turning these letters over to the police somehow felt ... wrong. An act of betrayal.

I absorbed—for the dozenth time—the perfectly cursive script and the red droplets that lined the torn edge, wondering what it all meant.

I bleed for you.

The wooden porch swing squealed as I pushed backward, sucking in a frigid breath that bit my throat. Slivers of sunshine creeping through the lattice work of Mom's front porch did little to warm my frozen cheeks. Winters in upstate New York were long, cruel crucibles that sent most of the town hibernating until spring.

I pulled my knees up to my chest, hugging them against the February chill, then closed my eyes, allowing the stiffness in my shoulders to lift with each breath. The headache I'd woken up with, the aftermath of a night of worrying, was finally beginning to fade. Clearing all thoughts, I let the sound of rustling leaves and the fragrance of lakefront air take me captive.

My gaze traveled back to the words. Not the writing of an average man, especially not one in Podunk, Nowhere, where farmers with Red Man-stained teeth and dirty overalls could barely make their Xs on orders down at the feed and seed—or so I fancied in my cynicism. This was definitely the work of a true romantic—someone steeped in good literature, someone with taste and breeding. A sensual poet, and I was his muse. The handwritten script curled and swirled across the page in perfect harmony, each word haunted with emotion. Although I gently clutched the paper, I didn't need to read it; I had memorized the note when it showed up in my mailbox this morning. No stamp. No return address. Just like all the others.

Just holding the letter between my fingertips evoked an intimacy with my secret admirer. He knew about my father's death. About my screenplays sitting in a dusty pile on my desk at home. About the fears that brought me to tears at night, the plaguing thoughts of loneliness and yearning. He even knew about my darkest secret—something I never spoke about, pushed deep into the crevices of my mind to rot.

He knew so much, and yet I knew precious little about him. But a picture was slowly forming.

Each letter left a deeper footprint on my mind. Each letter held a clue to his identity, a clue that I documented in my journal. I know, I know ... diaries were for children. But releasing my thoughts onto paper had always helped me cope with life's slings and arrows, so I continued to write well into adulthood. I'd even shared nostalgic excerpts with Mom and my sister Courtney when we got together, a rarer and rarer occurrence these days. Childhood memories of riding around the farm with Dad on his tractor, adolescent misadventures like getting caught drunk in the barn, sisterly battles over whose turn it was to use the bathroom first before school ... I'd read aloud while Courtney, Mom, and I would laugh until our chests hurt as they teased me about the drama queen I'd been back then—and still was, I suppose.

Over the course of a dozen letters, I profiled quite a character—eloquent, amorous, intelligent—but with each new message I found the reality disturbing. No one I knew fit the bill ... yet. But I would find him, just like he found me.

A faraway crow called from the wood line behind the house. Another cawed back. Below the cliff that sunk down into Lake Erie, I could hear the waves sloshing lazily against the shore. I imagined my mysterious devotee standing in the bow of a bobbing sailboat somewhere on that broad expanse of water, training a spyglass on Mom's porch. I was suddenly self-conscious of my body and pulled my coat tighter across my breasts.

The sudden creak of the screen door fetched me back to earth. Instinctively I shoved the letter under my blue-jeaned thigh.

"Hey, Mom," I said.

Peeking out from around the door with a coy smile that charmed everyone who met her, Gabrielle Montgomery's crow's-feet stretched from her eyes to her graying hairline. Unlike many of the local farm wives, Mom was aging gracefully. I chalked it up to good breeding, and the plain fact that living close to the land agreed with her. She reminded me sometimes of Sally Field in *Places in the Heart*, indomitable in the face of adversity, dainty and effortlessly pretty.

I wanted to tell her about the letters. Release the burden of this secret. I needed to tell someone ...

"Hale, what are you doing out here? I was looking all over the house for you." She shivered and wrapped her cardigan tighter around her chest. "It's freezing."

No matter how old I got, I was always her little girl.

"I'm fine." The words played on my tongue: *I need to tell you something* ... And yet they sat there, unspoken. "Just enjoying the nice morning."

She rolled her eyes at me. "Well, if you want to freeze your hiney off, that's your business. Did you get enough breakfast? Want another coffee to go?"

We had just finished an egg omelet breakfast together, a ritual that reminded me that I wasn't totally alone now that Courtney was off at college and it was just me and Mom.

Though I knew another cup would make me shaky, I nodded. "Sure, I'll take another cup. With cream and sugar—lots of it."

"Do you want me to pack you a lunch for later?"

So thoughtfully typical of her. Always sending me off with food. It was no wonder I couldn't lose the fifteen pounds that hung over my belt.

"No thanks, I'm fine. I might stop for fast food or something on my way home later."

She sighed in exasperation. "Honey, fast food will kill you. You may as well grab a handful of lard."

"As if your fried chicken is any healthier?"

She chuckled and shook her head, dislodging a few gray tendrils from her bun, then disappeared back into the house. No matter how much I protested, I already knew she'd return with a brown bag full of snacks.

Pressed between my leg and the seat of the swing, I pulled the letter back out, fingering its crisp edges and admiring the dusty rose color; none of the letters had been on plain white paper, but always in sensuous colors. More than once I wanted to tell Mom about the letters, though I probably never would. It would only freak her out to know her daughter was being courted by a stalker. But lonely nights had left the door open to online dating, which soon led to the letters. Fraught with danger, social media was like a cyber singles bar where predators stalked their prey. But what if it didn't feel dangerous? What if the excitement filled a void? Now I was hooked, despite the warnings that once buzzed in my head. Instead of heeding them, I mentally muted them.

Until I discovered the identity of my secret admirer, I couldn't—wouldn't—let it rest. Which was why my mother absolutely could not find out. Not yet, at least.

Listening to the sound of rusted metal grating at its hinges, a tinge of guilt over my secret pulled my focus to the house's deterioration: the wraparound porch that, like the rest of the two-story farmhouse, badly needed painting; the rusted porch railing; the rotting lattice and decking; the dangling shutters; and the rickety swing held up by two scarily loose bolts in the porch's moldy wainscot ceiling. The to-do list of repairs was never-ending. I imagined Dad shaking his head sadly at what had become of his legacy, but I couldn't make out his face. As the house fell into disrepair, my memories of him dulled with it. It was strange how memories worked—the feel of weathered wood could take me back in time to a distinct event with Dad, but I couldn't even remember how he parted his hair.

How could I let my mother live like this?

Money had been too tight for Mom to hire out renovations, and I lacked the time or energy to do it myself. Even Courtney was full of excuses on why she couldn't take a break from sorority parties and serial dating to come home to help.

It seemed like everything on the vineyard was slipping into ruin. A hopeless fate for many American farms. A fate my sender knew about:

I can make all your burdens lighter—free you from the debt that you carry. Let me prove myself to you.

A promise. A piercing ray of hope. Could this stranger really make our financial troubles disappear? It sounded too good to be true even to me, the eternal optimist, but he had reached out to me for a reason. I needed to know why. Why had he chosen *me*? And what if it was real? Could I afford to pass up an offer that could save my mom's livelihood?

"I'll figure you out eventually," I muttered to the vacant air.

A gunshot spurred me out of the swing, sending the letter fluttering to the floor. The porch afforded a panoramic view of the environs; no one was in sight. The shot had sounded way too close to be the far-flung neighbors target shooting ... especially at this early hour.

"Hello?" I yelled.

I listened for the crunch of shoes on dead leaves, the snap of a twig, anything to tell me someone was out there. Nothing but the wind whipping through empty branches and the distant cackle of a crow.

Our family's faded red farmhouse sat half a mile back from Route 5, the main road that passed through endless miles of farms—corn, grapes, and more grapes. Only a couple miles up the road and one would enter the heart of Westfield, New York. Nestled against Lake Erie, Westfield—my hometown and the only place I'd called home in my twenty-eight years—was a sleepy town known for grape farming and quiet living. As the Grape Juice Capital of the World, Westfield took special pride in its vineyards. Once upon a time Dad had been a master viticulturist; his years of experience and dedication ran through every vigorous vine, like a bloodline. But those days were long gone.

My love for Westfield had always been a double-edged sword. The village offered a wholesome quality of life exclusive to small towns, but it wasn't exactly prime breeding ground for an aspiring screenwriter. But it had its charm. Westfield represented the closest thing to southern hospitality north of the Mason-Dixon Line. Cars patiently waited at crosswalks for old folks to cross. Kids shamelessly wore hand-me-downs and said "please" and "thank you" with sincere politeness. Meals were home-cooked and families ate together at the dinner table. It was as if the days of *Leave it to Beaver* never left this close-knit lakeside community. Our family had been no exception.

Until my twelfth birthday, when everything changed.

The door squealed open again, Mom's eyes skimming

the yard. "Hey, did you hear that gunshot?"

"Yeah, but it's probably just the Campbells hunting."

"Sounded awful close," she muttered, then handed me a to-go mug and a heavy paper grocery sack. "There's no reason anyone should be hunting in our woods. Someone's liable to get killed."

"You worry too much."

"How can I not? There's so much to worry about these days. Every time I turn on the TV something horrible has happened." She pointed to the bag. "Make sure you eat, okay?"

"Unnecessary, Mom, but thanks," I said, lifting the bag.

"Go have fun at your screenplay class." Her words were tinted with disapproval. She'd never liked the idea of my Hollywood aspirations. She told me I was silly and naïve. I told her she was narrow-minded and boring. Maybe we were both right.

"Don't sound so enthusiastic," I said. "Do you realize that I'll be working with one of Hollywood's biggest producers? If he helps me sell one screenplay, that would be enough money to fix up this old shack, and bring the vineyard back to life."

Gabrielle shuffled to the swing and sat down. "It's not the money I care about. I just hate the idea of you heading off to Los Angeles. I'll never see you."

"You're getting ahead of yourself, Mom. But if it happens, it's my dream. I wish you'd support it."

"Of course I want your dreams to come true," she said, rising and bundling me into a hug. "But it doesn't mean it's easy for me to accept."

Wishful thinking hadn't worked yet, but I still clung to hope. After years of submitting proposal after proposal to any agent with a mailing address, and entering every contest and film festival I could find, I had tried to sell the rights to several screenplays. The pile of form letter rejections would have sent most other budding scenarists running for the razor blades. But not me. I was determined to find a way—no matter what the cost.

"You comin' over for supper tonight after your class? You can't have fast food twice in a day, y'know."

I shrugged. "Depends on what you're cooking."

"Who are you kidding? We both know your fridge is empty, Hale. And when was the last time you cooked a decent meal for yourself? You're all skin and bones, honey."

I chuckled. If I weighed 300 pounds, Mom would still say I was skin and bones. The pinch of my jeans was a depressing reminder that missing a couple of Mom's stick-to-your-ribs (and everything else) meals wouldn't hurt. But she had so few pleasures in life these days, I couldn't refuse.

"Fine. I'll see you later this evening." My teeth began to chatter as I checked my watch for the time. "I need to get going." Grabbing my knockoff brand hobo bag, I hoisted the strap over my shoulder, unaware of the letter that fluttered at my feet beneath the swing.

Pebbles crackled beneath my footsteps as I strode to my car. The sun's hazy rays bounced off the lake a lover's leap below the cliff that our family's vineyard sat atop. The slosh of whitecaps splashed against the boulders below, spraying icy droplets halfway up the rock face. Nimbostratus clouds, dark and distant, were making a steady advance. As the wind bit my cheeks and tousled my hair, I knew a storm was brewing, most likely bringing ice and snow with it.

Today was my first step toward a better future. For twenty-eight years I had lived in this indescribably boring backwater, my prospects about as promising as any one of the thousand tattered scarecrows dotting the landscape.

Until now. No more Lifetime movie-thons alone on the couch while single-handedly downing quart-sized containers of Cherry Garcia ice cream. My father had once told me to dream big and pursue my heart's desire, and today would be that day.

I tossed a quick wave good-bye to Mom, who knelt down near the porch swing. As I turned back to my car, it didn't occur to me that this action held any significance. I wouldn't feel the earthquake it created until weeks later.

Chapter 4

My fingertips tingled from the cold as I reached the car and tugged at the handle—stuck again. After a couple strong pulls, the door finally popped open and I slid into the stiff vinyl seat. Turning the key, the engine sputtered, then stalled. Three tries later, the engine finally groaned to life.

I vowed that getting rid of my 1997 Dodge Neon, a clunker held together by rust, duct tape, and prayer, would be my first priority, once I sold a screenplay. To replace it, I envisioned a cherry red Corvette convertible. It felt refreshingly good to believe it. Holding tight to dreams of breaking free from my mundane existence, every moment outside of my nine-to-five, gray-walled secretary's cubicle was spent putting pen to paper. It was my addiction, my escape. And the words came easy. I wrote about anything and everything from the time I first learned how to hold a pencil. I started documenting my simple thoughts and childish crises at the tender age of eight in a pink butterfly-adorned diary. My first entry demonstrated perfectly large-lettered penmanship, and more importantly, my dedication to my new confidante:

Dear Diary,

You are my new best friend. Angie Meyers used to be my best friend but today during recess she took back our friendship bracelet and gave it to Michelle Langdon. So now I am nobody's best friend. But at least I have you, Dear Diary. I promise to write every day.

A gold lock concealed the diary's secrets and I had used all my eight-year-old ingenuity to find the "perfect" hiding spot for the key: under my pillow, of course. Later I would discover that the lock could easily be picked with a hairpin. But even as a child, I dreamed of becoming someone special.

Since those days, the years rolled by quickly and quietly, like waves lapping the yellow sand beaches. Each day forgettably the same. Until destiny had intervened, and dropped Allen Michaels right in my lap. I couldn't believe it as I read the ad in last month's *Westfield Republican* promoting a screenplay class with the legendary Hollywood producer:

Are movies your passion? Producer/screenwriter Allen Michaels seeking enthusiastic, creative students. Learn all you need to know in this once-in-a-lifetime opportunity to build a career in the movie business. This four-session Saturday morning class will be held at Jamestown Community College. Inquire for details.

Allen Michaels was a bona fide Hollywood icon who cut his teeth on episodic television (mainly cop shows that I wasn't allowed to watch as a kid) and was now one of the most powerful movie moguls in the business. For the last decade, *The Hollywood Reporter* had consistently ranked him in the top twenty-five in its annual Most Influential People in Entertainment roster. As a movie buff, I was one of those pathetic people who stayed in her seat until the last credit had rolled, and I often found Allen's name, usually as producer or executive producer, sometimes as screenwriter. His action flicks, while not always favorites with the critics, were perennial summer blockbusters. While my dad, arguably the most un-starstruck human on the planet, wouldn't have recognized the name Allen Michaels, he was a huge fan of the cop series Michaels had produced and written in the 1980s: *Jack Ramrod*, a somewhat tongue-in-cheek chronicle of the crime-solving adventures of an eccentric ex-Green Beret.

Recently, Allen Michaels had made the front page of the supermarket tabloids after his wife Susan, a prominent socialite and his executive assistant, went missing, and the Hollywood gossip mill went into overdrive. But without a body, murder accusations eventually gave way to the latest Britney Spears or Lindsay Lohan drama. Despite his bad press, I knew Mr. Michaels would be my ticket out of Westfield. I could feel it.

Upon reaching JCC—as the locals called it—I hurried up the stairs of a mustard-colored brick building on the north side of campus. With the students still on winter break, the college looked like a ghost town.

After meandering through the hallways, I found a classroom where several people sat quietly reading or engaged in whispered conversation. The room number matched my sheet, so I headed inside.

A few seats were available in the back of the room, but I wanted to stand out among the early bird twenty-somethings around me. I took a seat in the front row and fumbled through my bag in search of a pen and paper. My heart beat a mile a minute; my stomach churned—the hallmarks of an all too familiar anxiety. I felt eyes watching me and looked up.

Eggshell white walls revealed clusters of cracks climbing spider-like up to the ceiling. A clock on the wall ticked down the minutes. The floor revealed black scuffmarks in contrast to the beige ceramic tile. My glance fell on a blond older man facing the class from the front of the room—his eyes creepily locked on me. His forehead was wrinkled with intensity. His skin was pale and hung loosely around his neck like a turkey wattle. A bony index finger reached up to push back into place the trendy glasses that had slid down his nose. I recognized him from *Entertainment Weekly* and, more recently, *The National Inquirer—the* Allen Michaels.

Big-shot Hollywood producer. Creative genius. Millionaire movie-maker ... and wife killer?

Chapter 5
Allen

Pushing his glasses up his nose, Allen Michaels glanced up from a scribbled list of story synopses as he waited for the last straggling students to arrive. After spending time getting to know Westfield, he found it the perfect setting for his next screenplay. The grind of producing blockbusters was wearing on him. He wanted a change of pace from shoot-'em-ups and high-octane thrillers, and was considering going back to his TV roots. A small-town murder mystery, or slice-of-life character study, packaged as a movie or mini-series, would play in Peoria, as the saying went. Lifetime or Hallmark would snap it up in a heartbeat. He hoped.

Self-consciously checking his collar, he straightened it out, then licked his hand and smoothed his thinning stray hairs into place—an obsessive habit since youth. His nerves had gotten the best of him this morning, but it could have been a combination of the spicy breakfast sausage he ate and his body's sluggish adjustment to the bitter climate. But getting acclimated to the northeastern winter wasn't the only thing on his mind today.

There was that dread that clung to him, always present, always following him.

The last laggard drifted in and noisily took a seat. Allen inhaled, rose from his chair, and formulated each word in his head before he spoke. He paced across the room, feeling the intense eyes peering up at him. He imagined what they were thinking: *Wow, am I really here, breathing the same air as Allen Michaels?* It was a massive ego stroke, knowing the hoi polloi would be hanging on his every word, worshipping him. And why shouldn't they? These kids didn't know how lucky they were, learning at the feet of the master. Allen puffed out his chest. What was there to be nervous about?

And then, there she was, right in front of him, in the flesh—a face he knew, that he'd admired from afar since he'd first arrived. After living among fake play-dough people—and having long been an unapologetic one himself—he instantly recognized purity when he saw it. Now Fate had smiled upon him and placed this wholesome goddess in his class.

His world had been turned upside down in the past few weeks. But after all that happened, this was the perfect diversion from the paparazzi. He could lay low, slip out of the spotlight, and start over. Maybe squeeze a good story out of this small town. He would take it day by day. And with this beautiful girl in his class, it just might be ... fun.

Was it his imagination, or had she smiled at him just now? There was no doubt. Not just a polite smile—a smile of adulation. After all his tribulations—a loveless marriage of convenience with a woman who turned out to be a cheating, gold-digging bitch—things were finally looking up.

That gave him all the courage he needed. He sat on the edge of his desk, folded his arms, and crossed his legs at the ankles.

"Welcome, class. If you haven't already figured it out, I'm your teacher. My name is Allen Michaels."

Loud applause broke out. Allen took note of a scruffy boy in the back with his legs sprawling in the aisle, who called out "woo-hoo!" more with derision than enthusiasm.

Allen held up his palms for silence.

"So," he said, peering over his Cutler and Gross designer eyeglasses that were too large and probably too youthful for him, "you want to be screenwriters?"

A pause, then a mumble of affirmations rose around the room.

"Well, you've come to the right place. Alfred Hitchcock once said, 'To make a great film you need three things: the script, the script, and the script.' Hitch was absolutely right; the script is *the* single most important single aspect of a movie. Without a good script, a director has nothing to work with, and the actors have nothing worth saying.

"In my class, you're going to discover whether or not you have the right stuff to be a top-drawer scenarist. But first things first. I want each of you to think of a single word that expresses *why* you want to be a screenwriter."

He waited for the shuffle of bags and whine of opening zippers to die down, then studied their faces. So eager and enthusiastic. It reminded him of his own hopeful beginnings ... until his life got sucked into a black hole.

The teaching venture first came to him several weeks back. Needing a break from Los Angeles and the acidic memories associated with it, he decided to take a brief sabbatical—at least that's what he told the press. Under normal circumstances he might have flown his private Learjet to Milan or a Caribbean island resort to soak up some rays, recharge his batteries—and, of course, sample the lovelies in a couple of his favorite brothels. But his latest emergency afforded him no such time. The weight of Los Angeles and its insatiable press suffocated him, and he knew if he didn't get out soon, he would choke. All he needed was a few weeks in hiding.

After considering all the options, he liked the idea of teaching. He thrived in front of an attentive audience. Since boyhood he'd been a frustrated performer and had been in a couple of high school productions. He'd had the good sense to recognize writing was his real talent, and parlayed his success as a TV writer/producer into a storied career as one of the titans of contemporary Hollywood cinema. The time was ripe to get back to his roots and impart his storytelling skills to a classroom of fresh-faced students that would hang on his every word.

So the next order of business was where. Far enough away to leave the past behind. By happenstance he'd come across an online posting for a second-semester creative writing professorship at a community college in a nondescript burg called Westfield in upstate New York. His application was enthusiastically accepted by the dean, who wasted no time in promoting the addition of "renowned Hollywood heavyweight Allen Michaels" to his otherwise lackluster staff.

Allen had then booked an extended stay at the bed and breakfast operated by one Edna Ellsworth, who, judging by the photo on her barebones website, was a sweet old lady who looked rather like an overstuffed chair. To cover his tracks he'd taken the red-eye (flying coach) to Erie International Airport and driven the forty or so miles to Westfield in a brand-new 2009 Mercedes E-320. The rental was the sole extravagance for a man on the run from a failed marriage, a sordid lifestyle—and from himself.

Allen glanced at the snowflakes drifting outside his classroom window. His shiny black Mercedes with beige leather interior was already covered in a dusting of snow and salty residue. He made a mental note to check on snow tires later that day. A cough from the back row signaled that the students were finished.

"So let's hear some of your responses. Just shout them out," Allen said with a dramatic gesture.

"Money!"

"Fame!"

And then the golden ticket answer. It was as if he had heard himself say it, or think it, but it came from the front row corner.

"Passion!" The girl who had commanded his attention moments earlier. "Without passion, nothing else matters. I mean, you've got to love what you do, right? It's not about the money or the fame. It's about writing something from your heart that other people can relate to, that means something to them personally. A movie isn't just a sequence of flickering images on a big screen. It's life— only better. It's people *doing* the adventurous and romantic things we wish we could do in our humdrum lives. It's people *saying* the things we wish we were articulate enough to think of. I want to write those words! The words that people will be quoting to each other on the way out of the theater. That they'll remember for the rest of their lives. I ..." She became aware she was ranting and lowered her face.

Allen planted himself in front of her desk. "Well, I can't give you any points for brevity, miss, for what was supposed to be a one-word answer, but you certainly demonstrated the meaning of passion. What's your name?"

She looked up. "Haley—Haley Montgomery," she said, her cheeks flushing. Embarrassed, she was even more attractive.

"Well, Haley Haley Montgomery, you've tapped into the key behind success. You could do anything for fortune and fame, but writing is about passion. And I'm going to help you cultivate that passion. Since this is a beginners' course, we're going to start with the basics. In order to begin, you must know your voice. What makes you tick? What inspires you?" He paused, shifted his gaze to Haley, and added: "What are your darkest secrets?"

She blushed, as he knew she would, and looked down guiltily. Allen paced the room, basking in his admiring students' rapt attention.

He proceeded with passion that almost felt real. But it was all fake, wasn't it? Because his own fervor had died years ago. In its place was an anger that bubbled and brewed, a resentment for what this life had cost him— what he had given up to keep living the lie.

"Before we dive into the art of writing screenplays, I want each of you to listen and listen good. Show business is not for the faint of heart. You probably think you've got talent to burn, that your story ideas are so unique, so fabulous, that every cigar-chomping caricature of a big-time Hollywood producer is just waiting for you and your inflated sense of your own genius to burst through his door. You probably think selling your first screenplay will be your ticket to easy street."

Here he noticed Haley Montgomery shifting uncomfortably in her seat. He directed a languid smile at her and continued.

"Well, I'm here to tell you you'll be lucky to get anyone important to even read your first screenplay, much less produce it. So if you've got any starry-eyed notions of the streets of Hollywood being paved with gold, and not with the broken dreams of kids *just like you* who expected to have success handed to them, instead of having to work for it, you're living in a fool's paradise. Writing a good screenplay, like any discipline, requires a toolbox of skills that you're not going to put together and master overnight. Your first screenplay will be a piece of shit. Your second, third, and fourth one too. If you learn the craft, and more importantly, if you learn how to write the kind of material—the lowbrow stuff, the exploitative crap, the fluff—that sells in the dream factory that is Hollywood, you might get your foot in the door. *Might*, I emphasize.

And then maybe, just maybe, you will write that highbrow screenplay brimful of importance and symbolism and deep meaning that proves your genius—good luck getting it produced, by the way.

"So, if you think you're God's gift to the written word, leave now. If you're not willing to admit you know nothing and have everything to learn, see ya. If you're not ready to work your ass off, there's the door!"

For several moments nobody moved ... or exhaled.

"Alright, that settles it. We're all in," he said with a clap of his hands. "Now that I've scared the crap out of you, I want to see your heart. Each of you will write a page about yourself, due next week. Get as personal and real and raw as you can. Tell me why you think you have what it takes to be a successful screenwriter."

He congratulated himself for the idea of teaching a writing class. Not only would it put some money in his emptying pockets—a result of a creative drought and lawsuit-happy ex—but the ego boost was always worth it.

"Does anyone have any questions so far?" Several hands shot up around the room. The scruffy boy in the back row Allen had noticed earlier spoke up without being called on.

"Uh, yeah, I was at the convenience store and seen you and your wife's picture on the cover of *The National Inquirer*." All eyes were riveted on him. He grinned wolfishly. "So did you, like, kill her or what?"

Allen took a menacing step toward him. "Get out of my classroom, you impudent jackass. GET THE HELL OUT NOW!"

"Dude, I paid the fee. You can't kick—"

Three strides later Allen gripped him by the collar. He dragged the troublemaker to the door and flung him through it. "Get your refund in the registrar's office on Monday ... now get out, and don't come back."

Allen slammed the door. He noticed Haley looking at

him with surprise and admiration.

"I apologize for that little interruption," he said, addressing the entire class. "Well, I see that my trials and tribulations precede me. No doubt many of you have heard that my wife, Susan, is missing. You might be wondering why I'm here, in your little town, rather than back in LA. It seems I was becoming a pest to the authorities in my efforts to aid them in solving Susan's disappearance. They not-so-subtly asked me to butt out. And my physician warned me, if I did not find some diversion from my woes, that I was headed for a nervous breakdown. When I stumbled upon this teaching opportunity, it seemed just what the doctor had ordered. I promise you, class, I will not let my emotional burdens interfere with being your friend and mentor."

Allen lied fluently and well. The class rewarded him with sustained applause. He returned Haley's shy smile. This girl was too good for LA.

Hollywood had been his single best friend and worst enemy. It embodied his next high, but the lows hit like a sobering rock to the skull. Although full of plastic people and fake smiles, it was where he felt most real.

"Moving on ... I'm passing out your syllabus." A couple of papers fluttered to the floor as he shuffled them from his desk into his hands. He clumsily bent to pick them up, only to lose several more in the process. A shadow of an overeager student passed over him. Glancing up, he was a gasp away from her now ... *the pink-cheeked Haley* ... and his fingertips trembled with the temptation to graze across her skin. Watching her gather the loose papers, Allen almost caught his breath when she looked up at him from her crouched position.

The face of an angel. She had captivated him from that first moment in passing on the street, but up close she was even more beautiful. Dark hair complemented her winter-pale skin. The innocence behind her emerald eyes, the lift of her soft lips, the coconut scent of her hair luring him closer. His gaze fell upon the alluring curves of her young body, tempting him to caress her flesh, to curl her hair around his finger.

"Why, thank you ... Haley. Would you mind passing those out for me?"

"You're welcome, sir," she replied with a shy grin.

"Please call me Allen."

She retrieved the last of the fallen pages and shoveled them into his arms. They momentarily stood eye-to-eye while he absorbed her radiance. She looked to be half his age, but that had never stopped him before in his many dalliances. He was drawn to the idea of a simple farm girl trying to better herself, who only needed a lover-mentor to show her how. His wife Susan had fit that profile too. Somehow he felt it would be different this time. That this girl was the real thing; that a conniving whore wasn't lurking behind those guileless eyes. She'd appreciate a man with his life experience. He was eager to play the Humbert Humbert to her Lolita.

Gently brushing past him, she headed back to her seat as a warm sensation spread through his body, pulsing each nerve. His icy blue eyes observed her as he passed out the papers. Something about her intrigued him, a mystery he couldn't solve. He knew that haunted look because it was his own. This green-eyed enigma was hiding something. He already knew some of her secrets, and he planned to unlock them all.

She was exactly what he had been looking for. If she didn't know it yet, she'd find out soon enough.

Chapter 6

"Ms. Montgomery—"

I spun around toward the sound of my name, but the wind drowned out the rest of his sentence. The lanky outline of Allen Michaels bounced across the parking lot toward me, his long overcoat flapping wildly in the wind and an overstuffed computer case bumping against his leg. He held out something—my bag. I glanced down at my side. Sure enough, I had left my bag under my chair. It wasn't the first time I'd forgotten it somewhere. My damn memory loved to play tricks on me.

"I think this is yours," he said between gasps, now within earshot.

His run slowed to a jog, then to a walk until he paused in front of me and my salt-covered car. Snowflakes danced around us as I waited, arm outstretched, for him to pass the purse over. Yet it rested firmly against his thigh, as if he had forgotten why he chased me down in the first place. When I gestured to the bag, Allen sputtered a laughing apology and handed it to me.

Our fingers brushed too long and I shivered. Not from the cold, but from something buried beneath his touch.

"Thanks," I said. "I guess I couldn't have gotten too far without it." I pulled my car keys from the purse and dangled them as I turned toward my car door. I waited for Allen to leave as I tugged at the stuck handle, but he stood there, watching me in awkward silence. Shifting a step or two, he hauled his briefcase strap back up on his shoulder.

"Damn thing keeps sliding off. That reminds me, I wanted to talk to you before you took off."

"Oh sure, Professor ... uh ... Mr. Michaels."

"Allen."

"I'm sorry. I forgot, Allen." I waited as the wind howled around us, my nerves sizzling. I had never chatted so casually with someone of his stature before. My intimidation left me speechless.

As the wind died down, Allen continued between labored breaths. "I just wanted to say I truly appreciated your input in class today. I can see you're pretty enthusiastic about this screenplay class."

My neck warmed at the praise. Even the bitter wind couldn't suppress the smile pulling at my frozen mouth.

"You have no idea how honored I am to learn from you. I mean, this is my dream, so to have you as a teacher is just ... well, I'm really excited about this opportunity. You have such an impressive background, it's humbling to be your student." I cringed at my nervous babbling.

"Well, that's what I am all about: opportunity, Haley. I bring opportunity where there is none. Because, and I hate to say this, you need more exposure outside of this quaint little town's walls if you want to make it."

Words I often reminded my mother of if I had any chance of success. But she didn't get it. She loved this quaint little town because it was home. But me—I needed more. It had long ago stopped feeling like home. My secrets trapped me here, and all I wanted was out. It was an impasse we'd never cross together.

"I'm certainly glad you decided to come here—to our quaint little town."

Laughing, he scratched his chin, penetrating me with an odd and discomforting stare. "Perhaps we can help each other. It's not easy being a stranger in a strange land. Maybe you can introduce me to the sights around here?"

"Well, except for the Barcelona Lighthouse, there's not a lot of sightseeing around here. It's a pretty small town, in case you didn't notice. We've got vineyards up the wazoo, but if you've seen one, you've see them all." I wasn't exactly coming across as a Westfield booster.

"I'm sure you'll come up with something noteworthy to show me." Then a wink I almost missed.

Was he insinuating what I thought he was? If he expected me to sleep my way to an easy A, he had another thing coming—like my fist in his face. I forced a grin.

"I'm not sure I'll have the time to chauffer you around. I work full-time, so maybe one of the other students can give you a tour. But I appreciate the interest, sir."

This time the *sir* was intentional. Maybe I'd allowed the boundaries to slip; I'd be damned if I didn't bluntly reaffirm them.

I glanced back at my car. "Well, I better get going." I aimed my key into the frozen lock and pushed until the lock popped open. A hand clutched my forearm a little too tightly.

"Before you go," he said, rushing his words and releasing his grip, "I wanted to offer you extra tutoring if you're interested in preparing for the final project coming up—the full screenplay you'll be expected to write over the course of this class." He paused dramatically. "It could give you an edge over the other students. I think it would be worth your while." Though the parking lot stretched empty around us, he leaned in and spoke in a conspiratorial whisper, his words tickling my ear. "But keep this between you and me."

The reek of stale coffee and halitosis lingered on his breath. I didn't want handouts … especially if they came with a price. But maybe I was judging Allen too quickly.

Maybe he just wanted to help. After all, what could it hurt?

"Uh, sure, I'd appreciate it."

Resting his palm on my car door, I suddenly realized I was cornered. My heart quickened, but I refused to react to it. Stay calm. We're just having a conversation ... alone in an empty parking lot, the harsh wind smothering all sound.

"Want in on a little secret? At the end of this course, I'm going to offer a chance for one screenplay to be presented to my Hollywood colleagues. A real shot at real money."

I wondered why he shared this with me.

"Over the next few weeks, I'm going to be assessing the best candidate for this golden opportunity based on creativity, natural ability, and of course a killer screenplay as the deciding factor. Consider this a heads-up."

Was I the only student privy to this "heads-up"? And if so, why? Maybe it was the way he leaned into me, or the way his eyes locked on mine, but I sensed a subliminal message from Allen ... something greedy in his cold blue eyes. I shook that thought away. I wanted something from him too, after all. A shot at this career. I decided then and there that if there *was* another motive behind his offer, I'd deal with it when it became an issue. There was no point judging a man I'd only just met, regardless of the way my skin crawled when he drew near.

"I assure you I'll give it my best shot."

"I can tell we're a lot alike, Haley. I'm already growing quite fond of you. Call me anytime."

Grabbing my hand, he pushed a business card into my palm. I glanced down at it, wondering if all Californians were as aggressive—and touchy—as Allen. Everything he did was big and bold, quite a contrast to Westfield, where most everyone was polite to a fault.

Would I have to fit that Hollywood mold? I'd spent my life practicing the invisibility of a chameleon—always changing my colors to blend into my environment. One color at work, another with my mom, another with friends. Hell, sometimes the roles got so convoluted that I ended up with no idea who I was anymore.

"Thanks, Allen, I'll keep that in mind."

He waved as I slid into my seat and closed the door behind me, relieved to finally put space—and metal—between us. As I pulled out of the parking lot minutes later, the familiar paranoia of being watched seeped into my bones. Glancing in my rearview mirror, there Allen stood, unmoving, his overcoat whipping around him as he watched me drive away. I couldn't stop the chill that followed me home.

Chapter 7

All through dinner with Mom, I sensed it ... the palpable feeling that something was wrong. The taut wire that we danced across, balancing our conversation as we wobbled back and forth like novice tightrope walkers.

As soon as I told her about Allen Michaels I instantly regretted it. Big-shot Hollywood producer whose wife has disappeared? Can't be trusted. At least that's what her tight-lipped grin confessed as I rambled on over dinner. Her stiff silence persisted through homemade pecan pie for dessert.

It wasn't in anything she said, more in what she didn't say. She was hiding something. I could always tell. Her awkward silence and distraction, worried eyes that avoided mine. Mom had always been an open book, a book that I spent nearly three decades reading ... and I knew the story well by now.

Her face had the same anguished look as when Dad got sick. The look that was born when she first lost hope. Something was up. Whatever it was, it was bad. Very bad.

As I grabbed the remaining tossed salad from the dinner table and emptied it into a Tupperware container, I trailed her to the kitchen. My socked feet slid along the laminate flooring as I tried to keep up with Mom's flitting from the counter, to the cupboard, then back as she searched for a Tupperware lid, then to the fridge, lastly to the sink.

"Mom," I finally blurted out, tired of playing the guessing game that she seemed determined to play. "What's going on? You're acting weird."

"Nothing, honey," she replied simply as she turned on the water, running it full blast. "I'm fine."

Liar.

"I can tell something's wrong, so why don't you just spit it out?"

"I'm thinking about your birthday coming up. What do you want to do? Go out to dinner or something?"

"Sure. That sounds fine."

She continued to wash the salad bowl, her hands mindlessly flipping the dish over. Rinsing. Sudsing. Rinsing again.

"We could see a movie in Erie if you want. I saw a couple good previews."

"Yeah, whatever, okay."

More sudsing. More rinsing. I remained quiet, waiting for it. It was coming ... I could feel it in the tension that snapped between us.

"I figured we could go to the mall and pick something out together."

Except she hated the mall almost as much as I did. We both knew this. What was she hiding?

"Mom, just tell me what's bothering you."

She paused in front of the sink as the water drowned out the sound of her heavy sigh. The rise and fall of her shoulders gave her away. The sigh always came before the storm.

Yet this time no irrational warning. No preaching. No ensuing argument about how she was being dramatic and I was *fine, I swear, I'm a grown woman and can handle myself.* Instead, she turned from the sink, took a step forward, and hugged me so tightly that I could feel her heartbeat drumming against my chest. She held me for a long moment, then released.

"I just want you to know I love you, Hale. But I don't want to go down that path with you again. I can't. I don't have the strength."

"What are you talking about? What path?"

She closed her eyes as if afraid to look at me—her own daughter. What did she see that I didn't? Then she turned back to the sink to continue washing the same salad bowl for the sixth time—I had counted.

"I'm not going to stop you this time. You do what you feel you need to do. If that's what you want, I can't keep monitoring you, protecting you from yourself."

Protecting me … from what? I didn't know where this was coming from, or why.

"Mom, I need a little more explanation than that. You're not making sense."

Suds filled the sink as she kept scrubbing. When her hands stopped sloshing in the dishwater, she looked up at me, her eyes glossy. "I'm sorry. It's nothing. I worry—that's what mothers do."

But it wasn't nothing. A ghost haunted my mother. A darkness hovered around us, and I didn't know how to dispel it.

"Just promise me you'll come to me if you ever need help, okay?" she added.

"Always, Mom."

I didn't know what I was agreeing to.

She shut off the water, grabbed a towel hanging from the oven door, and dried the salad bowl. Her gaze refused to meet mine as I watched her fold the cloth, smooth it, then place the bowl in the cupboard.

"How about some tea?" she offered with forced merriment.

I nodded hesitantly, wondering what had just happened.

"Green tea or almond?"

"Almond," I answered.

As my mother pulled down two mugs from the cupboard, a worry of my own wormed its way into my brain. This wasn't the first time Mom had acted strange recently. I flashed back to my grandmother's slow descent into dementia. Seeing my prim, proper, fiercely independent Grandma Rose become lost in the maze of her mind broke my heart ... and Grandma's spirit. Was this the beginning of the end for my mom?

Or was there a secret lurking between us that she wasn't telling me?

With the last of the dishes stacked on the drying rack, I turned off the kitchen light, passing the back door on my way to the living room. A light flickered in the darkness, illuminating a spot in the yard.

"Mom, come look at this."

Sidling up to me, she cupped her hands and peered out the window.

"Do you see that light?"

"Yes, that's strange. I'm going to go see what it is."

I thrust my hand out, stopping her. "Like hell you are. I'll go look. Stay inside."

Slowly opening the door to avoid making the hinges squeak, I slipped out onto the back porch. The planks groaned beneath me, but too softly for whoever was out there to hear. I tiptoed across a patch of brown grass, crunching with fresh frost. I crept close enough to make out a figure clad in red plaid. A man. A knit cap covering his head, his face hidden in the shadows.

"Hey!" I yelled.

Startled, he flicked the flashlight off before he bolted into the thicket. Jumping over the dead shrubs that separated us, I sprinted after him, my breath heavy and hot, until I realized I was chasing a ghost.

Chapter 8

Jake's eyes squeeze shut as he groans, moving back and forth on top of me. I watch him, full of love for him. And yet he closes his world off to me. Why won't he meet my gaze? Why does he shut me out as he deflowers me? Deflower. The word isn't mine, more like my mother's. And now my mother is here, watching from the corner. I glance over at her, a glare of disapproval shadowing her face as her firstborn loses her virginity.

Above me Jake's face reddens, glistening with sweat as he pumps. Unmoving and listless beneath him, it doesn't hurt like I expect it to. A little pinch at first, but I'm too excited and happy and full of love to stop.

A happy tear trickles down the corner of my eye, and I close my eyes to blink it away. When I open them again, Jake isn't Jake. Not the Jake I recognize. His face is rubbery, like a gray plastic film covers his skin. Eyes now open and dull, unseeing. A thick, scratchy rope wraps around his neck, and I think I hear the gasp of his throat being crushed. He's no longer moving, but falls on me, a dead weight.

Dead. Jake is dead, suffocating me as his body crushes the life out of mine.

**

I screamed, and my voice nudged me out of the recurring nightmare. But the memory, now in reach, stuck to me. The back of my skull throbbed where a hammer must have smashed into it. Another day, another headache.

Soft morning sunlight cut through the window at an angle, warming my cheek. It was too late to stay in bed, too early for coffee. I threw back the covers and stuck my feet in my slippers. Perhaps it was a touch of OCD, but I couldn't start the day with a messy bed. Morning after morning, every pillow had to be fluffed and every strip of floral bedding smoothed, a routine I found comfort in. That done, I padded to the glass-topped desk in my spare-bedroom-turned-office, and waited for the logon screen to pop up on my sleeping computer. The screen remained a lifeless black. I punched the power button to reboot, rolled the mouse, pounded a few keys, but the piece of shit appeared dead.

"C'mon, I don't have time for this," I grumbled, smacking my palm on the desk. I jumped up from the black leather chair and examined the back of the monitor. All wiring firmly plugged in. At least nothing was smoking.

"I hope Marc can fix you," I muttered to the screen, referring to Marc Vincetti—Westfield's only computer repairman. Though the computer had been showing error messages the past couple of days, I'd gotten by with a simple click on "okay." Not this time. Last night's toil on my latest film treatment—not to mention the one-page bio Allen Michaels had assigned—was lost somewhere in the bowels of a kaput computer. I had to retrieve it.

When I'd first hired Marc a couple weeks ago to fix my printer, he'd warned me that the green tint on my monitor spelled trouble. I should have listened to him.

I picked up the cordless and glanced at the sticky note clinging to the edge of the computer where I'd scribbled Marc's office number. Damn, he was hot, and my stomach fluttered as I conjured up a mental picture. I took a breath and dialed, nervously tapping the tabletop until his voice mail picked up, which I had expected at this early hour. I left a brief, frantic message.

There'd be nothing on cable other than the morning news, so I pulled out my diary tucked in the back of my desk, my pen hovering over the paper. I still had so many questions about my secret admirer—why the letters, who he was, what he wanted from me. I reached into my back pocket for the most recent letter, crinkling a gum wrapper but nothing else. I jogged downstairs to where my hobo bag hung crookedly from a dining room chair, then rifled through its contents.

No letter.

A burst of panic.

I needed to stay calm. It was just a letter, after all. Nothing to freak out about. Retracing my steps, I thought back to when I last had it. Yesterday morning. My mind rewound over each detail of the day.

On the porch. At Mom's house. My memory flashed back to the gunshot, then when I was driving off, Mom bent over, picking something up.

She must have found it.

This was getting worse by the minute.

But Mom hadn't mentioned it over dinner last night. If she had read it, she would have had a million and one questions. Questions that I didn't know answers to. Basic questions, like who was so fixated on her daughter. Or maybe Mom had said it all with her silence—the odd behavior, the elusiveness, the worry. It made sense.

I needed to put Mom's mind—and my own—at ease. I needed to figure out who it was, confront him, and end the games. I didn't know where to start. No name. No return address. All I could do was narrow down everything I knew about him so far. Based on the obvious romantic overtones, it could only be a *him*. Heading back upstairs, I grabbed my journal and padded across the hall to my bedroom, falling onto my meticulously made bed. Pulling the handful of letters from my bedside table drawer, I unfolded each one until I found the very first letter I'd gotten:

From the moment I laid eyes on you I knew I was in love. Perhaps you felt it too? If only I had the courage to call you, I would. But I'm hoping that this letter will prompt you to seek me out. You've seen my face, yet you know me not.

I've been watching you, waiting for you. I know the loneliness you feel at night as you gaze into the empty darkness of your house, just you and no one else. I know how you try to mask it with a smile, resigned to single life as a way to bear your cross. I know how you hurt, and about your fear of losing everything. I know how you miss your father—I read it in your eyes.

Let me make it all better. If you're willing, please write me back. Leave your reply in an unmarked envelope in your mailbox, and I will pick it up. I promise you that I can make your sadness go away.

I felt the unsettling wonder all over again as I read the words. I supposedly knew his face, but from where? Was he a local? And he knew about my father's death—how? Then the biggest clue: he had to live somewhat close by in order to have such easy access to my mailbox—did he live on my same street? Yet never once had I seen anyone other than the mailman drop by. Sweet old Mr. Jones was a widower, well into his sixties by now, and he used to give my sister and me AirHeads and Nerds as children, but the passion of the words … it couldn't be him. The man was a church deacon, for crying out loud.

Odd how my admirer managed to linger in the shadows. I thought of the lurking man with the flashlight at Mom's house. A tingle crept up my spine as my eyes darted to the nearby window. *Is he watching me now?*

I flinched at the phone's chirping and answered breathlessly.

"Good morning, Ms. Montgomery, this is Marc Vincetti calling you back." His voice sounded husky from sleep. "It's good to hear from you again—well, not so good for your computer."

"Haley—you can call me Haley." Did I usually sound so meek and girly? My neck warmed with embarrassment. "I appreciate you calling me back so quickly." I glanced at the time. "And so early."

"Rising with the sun today. Besides, working for yourself means 24/7 service, which isn't so bad when your clients are as pretty as you." He laughed awkwardly, as if aware that flirtatious comment could be misconstrued as sexual harassment. "So tell me what happened," he added, suddenly all business.

"I just tried turning on my computer and it's blacked out."

"Hmm. I had a feeling that would happen pretty soon."

"I know, I know. You warned me. Do you think you can fix it?"

"I'm thinking your monitor is dead, but it could be something else. Now, you're sure the computer is plugged in?"

"Do your customers usually not check that first?" I asked with a giggle.

"You'd be surprised."

"Wow, you get paid to plug in computers. Nice setup you got there. Yes, my screen is plugged in and yes, I rebooted everything just to be sure."

"How about I come over to check it out? I'll give you a free estimate before I do anything, and if I can't fix it, no charge. When would you like me to come by?"

"Anytime today works for me."

"Well, I'm available right now. Anything to help a damsel in distress." More flirtation, although a little archaic—but still sweet. "Remind me where you live again."

I wondered if he really didn't remember. It wasn't *that* big of a town; the village outskirts reached just under two miles from border to border. It took less than three turns to map it out for him—the yellow house a stone's throw from Main Street, the central road and hub of activity in Westfield—if one considered shopping at antique shops and a lone thrift store "the hub of activity."

"You can't miss me. I'm in the only yellow house on the block."

"Great. See you soon. Bye."

"Bye."

As soon as I hung up, I ran to the bathroom and jumped in the shower. I toweled off and threw on some clothes, then ran a brush through my hair. I reached for my blush then stopped short. No, it was ridiculous, primping for a computer repair house call. Though, maybe just a touch of lip gloss wouldn't hurt.

And I should probably put on something prettier than a sweatshirt and jeans, I thought, heading back to my closet.

Chapter 9

Twenty minutes later, the doorbell rang. Already in the living room pacing, I opened the door and studied Marc with fresh curiosity. Even if I wasn't interested—which I totally wasn't, I swear—I couldn't help but admire the way his short-sleeved polo shirt stretched over well-defined arms, and how his worn jeans hugged his thighs and flared where they covered his boots. A black nylon case hung over his shoulder, a shoulder I briefly imagined naked. His olive complexion accented intense brown eyes that seared me with heat. This dangerous man could disarm me with a smile. Yep, not interested at all.

"Thanks for making it out here so quickly." I stumbled back, tripping over myself as I walked him inside.

"No problem. I appreciate the business."

He paused in the entryway, then held out a firm, rough hand, easily dwarfing mine. It felt oddly reminiscent of Dad's hands—the hands of a man accustomed to physical labor. Then Marc squeezed, just as my father had squeezed my hand the last time I saw him alive.

I held on for a moment longer than I should have, letting the touch of his skin inspire a precious memory of Dad. Him carrying me on his shoulders through the vineyard, one hand on my leg holding me upright, the other picking grapes and offering them to me.

There was something familiar about Marc ... but I didn't know what exactly.

And I didn't want to find out.

Look, but don't touch, I reminded myself. Men were a distraction I couldn't afford. After one too many blind dates gone bad, I was happily resigned to singledom. Well, maybe *happily* was an exaggeration, but I was content. In the spring I had foolishly agreed to a blind date arranged by Shelly, my well-meaning friend from work. Shelly was a free spirit with a warped sense of humor. Though she would never admit it, I'm pretty sure she intended the setup as a joke. She was lucky I hadn't killed her.

Reeking of marijuana, this Neanderthal had showed up at my door with a bouquet of daisies in his grimy fist brazenly plucked from my own front porch planter. I couldn't decide which was more charming: his gold-toothed grin or his ketchup-encrusted porn star mustache. (At least I hoped it was ketchup.) It got even worse—if that was possible—when he insisted on dragging me to a seedy bar that night. The guy didn't even have the courtesy to upgrade me from the watery beer on tap to a mixed drink. And his foot fetish ... well, that was the last straw. No way I was going to let him play "this little piggy" with my tootsies. The pervert's rusted-out old pickup couldn't get me home fast enough.

The free meal (McDonald's—big spender!) and drinks weren't nearly compensation enough for the guy's beer-and-onion breath tickling my ear as he attempted to kiss me in front of my house. Grazing my cheek was as close as I let him get before I hotfooted it to my front door as if Freddy Krueger was chasing me. Never again. I'd rather be an old maid, social stigma be damned.

I gestured toward the staircase. "My office is upstairs." While leading Marc up the stairwell, I glanced back, finding him examining the cluster of pictures in matching cherry wood frames lining the wall rather than eyeing my ass. A true gentleman. There were several shots of Courtney and me as kids, a portrait taken when I was five, one of me straddling my father's knee when I was ten, each more recent as they climbed the stairwell.

"Are these you?" he asked.

"Yep, feels like forever ago."

"I know what you mean." He pointed to the latest family portrait. "Is this your family?"

"Yeah, that's them. Me, my sister, my mom, and my dad."

"I can see the resemblance between you and your sister."

"Unfortunately we aren't really close. She's in college now ... you know how that is. Too busy partying, I guess." I shrugged.

"I remember those days. We all gotta have our rebellious years, right?"

I chuckled. Was my rebellion now? Mom certainly seemed to think so.

"It looks like you had a fun childhood," he said, the stairs squealing under his shifting weight.

The conversation took an uneasy twist as my gut lurched. It felt too intimate, like an exploration of my soul by a man I hardly knew.

"Yeah, I did."

"This picture is really unique. That sunset ... breathtaking."

His fingertip traced the profiles of two small children holding hands, backlit by a brilliant orange sunset. The divide between water and sky disappeared into a strip of yellow. It had captured one of my favorite days with Jake *before* ... before the secret was born. Now I lived in the *after*, pushing Jake's ghost as far from me as possible. While I kept living, Jake was stuck at sixteen. Forever that goofy smile, that bowl haircut. I'd make memory after memory without him. I'd spent years trying to forget him, what happened, the aftermath. I shivered, clutching my chest. Jake was always smiling, always laughing. Until my words cut him so deep he never laughed again.

"Are you okay?" Marc's voice penetrated the black hole I had somehow gotten sucked into.

"Oh, yeah, I'm fine. Just got a chill is all."

"Sure?"

I nodded.

He returned to admiring the photo. "I happen to be a sunset enthusiast."

I grinned. "I didn't know there was such a thing."

"Oh, there sure is. Lake Erie sunsets are especially spectacular, as I'm sure you know."

The truth was, I was so wrapped up in my personal problems, and cynically despising everything about Westfield, I seldom noticed them anymore.

I shrugged and said, "They're okay."

"Okay? Well, that's a gross understatement. I designed my house around them."

"You built your own house?" What couldn't this guy do? At least that explained the rough texture of his hands; I didn't think they got that way from sucking the dust out of computer keyboards with a teeny-tiny vacuum.

"Yep, me and my dad, before he passed away. And the way I planned it, I wanted all the rooms to have a view of the lake, facing the west, so I wouldn't miss a sunset no matter where I was in the house."

Death—something we both understood. "I'm sorry about your dad. I lost my dad too. But at least you got to build a house together. And one with all those westerly views. How did you do it?"

"Let's just say it was an architectural nightmare."

"It's nice to meet someone who appreciates the simple things in life, like an unforgettable sunset," I said, smiling broadly.

Marc smiled back. "Maybe, uh ... maybe someday you can come over ... and, uh, watch one with me."

Why did his shyness have to be so gorgeous—not to mention the rest of him?

Remember, you're okay with spinsterhood. Right? Right. (I think.)

"We'll see," I said in a mouse voice.

After reaching the second-story landing, I led him into my office, pointing to the glass and chrome desk accented by black-and-white still lifes on the wall. "There's the headache of the day. I'm worried I lost an important file I was working on when it crashed."

"Let's see what we got here." Marc ambled over, dropping his bag on the floor before poking around in the wires under my desk.

I could only imagine the dust bunnies he was braving under there. "Sorry I haven't cleaned down there in a while ... or ever."

"Don't worry about it. Never met a client who does."

He peered out at me and winked, and a crippling claustrophobia swept over me. The room shrunk around me like a plastic bag, the temperature spiked. God help me not break out sweating right there in front of him. The longer he gazed at me with those chocolate eyes, the more intense it got. I needed air. Now.

"Oh, I'm a horrible hostess. Do you want anything to drink?" It was the only excuse I could think of to leave the room for a breath.

"I would love something. What do you have?"

I ticked the options aloud: "Water, coffee, more water. What's your pleasure?"

"Uh, water sounds perfect. Exactly what I wanted."

"Okay, I'll be right back. And I accept tips."

"Tip one is to not eat over your keyboard." He overturned the keyboard, spilling crumbs across the desk.

"I'm pretty sure I bought it that way—secondhand. Let me get that water before you find anything else in there that I don't want to know about. Be right back."

I traipsed down the stairway, wondering how giddily loonish I looked, but I couldn't help it. Marc was cuter and nicer by the minute, and those eyes! Deep brown, flecked with a hint of yellow. Forget sunsets—the sexy way they'd looked in the early morning light when he'd first arrived made me want to jump his bones right there in the threshold.

No doubt about it: I'd been in a sexual drought since … never mind. I needed to get me some. *Bad.*

I wondered how conspicuous it would be if I had another computer disaster. *Curb those hormones, girl! Don't give in to desperation.* I was only twenty-eight and in no rush to settle down.

How did that old playground rhyme go? *First comes love, then comes marriage, then comes Haley with a baby carriage …*

No no no, I had screenplays to write, Hollywood to conquer, the world waiting to be traveled. No flimsy crush on a small-town tech guy was worth losing all of that. There was no room in my life for love. But Marc was sure nice to drool over.

Opening the fridge to grab a bottle of water, I observed the bare shelves. My giddy mood vanished. Most evenings I spent eating dinner with Mom, so I admit I hadn't gone grocery shopping in weeks. The empty cupboard was as empty as my heart. Pathetic. As all my high school friends and co-workers married off, I was the perennial single gal that they offered to hook up with undateable losers—like that gold-toothed piggy fetishist.

One by one my single friends had flown the coop, leaving me to fill the void with Mom's cooking, television, and books. Every day served as a sad reminder that I had no special someone in my life who got me and accepted all my weird-ass quirks. Dinner for one had grown stale, and a roommate was out of the question, because being obsessively neat made it impossible for anyone to put up with me. Until I found it—a passion. A driving interest in something other than romance.

My screenplays. My shot at fame. My chance to be someone other than Haley Montgomery, the old maid from Westfield, New York.

Cold air seeping from the fridge reminded me that Marc was still upstairs. Upon reaching the top of the steps, I paused before making my presence known, eyeing his broad shoulders and back while his fingers moved furiously over the keyboard.

"How's it going?" I said, offering the drink.

"Oh, thanks." He accepted the water and took a swig. "I think I figured out the problem; it wasn't your monitor after all. Though you still should consider getting a new one before this one quits on you. You should be up and running in no time. You said you lost a file. Is this it?"

I leaned forward next to him, our cheeks nearly touching. "That's it. Thank God."

"I'm not trying to be nosy, but it comes with the job. I couldn't help but notice the file you were working on was a story of some sort. Are you a writer or something?" Marc's curiosity stirred something in me. Fear? Excitement? Probably a little of both, maybe.

I stood back up, took a safe step away. It was unnerving being so close to him. "Aspiring screenplay writer, actually. Right now I'm just a secretary; it's not really the most glamorous job."

"Screenplays—that's movies, right?"

"Yep, that's the dream, at least."

"I hope you achieve it. Life without a dream or passion is pretty boring, isn't it?"

"Exactly, especially in this town. Writing helps me feel like maybe I can do something bigger with my life, share a message, entertain people. My own mother thinks it's a waste of time. But we all remember the movies that touched our hearts—or scared the bejesus out of us. Like the first time I watched *Titanic* and sobbed my eyes out in my best friend's living room. Or the sleepover I had in high school watching *Scream* where we couldn't sleep the rest of the night. Or when my grandmother and I watched *My Fair Lady* and I wanted to be an actress like Audrey Hepburn. Hell, every girl remembers the first time she forced her boyfriend to watch *The Notebook* with her. That's what I hope to do—create a movie that will leave an imprint like that on peoples' lives."

"Wow—so you could be famous. Maybe I should get your autograph now." He grabbed a piece of pink heart-shaped paper and pen off my desk and thrust them at me with a forged starstruck urgency.

"Ha! We'll see. It's a cutthroat business."

"Hey, if you don't believe in yourself, who will? If there's one thing I've learned, it's that you should always follow your dreams."

Déjà vu smacked me in the face. My father's parting words. How did Marc know? The hands of my dad, the words he left me with ... it was as if a piece of my father lived inside of this stranger. I cast the childish notion aside.

So what kind of movies do you write? Comedies, thrillers ... Wait, lemme guess. Romance?"

My mouth dropped open in a mock gasp. "Just because I'm a woman doesn't mean I can only write emotional drivel. But yeah, you got me, that's what I'm working on. Enough about me. What about you? I can't believe poking around in computer innards is your passion. Maybe your dream is to create a coffee table book of Lake Erie sunsets?"

He laughed. God, he sounded sexy. "I'm still waiting for the lightning bolt to strike me before I figure what I really want to do. But this tech work pays the bills for now. Plus who can resist the perks of snooping into peoples' lives and illicit online activity?"

He laughed as he said it, but I detected a subliminal honesty in his joke.

"Give me five minutes with your computer and I'll tell you things about yourself you never knew." Leaning back in the chair, arms crossed, Marc looked up at me slyly. "I wouldn't mind knowing more about you, Haley."

Where the hell did that come from? I gripped the edge of the desk, holding myself up before my legs collapsed beneath me.

"Um, okay," I mumbled, averting my gaze to my feet and cursing myself for putting on those ridiculous bunny slippers. As much as I wanted to respond, my throat closed up. I was pretty sure my face turned every shade of red.

As Marc packed up his briefcase, I slapped a hand to my forehead. Stupid, stupid, stupid. What was wrong with me that I couldn't speak to this incredibly gorgeous man? Because he was an incredibly gorgeous man. Out of my league. Unattainable. Off limits.

Color flowed into the room through the window, creating tiny prisms on the corner of the glass desk. The deep reds and yellows illuminated Marc's handsome profile, casting an almost heavenly glow. I ached to run my hand over the light stubble on his chiseled jaw. He stood, faced me, meeting my hungry stare dead-on.

"You're all set, Haley."

I loved the way he said my name.

"Thanks. I won't ask what was wrong since I probably wouldn't understand it anyway. What do I owe you?"

"Oh, don't worry about it. It's on me."

"No, seriously, I insist on paying you for your time."

His hand rested on mine, still clutching the edge of the desk.

"Really, let me be a gentleman. I have sins to atone for."

"Um, okay, thank you. Should I ask about these sins piling up?"

"Probably best you not know. You might never look at me the same way again."

One moment I was held in his gaze, the next he sauntered toward the door, down the stairs, out of sight. Following in a trance, I reached out, tempted to grab his arm to pull him toward me. A silly over-the-top gesture they only did in romance flicks.

Marc was the exact opposite of what I needed right now, and yet the spark flickered so bright I couldn't look away. He waited at the front door for me, facing me now.

"I better get going now." He turned to leave, his hand on the doorknob.

One last chance. Say something! He beat me to it.

"I hope to see you around."

"Me too. Try to keep those sins in check."

"Never." He lifted my hand to his lips, brushing my knuckles gallantly with a kiss. "Adieu ... Haley."

I nearly swooned, because that's what a damsel in distress does when a handsome knight kisses her hand.

I watched him walk to his truck, ogling that exquisite butt (okay, so I'm a huge hypocrite) and wondering what would happen if I "accidentally" spilled a Coke on my keyboard—and how fast he'd come to my rescue this time.

Chapter 10

After forcing down spoonfuls of soppy oatmeal, I filled the rest of the day with writing, scrawling out checks for overdue bills, an afternoon nap, and cleaning. Pulling out the appliances kind of cleaning. I couldn't remember the last time I had wiped down the baseboards, but Marc's dust bunny attack inspired the sudden urge. I reveled in the satisfaction of a spotless house.

Grabbing two painkillers to alleviate a developing headache, I downed a glass of water and headed to my room. The pitch-black sky was speckled with thousands of stars twinkling when I detoured to my office to tidy up some stray papers before heading to bed.

I don't know how I missed it earlier, but there it was, like a flag waving at me. A piece of pink paper peeking out from under my keyboard. I pulled the scribbled note out from its hiding place, holding it up to the dim lamplight:

It was a pleasure seeing you today. I hope to see you again soon.

He must have written it when I was getting him water, but slid under my keyboard when I was straightening up. I read it again and again, my hand trembling with excitement. No, I didn't want to get excited, shouldn't get excited. It was nothing but a little note, nothing more.

Or was it more?

Something about the handwriting looked oddly familiar. Could it be? Bolting across the hall with the note in hand, I slipped into my bedroom and hastily grabbed the pile of anonymous letters I had tucked back into my bedside table. Placing Marc's letter next to the others, I rifled through the stack, comparing the script side by side. Sure enough, the similarities were striking. The curl at the end of the L, the roundness of the A's.

Was Marc my anonymous correspondent/stalker? Or was I overanalyzing it? I couldn't trust myself anymore, knowing what I knew. About my father, about Jake, about the past. But here it was, in tactile, readable proof. Perhaps the bigger question was: could I trust Marc?

**

I flipped over to face the clock on my bedside table, still wide-awake waiting for sleep to cloak me. Tonight it wasn't my usual anxiety keeping my brain in turmoil. It was something completely different.

Curiosity.

Fear.

Obsession.

A mental accounting of every detail since meeting Marc. I couldn't shove him out of my mind. It was crazy. A case of girlish desperation. But all the letters, and now this note ... how else could I explain it? The timing— receiving the letters shortly after meeting him for the first time. And the handwriting similarities. It couldn't be just a coincidence. And it was more than a little creepy. What did I really know about him? He seemed nice enough, but the intensity of his words justified my apprehension. Too much too fast—never a good sign.

But damn was he cute. It was hard to look past that mischievous grin and boyish charm to see the monster behind the mask.

As my brain turned somersaults, I wondered if Marc was thinking about me too right now.

Turning over for the umpteenth time, I settled on a view of the window where the moon hovered, a bright ball of white against an inky night sky. It was well after two o'clock; I had to be up at seven, which meant I'd get no more than five hours of sleep before work the next day. Just enough to function.

I fluffed up my pillow and sank into its downy comfort. I tried to make my mind go blank, but one thought kept intruding: Mom finding that letter. Then saying nothing about it.

Mom could hide her words, but she couldn't hide her thoughts. Not from me, at least. I read them in her expression, the worry creasing her face. I wanted to assure her nothing bad would happen, these letters weren't a dark omen of something terrible to come. It was romantic, wasn't it? A man sharing his vulnerability with me. What harm could possibly come from such an innocent gesture?

Unless it wasn't so innocent. Unless he wasn't so vulnerable. Unless he was a predator seeking out his next prey—me.

I *humphed* away the notion. Marc didn't seem like a psychopath. But how could I really know? I couldn't—not until it was too late.

I was tempted to leap out of bed and look Marc up online on one or more of those people finder search engines. But those sites seemed too sleazy and invasive to me, and you had to pay a fee for anything juicy, like divorce records and arrest reports. I decided against it; I didn't have that kind of money to throw away.

As much as I wanted to confess to Mom about the letters, Marc, my uncertainties, my secrets ... it was a conversation we could never have. The torn state of my heart had to remain my own burden. The past was buried.

No digging, no remembering. Leave the bones to turn to dust, the memories to wither and die.

And yet Jake's ghost still haunted my nightmares. With each year I had prayed he would give up, but again he would invade my thoughts, reawakening the pain with fresh cuts. I despaired that I'd never get over what happened, because it crippled me. Shackled me to the past. Most days I could feel life slipping away. Ticking away a chance at finding love, at having kids, at having hope for a fairy tale future. Not that I believed in fairy tales—not anymore. Though sometimes I dreamt them. That was all they were, though—dreams and nothing more. It was why *Hollywood or bust* was my new life motto. Screw love; I had bigger pursuits to chase after.

My eyelids drifted closed as Marc's face wafted into my mind, moments later transforming into a freakish demon that I couldn't escape.

Chapter 11
Allen

Sweet Mrs. Ellsworth. She had certainly lived up to the wholesome photo on her website, fussing over Allen with the same mother hen devotion Aunt Bee had always shown to Andy and Opie Taylor. She was convinced Allen was sad and lonely, and, being her only guest at the moment, took him under her wing. Tonight they had played four games of checkers in the bed and breakfast's parlor, surrounded by fusty antiques and hoary pictures of Mrs. Ellsworth's dearly departed kin, whose eyes followed Allen in a fashion he found most disconcerting.

Mrs. E was easy entertainment, though. Impressing her with details about the upcoming premiere for his latest film, he name-dropped to her excited squeals. He almost considered giving her one of the many complimentary invitations that he had no use for, now that Susan wasn't in the picture. He imagined the housedress-bedecked old lady lost in a sea of glitz and glamour, and chuckled. What a sight that would be!

At ten o'clock she cleared away the blue willow china cups in which she'd served elderberry tea (good for the digestion, she claimed), and what was left of the homemade shortbread cookies (they were tasty; Allen had eaten his fill), and said good night. Retiring to his own room, Allen reflected on the fact that Westfield was a Mayberrian utopia of genuinely warm, friendly, hardworking people. He had never imagined such a place could actually exist, except in reruns.

He sat cross-legged in the cushioned armchair alongside his bed, with notebook in hand. The page was blank. Inspiration wouldn't come, not with Haley Montgomery haunting his thoughts. *Haley Michaels.* Ah, the name had a certain a ring to it.

He stood up from his chair and tossed his notebook on the bed. A walk seemed the only solution for clearing his head tonight. Perhaps the chill of fresh lakefront air would spur his creative juices. He grabbed his coat, stuffed his cell phone in his pocket, and eased the door open. The joints of the house and original maple flooring groaned more than a woman in labor. With stealthy steps he descended the massive stairway and slipped out the front door. The shock of the freezing cold would make this a short walk.

Allen lumbered down the sidewalk, mindful of the treacherous bulges in the slabs made by the roots of a northern red oak, bare and spidery under the blush of a streetlamp. He considered all of the feet that had trod this path—the unnoticed footsteps of unnoticed lives. What a contrast to the forecourt of Grauman's Chinese Theatre, 2,500 miles west on Hollywood Boulevard, where tourists pay homage to the handprints of the stars immortalized in wet cement. All his adult life he had worked for the fame that those concrete memorials represented, but there was something serenely beautiful about the anonymity of unnoticed steps here in this small town tonight.

The sidewalk turned a sharp corner, heading further into the cozy neighborhood of two-story homes safeguarding children snug and warm in their beds. His mind drifted back to his own childhood in Denver, Colorado. His father had been a dreamer, always either entering into another get-rich-quick scheme, or recovering from one. One day he'd set off on another of his quixotic quests and never came back, leaving Allen, his little sister, and his ill-equipped mother to fend for themselves, and saddling them with a mountain of debt. A progression of psychotic boyfriends culminated with an abusive stepfather who punched, backhanded, and whipped Allen into isolation until his bedroom became his only safe house and movies his only escape. Every waking moment was spent fighting for his and his sister's lives, though she was spared their stepfather's iron fist.

Allen was special, after all. Bookish and creative. A "sissy" his stepfather had branded him. "Thinks his shit don't stink," he'd said, fumbling for words to explain the boy's aloofness, which was in actuality a shield. In other words, the perfect target for a self-loathing bully.

Growing up awkward and introverted, Allen took solace in his studies. In high school he exhibited a flair for creative writing, which earned him an academic scholarship to college. He quickly grew bored with traditional education and dropped out in his sophomore year, setting his sights on Hollywood, where he hoped to follow in the huge footsteps of some of the celebrated screenwriters he admired: Billy Wilder, Preston Sturges, Ernest Lehman, Dalton Trumbo, Paddy Chayefsky.

He kicked around town for several years, landing menial jobs at various studios, studying the rigid hierarchy and trying to figure out where he fit in, all the while pounding out scripts he hadn't yet grown the balls to show to anyone. His "foot in the door" came when he was hired as a production assistant for Stephen J. Cannell's company. It was television, not the movies, but it was a start. Allen finally got up the nerve to show Cannell, who was the hottest writer/producer in TV at the time, some of his scripts. Impressed, Cannell asked him to try his hand at writing an episode of *The Rockford Files*, an immensely popular show at the time. His script went through numerous drafts, as was typical. In the end another writer received the on-screen credit, which was also typical. But Allen received a "story by" credit, which entitled him to join the Writers Guild. He was on his way.

But Susan—she was his real turning point. When he met her, she was an Iowa farm girl who had just fallen off the turnip truck, in awe of Hollywood's bright lights—and of him, an up-and-coming golden boy. She was sweet and beautiful; he couldn't resist her corn-fed charm. After a fairytale wedding, they used each other to claw their way to the top, an ascent marked by deception, greed, moral ambiguity, cynicism—all the ingredients of a Hollywood *film noir*. Susan gave an Oscar-worthy performance as the *femme fatale*. She became pregnant with another man's child, mocking his longtime desire for fatherhood. The death blow came when she'd filed for divorce, threatening to take away his money and destroy his mystique.

Allen didn't like being made to play the role of the chump.

He had attempted to blot out the stain of their loveless joke of a marriage in a single cruel act. An act that drove him out of Sodom to this latter-day Mayberry. He'd hoped that exposure to the wholesomeness of ordinary people might act as a balm for his wicked ways. Yet guilt had a nasty habit of following one … and it never needs a map.

He couldn't escape the angry specter of his wife, but he could find a beautifully naïve distraction.

Chapter 12

Marc

She taunts him in his dreams. Only in the safety of dreams is he permitted to reach her, though. In real life she is as elusive as a rabbit, cute to look at but impossible to catch.

In a foggy faraway place she sits, behind glass that his breath had frosted. Wiping away the dewy moisture, Marc's gaze locks on her. Sitting at a booth in a fancy restaurant with another man. Her outfit—diamond spaghetti straps, tight-fitting bodice, black fuck-me stilettos—is stunning. She looks sexy but refined. And relaxed. Dangling one leg over her other knee, brushing the tip of her shoe against his foot. Laughing that delicious laugh that had once charmed him. Now she charms another man with it. Her hand rests on the man's shoulders—a man Marc recognizes, but not by name. A thick face, smoothed by fat. Nice suit—a businessman.

Marc tears up as he can't pull away. She looks up, spots him, and for a long moment they speak with their eyes. Him questioning why. Her answering that it is over.

The man dangles his arm around her possessively. He knows the truth as she leans into the crook of his arm. Marc turns to leave as she turns back to the man. Then he feels shards pinching his skin, watches his world shatter, the glass house he never knew he lived in crumbling around him, slicing him open as it falls …

**

While the dream faded into morning, the tears hung around. Wiping them away, Marc sucked in a breath to clear the dream from his head.

"Stupid bitch," he muttered. The words helped him hold on to the grudge.

The week trickled down to another Friday at a grueling pace. Peering out from under the covers, Marc Vincetti watched dark clouds scudding across the sky through the wall-to-wall window that reached across the bedroom. He groaned. Another gray day. He moved his leg and gently nudged at the sleeping form next to him, cocooned in the bedding. He could chase her from his bed, but he hadn't the heart. How could he resist those big, brown puppy-dog eyes? It was too late—she had cast her spell on him.

"Time to get up, Sheba," he said, patting her rear.

Marc rolled out of bed and stared at his chow-chow shepherd mix. Her curled tail began to wiggle. It wasn't quite long enough to wag.

The dog lazily jumped down and followed him as he led her through a maze of yesterday's clothes and shoes scattered over the braided area rug. Neatness wasn't his strong suit. But that was the luxury of being a bachelor. He got to do what he wanted, when he wanted, and no one could tell him otherwise. That's how he liked to organize his life: by *his* rules.

Marc's stomach grumbled as he made his way through the loft bedroom, down the open stairwell that overlooked the heart of the home, and past his sparsely furnished living room. What more did a guy need than a leather sofa and big-screen television? Padding across the rich, textured wood floors in bare feet, he remembered that excruciating summer with his dad sanding, staining, and applying polyurethane until they glowed lustrously in the sunlight. The house was a showplace, inside and out, even if the westerly views in every room suggested M. C. Escher had been the architect. Its construction had been worth all the blood, sweat, and tears, and stood as a testament to the ultimate father-son bonding project.

The high ceilings showcased knotted beams with recessed lighting that was hardly ever used, as the picture windows on every wall permitted more than enough light. His favorite touch was the open fireplace purposefully positioned between the living room and kitchen, with multicolored stone facing on both sides, adding simultaneous warmth and atmosphere to both rooms. He even mounted a cooking fixture to the kitchen side of the hearth in case he lost power. Hell, sometimes he'd cook over an open flame just for the fun of good old-fashioned rustic living. Nothing beat the taste of smoked meat, his father always said.

He paused on his way to the kitchen to flip through the junk mail piled on the dining room table. The mailman had a tendency to insert important bills within the sales circulars, and on more than one occasion Marc unknowingly threw the pile—bills and all—into the garbage.

The ex-who-could-not-be-named had been the more organized of the two and took care of his bank accounts and bills since college, after the engagement. But since their break-up, whenever he'd make a late payment or bounce a check, he imagined the torrent of invective gushing from her snarling lips. It wasn't exactly an amicable split. Considering she left him for a big-time CPA, he could bitterly joke now that they were a perfect fit.

He pressed his fingers against his temple; a headache persisted, triggered by the past week's craziness. Work consumed more than seventy hours a week, which wasn't unusual for the first year of a startup. But he'd been in business for three years now. Each year he assured himself it'd get easier, but the long hours were still wreaking havoc on his social life.

He dropped the stack of mail and turned the corner into the kitchen. Stepping onto cold ceramic tile, his body trembled and a chill burrowed into his bones. Opening the fridge, he palmed two eggs and the butter dish.

"How about some eggs, girl?" He glanced down at his furry shadow. "You have the life, sitting around getting waited on hand and foot."

Sheba cocked her head, looking up at him curiously.

"I'll never forget when you showed up on my doorstep, fur all knotted and tangled, covered in fleas. Remember that, girl?" Her tail wagged in agreement. "I never realized how slippery a wet dog could be until you came along." He'd gotten wetter than she did during her first—and last—bath.

Rubbing her ears—one was always alert and perky, the other lay flat—he chuckled as she gazed at him like she understood his every word.

As he moved to close the fridge, Sheba followed at his feet. It hadn't taken long for her to get comfortable with him; she rarely left his side. In the kitchen, she was there. In bed, she was there. In the bathroom, well, the bath thing wasn't a hit the first time around, so she waited at the base of the tub.

Most days he felt guilty when he headed off to work and caught a glimpse of her intently watching his departure from the living room window as he pulled away. Hours later, when his Ford F-150 rumbled up the driveway, she'd be planted exactly where he left her, jiggling her twisted, fluffy tail. He could barely get a moment's peace, but he didn't mind. She was his and he was hers. Such loyalty was hard to find.

As he cracked the eggs into a buttery pan, Sheba whined, a nose-length behind him.

"You gotta pee, girl?"

She barked.

Five minutes later, with toast buttered and eggs resting on top, he shrugged on a coat over his bare chest, stepped into his boots, and headed outside to the back deck. Sheba took off for the woods chasing a squirrel.

Now *he* had to go. "When nature calls ..." Another perk of being a guy—the conveniences. "Thar she blows!" he cried, whipping out his willy. He took a leisurely whiz between a pair of balusters, admiring the golden puddle he made on the ground ten feet below.

The porch's sweeping view of Lake Erie was a doleful reminder of how he'd acquired the property. Being his great-uncle's next of kin, Marc had inherited seventeen acres after the man's untimely death when Marc was still an indifferent teenager. The land sat vacant for a number of years when he ran off to the "big city" of Buffalo, New York, to study computer science and chase love with the woman of his dreams: Julie Carter. Julie epitomized the ideal woman for most guys. Blonde and gorgeous, with green eyes that would put Jennifer Connelly's to shame. And her smarts were just as dazzling as her looks. Marc had fallen hook, line, and sinker for the pretty package and seductive lies that masked a cheating ballbuster. A broken heart could mend. A crushed spirit seldom did.

As he sat down with his plate at the picnic table, he found he had a heaping helping of regret to go along with his toast and eggs. He lost his appetite. He was tired of being the victim. Tired of playing the hero. For once he wanted to be the villain, to do the hurting, stop the bleeding regret.

There was only one thing that could salve regret, and that was revenge.

**

June 1996

Even at age seventeen he would have married her in a heartbeat. He had told her so, many times. But despite Julie's promises that they'd figure out a way to make it work, the truth shattered any hope. Today was the end.

For most kids, summer promised tanned, half-naked bodies baking on Lake Erie's beaches and frolicking in the lapping waves. For Marc, it offered nothing but pain. As he stood at the airport gate, clutching Julie's hand, tears coursing down his cheeks, he didn't even bother to wipe them away. He wanted her to see how he hurt, masculinity be damned.

"Why do you have to go to Florida?" His choked words pleaded with her, even though the answer would remain the same as always.

"You know why, babe. My dad has part custody. I'll be back for school in the fall."

It wasn't good enough for Marc. He needed her here, now.

The loudspeaker announced her flight number, instructing passengers to board. Gripping her hand tighter, he pulled her into his arms. "Please don't go. This summer's gonna suck without you."

"You can always come visit me," she muttered against his chest. "That's my flight. I have to go. I'll be back before you know it. I love you. I'll call when I get there." With a kiss on his cheek she was gone.

As the love of his adolescence walked the ramp toward a new life without him, Marc stood helplessly watching, a statue among a sea of swarming people. In his hand a dozen red roses reminded him that like the flowers, there was no room in her life for him as hundreds of miles separated them. Driving home in his dad's car, he almost tossed the roses out the window, but something stopped him. A teenage boy's wish. A watery prayer that Julie would come back for him. That they'd have their happily ever after.

That day was the first time his heart had broken, but not the last.

That day was the first time Marc had felt the monster awaken, but not the last.

Chapter 13

Everything's changing and yet nothing's changed. I've been taking a screenplay writing class; it's a game-changer for me, at least I hope it is. I've learned so much from the teacher— Allen Michaels, can you believe it? All I've ever dreamed could come true ... but until Hollywood actually happens, I can't help but feel guardedly optimistic. What if I screw it up? Because that's what I do.

Aaaand, I just looked at the time.

Can't write much longer. Have to shower before work. Woke up late again. Another restless night. I got another letter yesterday—makes three this week. Every moment of every day he's there, in the recesses of my mind. Relentless.

I have a speculation about the mysterious author: Marc Vincetti. Gorgeous, sweet, kind ... did I mention gorgeous? Do you think it's coincidence that the clues point to him? The day after I met Marc the letters started. Same penmanship as a note he left me. Coincidence, or a figment of my imagination? I want the letters to be from him, but it's creepy, isn't it? Anonymous notes—that can't be normal. But I think I'd be disappointed if they stopped.

There's something incredibly romantic about someone pursuing me so fiercely, knowing me so deeply. I should be scared. I'm not. Is it safe to be so vulnerable? I think back to all of the secrets we keep, and it's frightening to imagine someone capable of accessing all those moments we hoped to take with us to the grave. Even Dad didn't know Mom's secrets. I know why she couldn't tell him. It's not something a man wants to find out about his family before he dies. Though I wonder if him knowing would have changed anything.

Maybe secrets are meant to be told.

Shit—now I'm officially late for work.

**

Friday got off to a bad start as I managed to speed-shower, speed-dress, and speed-eat a dry piece of toast on my way out the door without realizing I wore two unmatched socks. It wasn't until I stepped into the car when my pant legs rose up enough to show one snowflaked sock and one Santa sock. I'd pretend it was intentional, maybe start a new fad.

With three minutes to clock in at work and five minutes' worth of traffic and stop signs to get through, I rushed into the law firm office looking like a bedraggled cat, a casualty of the icy wind blowing off Lake Erie as I trudged from the parking lot to the front door. Spotting my cubicle-mate Shelly, I anticipated a juicy morning gossip session as I tried my best to tame my Sideshow Bob hair with my fingers.

Carrying a mug of black, burned coffee from the breakroom, I strutted down the short corridor to where the two other legal secretaries sat typing away, the faint *tap-tap-tapping* the only sound in the hushed office.

"Hey, Shelly. TGIF."

Shelly smiled up at me from her cluttered desk. Our bosses were stuffed-shirt attorneys who demanded decorum and neatness, but Shelly, by virtue of being whip-smart, excellent at her job, and no one's lap dog, got away with murder. A sign on her cubicle wall bore the slogan: LET ME CHECK MY GIVEASHITOMETER. NOPE, NOTHING. None of the attorneys had the balls to challenge Shelly on the appropriateness of this decoration. She fended off their infrequent amorous advances (most particularly at the office Christmas party, when they got stumbling drunk) with a withering glance or remark and never worried about getting fired. She was as much an office fixture as the water cooler, popular, indispensable, and irreplaceable.

Four years ago she'd taken me under her wing, a mother figure to all the new girls—a young, hip mother. Though Shelly's subtle creases showed she was nearing her late thirties, the woman dressed trendier than some teens, and her slim figure pulled it off well.

"I have a feeling it's going to be a slow day. Practically no one's in today. I already went through the paperwork for all our cases and it looks like we're all caught up."

"That's good to know. I got practically no sleep last night. I feel like shit."

"You look like it too."

"Gee, thanks for that vote of confidence."

"Don't mention it. So got any plans this weekend, birthday girl?"

I wagged my finger at her. "Hold off on that birthday talk. It's not until tomorrow. Let me bask in my youth while I still have it."

"Whatever. You're still a spring chicken. Just wait until you hit thirty—it's all downhill from there."

"You can't talk. Look at you, Shel. You look better than I do and you're happily married to the greatest guy on earth. It doesn't look too downhill from where I'm standing."

"Don't worry, sweetie. Your Mr. Right will gallop into your life on his white steed and all that shit." She winked, her eyelid coated in silver and purple eyeshadow.

"I wish."

Tossing an embarrassed sideways glance, I wondered if it was safe to tell her that perhaps Mr. Right was already in the scene.

"I know a guy who'd be perfect for you. Maybe we could do a double-date?"

Laughing, I shook my head. "After foot fetish guy? I don't trust your judgment anymore. No thanks. Besides, if I do decide I want to date—and that's a big *if*—I think I may have met someone."

"What?" Shelly's audible gasp drew the attention of two legal assistants sitting across from us before I shushed her. "Tell me everything!"

Of course I wouldn't tell her everything. Just enough to make it appear normal. "It was a couple weeks ago, this guy Marc fixed my computer. I didn't think much of it, until I had another issue and he came back. He made a couple flirtatious remarks. He even kissed my hand."

"Kissed your hand? Honey, nobody does that these days, but it's romantic as hell."

"I know, right? And he wrote me a note. Hopes to see me again. Am I reading too much into it? Be honest."

Shelly's eyes widened with excitement as she scooted her rolling chair closer to me. "Haley, that's definitely interest. He wants to bone you, girl."

"Stop." I scrunched up my nose as if the idea were repulsive, when I considered it anything but. "So it's promising?"

"Hell, yeah! You gotta call him, ask him out, and make sure to shave your legs. You don't want him to mistake you for a porcupine during your first time together."

"Shel, first of all, I'm not going to sleep with him ... yet. Secondly, I'm not asking him out. Call me old-fashioned, but that's the man's job. Besides, I just want to get to know him first."

"All I'm saying is you gotta act fast. A single guy in this town won't last long. And he left you a note, so that's pretty much an invitation to call him."

"I dunno ..." Calling Marc out of the blue, no ... I couldn't do it. It required girl-balls I never had.

"Haley!" The tone accompanying that single word held the reprimand of a hundred words. "It's the twenty-first century. Girls ask guys out. Take my advice—what do you have to lose? If he says no, then his loss. Move on."

"Easy for you to say," I muttered. I'd never been confident like Shelly. My pants squeezed my thighs like two stuffed sausages, and my belly poured out from under my too-short top that had fit me nicely three months ago. If I wasn't hard-core dieting, I gained weight simply by looking at food. I could never have the self-assurance of a skinny, beautiful woman because, well, I wasn't one.

How did a timid, self-conscious woman tell a man out of her league "I like you" without saying "I'm desperate"?

By three o'clock half the staff had cut out early for the day. A mild, sunny Friday in February was a rare treat, so we took advantage of it when we could. I decided to clock out, grab a late lunch, and head to the town square to eat.

The white gazebo nestled between massive naked maple trees and surrounded by red-berried holly shrubs provided a charming, idyllic setting reminiscent of Stars Hollow from *Gilmore Girls*. I sat on the bench eating a chicken wrap from a local sandwich shop, enjoying the chirp of sparrows waiting for my crumbs, when I heard a whisper.

"Haley ..."

The sound was distant, like an echo in my mind. I glanced around the empty lawn behind me. Nothing.

"Haley ..." the whisper came again on a breeze.

Was I hearing things?

As I turned to search behind me, several taps on my shoulder startled me out of my seat. Pivoting the other direction, I glanced down to find Marc, hunched below the edge of the gazebo, gazing up at me, a boyish grin plastered on his face.

"You ass!" I sputtered. "You scared the crap out of me."

"That was the whole point." The words scattered amid his laughter. "I almost thought it wasn't you. That would have been awkward."

"You're such a child." And yet I found it utterly endearing.

"Mind if I join you?"

"Sure, I'm just having lunch." I held up my half-eaten wrap.

Marc effortlessly climbed over the railing, falling onto the bench beside me. Eyes twinkling with mischief, he captivated my heart.

I felt it all in that moment. A dance between confession and restraint. I wanted to tell him, but I couldn't. I wanted to ask him, but I wouldn't. It needed to come from him, if he was the man behind the mystery, the author of the letters. The one who sought to rescue me.

But did I really need rescuing?

Maybe I did and didn't know it.

"Beautiful day ... for February. It's the first time I haven't seen my breath so far this year."

"I know, I think we're actually above freezing. I figured I'd take advantage of it and eat outside. It's actually kind of warm in the sun."

"You look ... different. No fuzzy slippers today."

I chuckled. "I thought I saw you eyeing them when you were at my house. Sorry, but they don't come in your size. So what brings you here?"

"I saw you and figured you could use some company."

"Because I'm a single woman sitting alone I need company, huh?"

"No, I didn't mean it like that—"

"I'm messing with you. I appreciate you stopping by to give me a heart attack. I can't imagine any woman turning down a chance to eat lunch with you," I teased.

"I can think of one."

I leaned forward with interest. "Do tell."

As he faced the street, I watched the life drain from his features. A silent pain burrowed within him—one I recognized. A familiar friend of mine.

Finally he spoke, the words curt and cruel. "My ex. A real bitch. Broke me twice, as if the first time wasn't enough."

"I'm sorry." It was a whisper, and I wasn't sure he even heard me until he turned to me.

"Thanks. It's in the past, but I still feel it, you know? I was so blind back then—thought it was love. She really had my heart in a chokehold."

"How far in the past?" I hoped my question wasn't too invasive, but I watched his shoulders relax from having someone to unburden himself to.

"We were high school sweethearts. She was the honor roll student, I was the C-average athlete. A totally mismatched pair. Julie was way out of my league. Hell, when I asked her out on a date she thought it was an April Fool's joke ... but she said yes. Then one day she leaves for Florida to live with her dad and never contacts me after that. By the time she came back, I was starting college, but I hadn't gotten over her. I guess love will make you do stupid things."

"You dated again in college?"

"Worse. By a twist of fate we ended up engaged. That's when she cheated on me. Had to gouge the knife a little deeper just in case I hadn't been scarred enough."

His jaw clenched at the recollection. The heat of his anger climbed up his neck. Silent, I regretted slicing open his wound. I was all too familiar with hidden wounds. The uncomfortable lull passed and he continued, more matter-of-fact now.

"We were inseparable, moved to Buffalo together. I was miserable. It was all too fast-paced for me. A demanding job I hated, constant travel, knee-deep in meetings. The more I worked, the more distant we grew. We started to get on each other's nerves. Her domineering side reared its ugly head. She found fault with everything I did or didn't do, especially when it came to our finances.

"Finally I couldn't take it anymore. Corny as it sounds, I was homesick for boring old Westfield. What's that old saying? It ain't much, but it's home. Apparently I was too late. While I was killing myself at that job, she was stepping out on me. I caught her on a date with some guy and decided then and there to walk away."

I imagined Marc gazing through a frosty window, watching his fiancée cuddled in the arms of another man, his breath clouding the glass. The image shattered into tiny pieces as I heard my name.

"Haley, I'm sorry for dragging you through my shit. Even though I'm over it, I still wish I could have said something. Had the last word. I don't know. Maybe it's best I didn't."

"You never confronted her about it?"

"Nope. I never called her, and she never called me after that night. It was like nothing had ever happened between us, like nothing ever was real. Like it was all a dream ... or a nightmare."

I hadn't noticed the chill until now. Wind nipped at my cheeks, and I felt my fingers start to tingle. The gray-blue sky darkened as the afternoon slipped by.

"We all make mistakes. But that doesn't mean something better isn't around the corner."

"Do you ever wonder if nothing you feel is real? Like you're stuck playing someone else's game?"

The question both alarmed me and aroused my compassion. Because I understood exactly what he meant. I wanted to comfort him, show him that not all women were bitches. Yes, his ex had been one big ugly mistake. But I could make him forget it.

Chapter 14

I sensed it the moment I stepped into my living room. Dread. Across the polished hardwood floors, the lavender-scented space, the red flicker warned me.

Four messages on my answering machine. I never got four messages. I never got one message.

Before pressing the button to listen, I already knew it was Mom. She was the only person who called. Shelly and I didn't talk outside of work. I wondered why Mom would have rung while she knew I wasn't home, but Mom didn't always follow logic. Sometimes her mind was a knotted ball of yarn I couldn't unravel. Best just to toss it aside than spend hours picking it apart, only to end up frustrated.

The first message wished me a happy birthday. The second reiterated our plans for dinner. The third one listed the movies showing at the Spotlight Cinema. And the fourth one just rambled, her words strung together like Christmas lights. Though she hadn't specifically mentioned the letter, her voice betrayed the warning tone of an overprotective mother. I recognized it well. It was probably why I was still single.

I didn't want this conversation hanging over me, so I dialed her back, ready to argue.

"Hello?" Mom answered on the first ring, singsongy sweet.

"It's me. I got your messages."

"I just wanted to make sure we're on for your birthday dinner tonight. That's all."

"I know you didn't leave me four messages about my birthday dinner. So what's bugging you? Just tell me."

Flat silence. Then finally, "Haley, honey, we need to talk. In person. This isn't a conversation for the telephone. Can you come over and we can talk in the car on the way to Erie?"

"I'm guessing you read the letter I dropped," I said.

Her sigh confirmed my suspicions. Confession time.

"Yes, I did. And it's worrisome. I think you know why."

"No, I don't know why. Some people would call this romantic."

"This isn't about romance. It's about secrets."

My grip tightened on the receiver. I fought the urge to slam it down on the cradle. "Mom, you invaded my privacy and now you want to lecture me about secrets? Don't you have enough of your own to worry about?"

"Honey—" She fumbled for an answer, but we both knew there was none. "That's not what I'm trying to do. I'm just trying to protect you."

"You need to stop making a big deal about this. They're nice letters from a nice guy."

"A nice guy? Oh, Hale, you know better. And this *is* a big deal! I know I promised to butt out, but after everything that you've been through, don't you think it's time you opened your eyes to what this is really about?"

Here they come, Mom's trademark doomsday warnings. "And what's it about, Mom? Go ahead and tell me."

"It's about you. And your need to feel fulfilled. But this isn't the way to do it."

"Isn't that what life is all about? Fulfillment? Love? Relationships?"

"Real relationships, Hale, not like this. And of course I want you to be fulfilled and happy, but this isn't it. I understand having a secret admirer satisfies your desire to be wanted and loved, the same as any girl, but some of the things he wrote ... well, they're just plain *creepy*."

"They may seem creepy to you, but to me ... it's like somebody finally *gets* me."

"But your past, Hale—you can't ignore that."

And there it was. The *painful past* card. Her default move when I wouldn't budge. To Mom, I was damaged goods, too broken to glue back together.

"I'm not going down this road with you again. Let the dead rest in peace."

"That's exactly the problem—they'll never rest in peace! I know they haunt you, just like they haunt me." The apocalyptic overtones sent a shiver up my spine.

"Are you referring to Jake?" Jake, my best friend. Jake, who loved me. Jake, who killed himself. For me. Because of me. "Mom, that was forever ago."

"Yes, I'm talking about Jake, but also about ... well, *you*."

It slapped me across the face, the accusation in that one word: *you*. Stinging, spreading its toxic venom, poisoning my body with the memory all over again. As if it was my fault what happened with Jake. As if I tied the bungee cord around his neck, tightened the knot, dropped him from the hayloft, his body dangling from the oak beam in my father's barn.

"Mom, how can you blame me for that? We were teenagers. I didn't know he would do that."

"I'm not blaming you, honey, but we both know that there were a lot of other issues surrounding that situation and I don't want to see you go through that again. I think you've been through enough, don't you?"

For once I had a chance at a happily ever after—or at least a happily ever now—but the past kept spilling out of the box I hid it in. No matter how deep I shoved that box of pain under the bed, the contents always managed to scatter across my life.

"Mom, I have to move on with my life, and I'm not going to live in the shadow of what happened anymore. It's time to let go."

"How do you outrun a ghost that's chasing you?" Her voice was a whisper against dead air.

The line clicked. I had no answer. Some secrets I would never outrun.

Chapter 15
Marc

If Friday was any indication of how hectic Marc's weekend would be, he would have rather skipped straight ahead to Monday. His day had been a blur of house calls, playing catch-up on client billing, and running long delayed errands.

To end the day on a high note, Campbell's soup with an extra buttery grilled cheese sandwich for dinner. Nothing like the metallic taste of canned tomato soup to get the taste buds excited. But it didn't bother him tonight, because something—rather, someone—bothered him much more. A poking thought that tunneled deeper into his brain, until he was forced to entertain it.

One phone call. That was all it took for her to twist him around her finger, to seduce him with her magic. There she was, plastered on the wall of his mind. No matter how much he tried to paint over her face, her Mona Lisa eyes watched him.

He had given himself enough time to weigh the pros and cons of getting back into the dating arena. If he ever wanted his heart whole again, he'd need to take a chance. On himself, on her, on love.

If Marc were to be completely honest with himself, he wanted to see her, hold her, kiss her, love her. It was what he always imagined finding. No matter how detached and macho men acted, they wanted the same thing women wanted: Someone who completed them. Someone to drive away the loneliness.

As he sat at his dining room table, he watched the climax of yet another incomparable sunset through the wall-sized picture window—deep blues mingled with yellows, highlighting billowing clouds. He hadn't stopped thinking about her since he first laid eyes on her. When she called him out of the blue, he had no idea his life would be changed from that moment on. It was quite unexpected, because he had forgotten what being in love felt like. The swarm of butterflies in his stomach. Smiling for no reason. Saying her name out loud just to savor the sound of it. She was a fireworks show against his empty sky.

When he closed his eyes, he saw her. Still smelled the sweet scent of her hair. Couldn't stop himself from replaying her impish grin over and over in his head. He knew her inside and out. How, he didn't quite know. He just did.

He'd driven past her house more often than he cared to admit. Already he'd made four phones calls to her house, each time hanging up before the first ring. Was he being too presumptuous by calling so soon? Time was subjective when feelings were involved. Twenty-four hours felt like twenty-four days. And what would he say when she picked up? With her, cool-calm-and-collected Marc was reduced to a bumbling ball of nerves. While he hated being so vulnerable, he couldn't resist the urge. The obsession. It overpowered his weak will.

Without assurance that she shared the same feelings toward him, he needed to see where she stood without asking as much. Nothing obvious. Just a way to test the waters. Not that understanding women was ever an easy feat.

Darkness settled in, and the clouds parted, opening the sky to millions of stars twinkling in all their glory. A shooting star streaked across the blackness, leaving tiny sparkles in its wake. The cold air began to shroud his home. Close by, Marc heard the lonely hooting of an owl. He counted the seconds until, much deeper in the surrounding forest, he heard the answering call of its mate. Marc smiled.

A thought raided him fully shaped and apparent. He needed to see her again. But how? And where?

And if it didn't go as planned? Well, Marc wouldn't end up the one hurt. Of that he was certain.

Chapter 16

It still hurts. Years later, and the memories still slice through me like a box cutter. Sometimes I feel like I've taken a tenderizer to my heart. Maybe one day it won't hurt so bad. Or maybe I don't deserve that freedom.

And now I'm supposed to celebrate. Life's got a cruel way of.

I got a birthday card from my admirer this morning. And red roses, propped up against the mailbox. The flower of love. I'm smitten and I don't even know with certainty who I'm smitten with. How pathetic am I? I spent more time pining over my flowers than I spent on my assignment for the screenplay class I'm taking—actually sitting in at this very moment. I'm supposed to be working on a script, but I can't stop thinking about who is behind the letters. He's destroying me. Shattering my focus, invading my dreams, stealing my heart. I want to steel my resolve against his thieving words, but I'm addicted.

He's a blank canvas giving me freedom to paint him with any color. Right now, he's who I want him to be. But what happens when I find out who's behind the beautiful words and poetic musings. That's what scares me. He might not be who I want him to be.

What if he's a monster hiding behind his pen? A wolf in sheep's clothing, hungry for blood?

"Haley, have you finished yet?" From behind his desk Allen's voice broke my concentration, making me abruptly aware that everyone else had already left the classroom.

"Oh, I'm sorry. I was lost in my head." Hastily closing my journal, I shoved it in my bag.

"It happens to the best of us. Mind if I take a peek?"

"It's not ready yet." At the rate I was going, it might never be ready. I hefted my bag over my shoulder.

"Well, time's a-ticking. Have you given any thought to my offer to work with you on it?"

In fact, I had. The temptation to work one-on-one with him outweighed the fear of what might be expected of me in return. I didn't know what Allen's help would cost me, but everything had a price.

Pieces of last night's conversation with my mother had echoed in my mind all night, keeping me awake until a sleep-aid-painkiller concoction knocked me out. She had that effect on me—a constant pain in my ass *and* head.

"My screenplay class teacher offered to tutor me. Do you think I should?" I had asked her between bites of fried chicken and homemade biscuits.

"Tutor you—alone? That doesn't sound wise, dear. What if he takes advantage of you?"

"Advantage of me how? He's a professional. I'm not the only one he's offered to tutor." It was a lie the moment it left my lips, but worth it if it shut her up.

"I Googled him, Hale. You know his wife is missing? He's currently under investigation. Did you know that?" I eyed her skeptically. "Yes, I know how to Google. I'm not *that* old." Her hand had rested on mine, but I pulled away.

"Seriously, you Googled my professor? That's a new low, even for you."

"Apparently someone has to. The man may have murdered his wife and here you're talking about private tutoring with him. Meanwhile you think it's perfectly all right for some stalker to send you strange letters. What's happened to you, Haley? Don't you know what happens when you play with fire?"

The echo had drummed against my skull all night, was still drumming. Mysterious letters from an anonymous admirer. Private tutoring with a man who may or may not have killed his wife. A crush on a man I hardly knew. Maybe I was playing with fire. But it felt damn invigorating.

I had a shot at creating something amazing, a dream growing bones and sinew. If I said no because of a fear of getting burned, I'd stay a nobody stuck in a nothing town.

Tons of people slept their way to the top. I wasn't about to do that, but was it so bad if I harmlessly flirted a little to boost an old man's ego to get ahead? Allen would pitch the best final project to a producer colleague in Hollywood. A huge break, a once-in-a-lifetime opportunity. Hollywood, here I come! If only my father could see how close I was. He'd be proud ... wouldn't he?

But there was no denying there was something strange and unsettling about Allen Michaels. The media rumors, his odd mannerisms, his egotism. But there was something else. Something deeper, darker, more villainous I couldn't quite put my finger on ...

"Earth to Haley!" Allen's voice. "I asked you if you'd thought about my tutoring offer."

"What? Oh, yeah. I've thought about it ..."

"And?"

I was surprised to hear myself say, "I would be honored to be tutored by you."

To get the ball rolling, we made dinner plans for that evening, despite the shitty weather. I'd recommended a place sure to be packed with patrons, a popular diner on the corner of Main Street and Holt. Vine City Restaurant boasted several huge oak tables, wide enough for us to work while eating from oversized serving plates full of fish and a double helping of fries—one of my personal favorites. Locals joked that the building was so bound to its history that one could still hear the clink of milk bottles that once filled the rooms of this former dairy.

I pushed through the heavy exit door that led out into the college campus parking lot. The northern February weather was as bitter as ever. As I rushed to my car, battling fierce wind, I glanced up and noticed ominous storm clouds scudding across the sky and quickened my pace to a run. Angry clouds hovered overhead, ready to throw icy darts. I hoped to make it home before sleet carpeted the streets.

Once inside the calm of my car, I revved the engine and blasted the defroster. Over the past couple of hours a glaze of ice had encrusted all the windows. Reluctant to get out again to scrape them, I sat and waited for the ice to melt, scrolling through radio stations for anything without commercials.

After tossing my bag in the backseat, a sudden rattle startled me. A figure blurred by the icy haze pried at my door. When a fist smacked against the window, I frantically pushed the lock down, thankful that my car door had a knack for sticking during winter's hostile temperatures. The person was screaming, but the roar of the defroster muted the voice.

By the time I cranked the lukewarm heat down a couple of notches to a low hum, I could make out my name.

"Allen!" I said, rolling down the window partway. "You scared me half to death."

"I'm sorry. I thought you might be having car trouble so I figured I'd check on you."

"No, I'm just too lazy to scrape my windows. I'm fine, thanks."

"Hey, I brought something to class for you but forgot to give it to you earlier." He pushed a rumpled brown paper bag toward me through the small opening in the window. I hesitantly accepted it and looked up at him questioningly.

"Go ahead," he prodded, "open it."

Opening the bag, I pulled out a book. A dark hooded figure aiming a gun at the reader stared back at me from the cover.

"What is this?"

"It's my autobiography. I thought you might like a copy."

A shiver crept up my spine as cold, lifeless blue eyes leapt off the book jacket.

"This is you?"

"In a former life, yes."

"Is that a real gun?"

"Yeah, but don't ask if I used it. Just read the book."

I arched an eyebrow, realizing I knew so little about this man, really. This cover picture depicted a menacing killer, not a professional screenplay writer. Who was he really?

"Thank you very much, Allen," I finally sputtered, at a loss for any other words. I was terrified to find out what exactly the book would reveal about the person I'd be dining with this evening.

A mesh of slush and rain fell in heavy drops now, slipping through the crack in my window.

"Well, we'd both better get home before the roads get worse," he said. "I'll see you at seven o'clock." His coat flapped behind him as he ran into the icy miasma.

"See you then."

After Allen disappeared from sight, I pulled the book out once again and stared at it, letting its alarming picture burn itself into my mind. While Allen's past was apparently an open book, his secrets were well hidden.

Chapter 17
Allen

When Allen got back to his one-room rental, he searched through his tiny yet meticulously organized closet looking for the perfect attire. Deciding on a plaid Brooks Brothers brushed oxford sports shirt and a pair of 501 Levi's, he carefully laid the clothes out on his bed. He was pleased with himself: offering tutoring sessions to score a dinner date with Haley.

So far everything between them remained cordial but distant. He had hoped they'd be more personal by now, but time hadn't permitted it just yet. With not nearly enough time to woo her into following him to Los Angeles, he suspected that a career opportunity of a lifetime would do the trick. It didn't matter that none of it was real. An illusionist dealt in sleight of hand, of which he was the master.

All Allen knew was that he had to have her—no matter what it cost.

At first it was purely physical attraction, but now he was ready to get to know this beautiful creature on a deeper level. Every day since he first laid eyes on her heading into Westfield Main Diner, a throwback to the 1950's soda shop, Allen sweetly surrendered to visions of Haley. Everything she did and said reinforced one thing in his mind: she was perfect. Perfect for a broken man like himself.

She would be an ideal match—genuine, kind, and obviously enamored of his success and glamorous lifestyle. When she bounced into his classroom, her step was full of life. Yet she was submissively shy, too. Quiet, the type to stay out of his limelight, and enough of a follower to let him do the leading. Unlike his attention-starved ex who couldn't resist competing for all the glory, Haley was exactly what he had been looking for: passive yet passionate. And at this stage in his life, he needed a zealous counterpart to carry on his work. The way she hung on his every word made it clear that she would happily carry out that task. She was the one.

Allen was determined to know every little thing about her—from her morning routine to her bedtime habits—and had gone on numerous reconnaissance missions, always parking his car a discreet distance down the street and "passing by" under the pretense of being out for a stroll. He'd been careful to wear a scarf and hat, though even those couldn't withstand the glacial climate, and was not apt to draw anyone's scrutiny.

As he observed Haley, the little details about her fascinated him. Like how she was perpetually fifteen minutes late to everything. She always ate on the run, except for dinner when she'd usually eat at her mother's house. She went to bed well after midnight, her schedule like clockwork.

Eventually he would reveal in person how he felt, in hopes that she would reciprocate the emotional attachment brewing inside him. Surprisingly, he wasn't afraid that she would reject him. And if he wrong about her? Well, he was never wrong.

Examining himself in the full-length cheval mirror that, like everything else in Mrs. Ellsworth's B&B, was a family heirloom, he pulled at the skin on his face. He had aged significantly in the past year, appearing much older than he actually was. Stress would do that to a person. But that part of his life was over now. His past was far behind him. How quickly a little joy could heal past wounds. Watching Haley develop her creative and artistic abilities could vicariously grant him a whole new life. Energy, excitement, pleasure—all of life was his oyster and Haley was his pearl.

It was as he met his own stare in the mirror when he had an epiphany: Haley was the reason he left Los Angeles, and the last few dark weeks, behind. She was the reason he taught that class. All this was finally clear to him. He hadn't known it before now, and she would find out soon: they were meant to be. Only one thing stood between them—his little secret.

With a couple hours to kill, Allen plopped onto his bed and flicked off his bedside lamp. Perhaps a little meditation would settle his nerves. He folded his arms under his head and stared up at the darkened ceiling, filling his imagination with visions of Haley. He wasn't worried about sweeping her off her feet. Girls like Haley, simple small-town girls, appreciated confident, successful men like him. If only he could find the perfect way to show her how much he adored her.

He saw her hunger, her appetite for life. That had been him at one point in his life, but that was so long ago. The artificiality of Hollywood sucked the life out of everybody eventually. Yet Haley reminded him of what it felt like back in the beginning, and he would do anything to win her, to offer her the world. And he would follow through in due time. But time was growing short.

Tonight the plan would begin.

Chapter 18

I was fascinated yet afraid.

I couldn't understand why Allen had given me a copy of his book, until I'd devoured my way through it that afternoon. It left me drunk on a cocktail of curiosity and fear. After all, he chronicled a childhood of abuse and neglect, his rise to power, then ended with the disappearance of his hateful stepfather one rainy, summer night.

Was Allen behind it and this his passive-aggressive confession? I would never know, would I? Maybe there were no lines to read through. Or maybe there were.

What do you say to a man who can make people disappear, that same man you've agreed to meet alone for dinner?

I was still working that out.

I arrived at Vine City Restaurant a few minutes after seven o'clock. My boots left a trail of gray slush all the way from the front entrance to the table where Allen sat waiting.

"You made it." Allen stood and greeted me, arms open in an expectant hug.

I allowed him a quick half-hug then sat down, wanting as much space as possible between us.

"Have you been waiting long?" I felt like my voice boomed against the relative quiet. I noted the small number of patrons for a Saturday evening, probably because of the storm and black ice.

"Just a few minutes."

Our waitress hustled to fetch two glasses of water with lemon after dropping off our menus.

"I've been wanting to talk to you about the final project, see where you're at with your screenplay. I really would love for you to be considered for that trip to Hollywood, Haley, if you're serious about being a screenwriter. Are you?" His eyes bore into me.

I nodded. "Of course."

"Are you willing to do anything to get to the top?"

What kind of question was that? "Anything? I don't know about *anything* ... but working hard, yes."

His question shot an awkward sensation all through me; I had to look away. A family of four sat in the center of the restaurant, their two children gabbing loudly, while an elderly couple in the corner held hands from across the table. I caught Allen's glance over at the couple and the tiniest smile cracked his typically somber appearance.

The lighting bathed his pallid skin in a harsh white, accentuating the bags under his eyes and the deep furrows etched across his forehead. For the first time I noticed his marionette lines and the jowliness of his jawline. But oddly, he looked less haggard than when I first met him. Perhaps it was his eyes; they didn't look so vacant anymore.

"Hard work, yes, that's a given. I'm talking about stretching yourself, pushing your limits, seeing what you're capable of." He raised a blond eyebrow as he leaned in.

If only he knew just what I was capable of, it would scare him. I scared myself sometimes.

"I understand, and I'm willing to push myself. Whatever it takes."

And I meant it.

"Great. Let's see what you've got." Allen slapped the table twice.

Pulling my bag to my side, I rifled through the papers and retrieved a yellow legal pad along with my typed half-written screenplay.

"Okay, here's my first draft." I handed the paperclipped screenplay to him.

As his eyes darted over the pages, I anxiously tapped a nail against the notepad, waiting for him to finish.

"Hmm ..." he grunted. "A romance story. Nice. But the main male character—Marc—I'm not sure I like him. Italian, gorgeous—he sounds a little ordinary if you ask me, Haley."

"I guess he is ordinary. An everyday relatable love interest."

Allen's upheld index finger shushed me.

"Stop. Before you say anything more, let me ask you something. Do you remember at our first class when I asked everyone to write about why they believed they had what it takes to be successful in the movie industry?"

I thought back to that assignment ... that endless night of self-realization. The night I reflected on my life— my yesterdays, todays, and tomorrows—and how writing gave me meaning and purpose through all those years. That night I had decided I was all in, even at the loss of love. I'd seen what love did to my mother, to Jake, to me. Writing was safer, a fabulous career was safer. It was all I had, and I had determined that night to fight for it. That's what I had written.

"Yes, I remember."

"I recall what you wrote too. Writing is everything to you. When you create a script, you know the characters personally and experience the action and envision the scenes in your mind. You said that your screenplay is a part of you. I was inspired by that, Haley. And I'm inspired by your work. But this meeting isn't about the details of your final project. It's about the bigger picture."

I folded my hands on my lap, wondering where he was going with this.

"Would you sacrifice your life as you know it for this dream?"

It was the million-dollar question. When it came down to it, would I throw away everything in pursuit of fame and fortune? Was success worth the cost of everything else— Mom, my comfortable job ... Marc? I had never considered the ultimatum; no one had ever asked me to choose between my dream and my reality. If I pursued this career head-on, any possible chance with Marc would be left in the dust. Or could I have it all?

Across from me sat an honest-to-goodness Hollywood producer who personified a fantasy I had envisioned since youth. Allen invited me into his world—a clique so small only the best could get in and only by invitation. Me, a small-town no-name having dinner with destiny. It all seemed so surreal, so ... impossible. Was I, a country girl, really worthy of standing in this man's shadow? Or the bigger question, was he not everything he proclaimed to be?

"Yes," I decided right then and there. "I would sacrifice everything for this. It's what I've always wanted, and I couldn't throw away this opportunity."

My voice sounded so tiny, choked with anxiety and anticipation. Was I being honest with him—or with myself? Could I really give up a chance with Marc for the sake of a fantasy? There was only one way to find out.

Chapter 19
Allen

Writing is both mask and unveiling. The quote by E. B. White was one Allen lived by, though he preferred to remain masked.

Words had always been his vice, no matter how dangerous. Once they're out in the open, there's no taking them back. They can be the death of a man like Allen.

He wanted to tell Haley everything in his heart. He wanted to tell her what he was running from, what he wanted to run to. But it would be too much. Her aloofness told him she wasn't ready to hear his secrets or meet his demons. He needed to build her trust first and ensure she'd be willing to embrace everything he had to offer, including the shadows his past lived in. Unspoken words ached to let loose; he needed to say it all out loud, just to cool the emotional furnace burning deep inside of him. He knew he would feel better after unveiling every part to her. But instead he tightened his lips. Too soon. As quickly as he was prepared to tear down his wall, he built it back up, brick by brick, secret by secret.

Allen wasn't sure where to go from here. As he examined Haley's face, her intense green eyes saw through his mask. Her chin perched on her hands, resting comfortably as he talked. It was magnificent being alone with her. Better than he imagined it would be. He pictured leaning over and kissing her, her lips soft against his, allowing himself to be carried away in its promise of bliss. It was so real that he could almost taste her.

"Haley, there's something I want to tell you."

Tell her the truth. Unleash the beast. But logic warned him otherwise: if he told her, she'd run.

"Sure, what's up?"

Damn logic to hell. Time was growing too short to wait.

"It's not about class. It's something personal. And the only reason I want to tell you is because I feel like our friendship is starting to develop and, well, friends share things about themselves, right?" He'd never had any real friends, and certainly not in the dog-eat-dog movie industry. He'd lived a lonely, solitary existence ever since things with his wife began to unravel. A bone-jarring shiver ripped through him as he recalled the last time he'd seen Susan Michaels—alive.

"Friends, yeah." There was a sharp edge to her voice.

"As you know, I'm in the middle of a messy divorce. Anyway, my soon-to-be ex-wife took our breakup much harder than I did. She was really disturbed over it, told me she'd kill herself if I didn't take her back."

Lies. All lies. Susan had left without so much as a backward glance. But it sounded believable.

Haley gasped. "I'm so sorry."

He detected sympathy, possibly genuine, though he could never decipher emotions, real or fake. A touch drew his attention, her hand cupping his, stroking his knuckles tenderly. The smooth flesh of her fingertips delivered tremors to his core. He felt an erection stirring in his pants—the first woody he'd had in years without the aid of Viagra. He fought the strong urge to grin in triumph.

"There's more," he added. "After her suicide threat, I knew that things would escalate, so I was forced to make a decision. A decision no husband should ever have to face—"

"Can I take your order?" A ponytailed server stood over them, leaning her hip into the edge of the table with pen and pad ready. Allen sighed at the intrusion, rethinking his confession. He had shared enough for one day. He'd revisit the conversation when they were alone ... when he knew he could trust her.

They both placed their orders; Haley ordered the fish and chips, and Allen selected a chicken sandwich. Making a mental note of Haley's preferences, he began documenting in his mind the things he knew about Haley. And everything about her, so far, was perfect.

A perfect replacement for Susan.

Chapter 20
Marc

Marc waited in his F-150 while it idled, gaze fixed on the entrance. He had gotten there early, as usual. "Fashionably late" wasn't part of his vocabulary. Only one person mattered right now, and she hadn't yet arrived.

He watched as Westfield's movers and shakers hustled inside the Episcopal church from the cold; they were probably milling about inside, chatting in the lobby while waiting for the town meeting to commence. With Sunday's after-service coffee hour cleaned up by now, Marc anticipated a packed recreation room, with a couple hundred townsfolk present. Knowing that her mother was a councilperson on the town board, he hoped she would have been dragged along for the fun. Now if only he could swallow the lump that lodged in his throat every time he thought of seeing her again.

As flurries fell from a dismal sky, Marc grumbled at the clouds to go the hell away. He was tired of the gloom and needed a burst of sunshine to energize him. Relying on less than four hours of sleep, he felt like the walking dead, looked it too, with his disheveled hair that refused to lay flat. While he fussed with it in front of his bathroom mirror earlier that day, like a self-conscious teenager, he rehearsed what he would say when he saw her today. God willing she showed.

A simple *hey, it's great to see you,* sounded appropriate enough to start.

What are you doing here? she would probably ask.

His smooth reply would go something like, *I've always had an interest in town politics and like to get involved whenever possible.* Then she'd be impressed with his responsible citizenship and invite him to sit with her. She would gladly accept. Emboldened, he would ask her to lunch afterward. She'd graciously agree and the rest would be easy as he wooed her with his natural charm.

Or it could all fall apart before it even began.

He wouldn't let that happen, though. Not this time.

Mustering his courage, Marc headed into St. Peter's Episcopal Church ten minutes before the town meeting was supposed to start. He pulled open the heavy wooden doors, where greeters guided him down the hallway. Self-consciously reaching up to smooth the back of his amply-gelled chestnut hair, he could feel the cowlick sticking straight up. Muttering an oath under his breath, then apologizing to God for swearing in church, he shuffled awkwardly into the lobby area waiting to see a familiar face.

St. Peter's origins dated back to the 1830s. The ornate interior detail had survived the ages in remarkable condition, down to the baroque patterns on the pews. It was an aspect of the building that Marc appreciated more than most, being a craftsman hobbyist. Stained glass windows in vibrant colors lined the sanctuary walls, picturing the various aspects of Jesus Christ's life, death, and resurrection. The thorns, the pierced hands, the vivid scenes—visitors came from far and wide to admire the artisan's handiwork.

For a fleeting moment Marc considered how he had felt so dead and broken for so long, but now it seemed like he was given a second chance at life, at love. Lost in thought, a traffic jam of people built up behind him.

A sharp "ahem" snapped Marc back to the present. He followed the crowd past the sanctuary entrance toward the recreation hall, where a friendly old lady passed out meeting agendas. He passed through clusters of individuals chatting and exchanging small talk. Searching her out among the crowds, he plastered himself against a wall, pretending to be reading the agenda.

A knot of women were stuck to the wall across from him like wads of old chewing gum. He recognized several of them—Mrs. Miller. Mrs. Montgomery. Mrs. Ellsworth. Mrs. Carter. Hiding his face behind the agenda, he had hoped she'd be with her mom, but she wasn't. She was probably close by, though.

It wasn't more than a couple of seconds later when she walked in. It was as if the sunlight chose at that very moment to peek out from behind the clouds and shine brilliantly on her, making her appear more radiant than he remembered. Of course, it could have been his sleep-deprived imagination, but damn, did she look good. Catching his breath, he needed to make sure she saw him. Stepping away from the wall, he walked directly into her path.

Just then, a bump from behind knocked him into a small table. Agendas went flying. Marc bent down to collect them, knocking skulls with someone next to him.

"Shit," he said, massaging his stinging scalp.

"Language, young man," he heard a familiar voice say.

He was about to apologize, until he saw who it was.

"Hey there, fancy meeting you here," he said with mock surprise to camouflage the truth that he'd been obsessively watching for her.

"Marc, I had no idea you'd be here today. Do you always come to these meetings, or did I just get lucky?" She flashed a red-lipped smile that made gelatin out of his legs.

Damned if he could remember the lines he had practiced. "I come for the cookies." It had flowed so much easier when he was talking to his reflection, but at least he scored a laugh.

"I'm glad we ran into each other. I've been meaning to call you." Her hand rested on his shoulder.

Dumbfounded, he still clutched the pile of papers while a small huddle of attendees waited awkwardly for him to pass the agendas out. Realizing they thought he was one of the ushers, he quickly handed out a couple sheets and put the rest back on the table. What had she just said?

"Oh, yeah, um, me too. I mean, I was going to call you too."

"Really? I find that hard to believe."

"I know how to pick up a phone."

"But do you know how to dial? That's the key," she said with a wink.

"I could always learn. Where are you sitting? Want company?"

She winced. "My mom is saving me a seat, so I really should sit with her."

An intercom announced that they had two minutes before the meeting started.

"Looks like it's time to head in," she said. "I'll talk to you later?"

"If I figure out that whole dialing thing."

With a half-wave they headed in different directions— her to her seat, him to the restroom. The single stall was occupied, so Marc waited by the lone sink staring himself down in the mirror. After splashing water on his face, he mumbled expletives to himself for not closing the deal. One lunch—that was all he needed to ask for. What the hell was he doing? Playing with fire always got him burned.

The flush behind the partition spurred him to exit. The last thing he wanted was to be spotted talking crazily to himself. He debated whether he should abandon the meeting but knew she would notice if he went AWOL. Besides, maybe he'd get a chance to rectify things and get that lunch date after all.

He entered the recreation hall and headed toward a section of empty folding chairs in the back corner. The meeting had already begun, so he plopped into the nearest seat and pretended to pay attention while searching her out. There she was, seated to his left. From the corner of his eye he held fast to her, oblivious to his gaze.

The meeting felt like an endless torture of boredom as Marc awaited the closing remarks. Small interruptions stole his focus on several occasions, thank God—Mrs. Ellsworth's snoring, Jenny DeMarco's red-faced crying baby, George Turner's absurd hairpiece. The man was completely bald, and anything would have looked better than the furry monstrosity perched atop his head like a roadkill squirrel, but no one ever said anything to the ninety-two-year-old, figuring he'd earned the right to look as ridiculous as he pleased, checkered pants and all. Marc wondered if he'd someday be as confident in his fashion senselessness at that age.

When the moderator dismissed the meeting, Marc searched the empty seat where she had been sitting. Had she snuck out when he wasn't looking? And why so quickly? Was she intentionally avoiding him? The sea of bodies poured out the back entrance, but he couldn't find her among them. At this point there was nothing to do but shrug it off and go home.

As quickly as his hopes had risen, she struck them down.

Chapter 21

I kept a close eye on Marc while the meeting concluded, counting down the minutes until it was over.

I remembered being a kid dragged to these dull meetings, whining and fussing from the time we left our house until the moment it ended. But as an adult I was held to a higher standard, so I bit my tongue to appease Mom for the two grueling hours they discussed the same issues over and over: upcoming town events, new members of the council, assigning various duties for the ICE Festival, blah blah blah. The only saving grace was that Marc showed up.

As the meeting came to a close, I slipped out of my chair, stepping on a pair of feet and someone's purse on my way out of the aisle, hoping to avoid the mad rush of people leaving. It was late afternoon by the time the meeting adjourned, and a chatter of lunch invitations filled the large room. Sliding through the rows of chairs until I found him, he faced the other direction, neck craned. I reached over and gently grabbed his elbow.

"Hey, you. Looking for someone?"

Marc spun around, mouth agape in a surprised O. "Hey there. What'd you think of the meeting?"

"I wasn't paying attention. I was too distracted by George's hair."

He laughed. "Should I be jealous?"

"Yeah, women love men with bad toupees. Very sexy."

Again, that deep laugh I could listen to all day.

"I heard them call your name for the ICE Festival committee," he said.

"Yeah, I'm taking pictures of it for the local paper. You going?" I mentally crossed my fingers for a yes.

"I go on opening night—when they have the biggest bonfire." He twirled an imaginary mustache. "I guess there's a bit of pyromaniac in me."

Now it was her turn to laugh. So he would be at the ICE Festival. Now *that* was good information to know. "Maybe I'll see you there."

Maybe? Wild horses couldn't keep me away. Why was I being so cagey when I felt like I was walking on air when I was around him? The stupid things we do when we're in love ... or something like it.

The Ice Castle Extravaganza—popularly known as the ICE Festival—was held annually over Presidents Day weekend in Mayville, the seat of Chautauqua County. The family-friendly event offered wintry activities to suit every taste, ranging from snowman-building and snowball-throwing contests, to a gigantic snow slide and a fiercely-contested broomball tournament. More leisurely activities were on hand as well, such as carriage rides, a petting zoo and pony rides for the kiddies, and of course, ice-skating on the lake.

A gargantuan ice castle—fifty feet long, twelve feet high—was the Festival's focal point. Volunteers typically spent two weeks constructing the castle, made from blocks of ice cut from Chautauqua Lake. On closing night patrons thrilled to fireworks, a bonfire, and the lighting of the ice castle. To quote a certain band of mop-topped Liverpudlians: a splendid time is guaranteed for all.

The ICE Festival was exactly what it sounded like—an event highlighting ice decorations and all things winter, things I could easily do without. Sculptors chiseled out large blocks of ice from nearby Lake Chautauqua to create life-sized structures that were placed strategically off the shore of the frozen lake. Since Lake Chautauqua wasn't nearly the size of Lake Erie, early February temperature lows guaranteed parts of it would be frozen enough for the ice sculptors to cut blocks of ice.

Chautauqua was a popular summertime vacation destination. Rustic bed and breakfasts lined with rocking chair porches, boating excursions, stately historical homes, and the ferry were just a few of the attractions that the picturesque village offered to tourists. Chautauqua was virtually empty this time of year, however, as the snowbirds migrated south for the winter. For six months out of the year Chautauqua resembled a wintry ghost town, but during the ICE Festival it came back to life.

As the ushers started to nudge everyone out of the hall, it was now or never. "You got lunch plans? My treat. I never got to thank you for your free services the other day."

"You know, that sounds nice, thanks. Consider us even, then," Marc said. "Got a preference?"

As I flipped through the limited romantic options in town, Mom beckoned me with wildly waving arms across the room. I had an idea—a good one or not, I wasn't yet sure.

"Would you want to join my mom and me at her house? I'm sure she'd love to have you over. And she's a great cook."

While being alone with Marc was obviously my preference, if anyone could charm a man into the family, it was Mom. Gabrielle was irresistible in every sense of the word—no one could tell her no. When she hosted meals, strangers became family, if only for the afternoon. And, in her capacity as a town councilperson, she had an uncanny knack for talking favors out of anyone; before you knew it, you had volunteered to de-litter the town square and repaint the gazebo. It was that same charisma that drew people to her, and if anyone could win Marc over, it was Mom.

"How can I say no to home cooking?" His palm grazed my lower back, guiding me along the stream of people leaving. The pressure of his fingers against my shirt shot a tingle up my spine.

"I'll warn you now—my mom will probably pull out the old picture albums of me as a kid. If you have a heart, you're not allowed to tease me about them."

"So you're saying I could find some good blackmail-worthy material in those albums?" He winked. I melted.

"I'm saying if you dare make one joke about my fifth-grade bowl cut, huge glasses, and braces, you better sleep with one eye open, mister. Because you will not live to tell about it."

His laugh was the most amazing sound I'd ever heard.

"I'm sure you look adorable wearing big glasses."

"And a spaceship shirt I wore every Friday. I was the queen of style, you know."

"Oh, I bet you were. The coolest kid in school."

Cool was something I had never been accused of.

As I headed to the parking lot with a skip in my step, I had a feeling things were about to get real.

Chapter 22

Two hours of embarrassment later, Marc and I were finally alone in the breakfast nook away from Mom's prying eyes and those damn photo albums that captured a variety of bad hair days and poor taste in fashion that I'd lived through. I hadn't exaggerated about the shirt adorned with cartoonish Martians and spaceships, or the hideous bowl haircut that took forever to grow out. The evidence was in page after page of laminated pictures that Mom and Marc took too much pleasure in, if you ask me.

After a round of jokes on me as Marc and Mom's coffee klatch erupted into gales of raucous laughter, I could see Mom falling for him almost as much as I was.

It felt as if Marc was already family.

I unbuttoned my pants, my stomach overstuffed from an exquisite lunch that started off with a salad of fresh greens doused in hot bacon dressing. After that, I finished half a plate of homemade macaroni salad, two tea-sized sandwiches, a bowlful of homemade beef stew, and satisfied that tiny empty spot with homemade apple pie. It was good cooking at its best, and my diet was nowhere in sight. I hadn't felt shy about eating like a pig in front of Marc. For some reason—I guess because he seemed like such a down-to-earth guy—I thought he'd appreciate a girl with a healthy appetite, as opposed to one that ate like a bird.

Leaning back in my chair, I had been trying to decipher Marc's mannerisms all afternoon. Did he want to leave? Did I annoy him? Did my childhood ugly duckling syndrome repulse him? I couldn't tell for sure, but he smiled a lot and made jokes and small talk, so that had to be good.

"Does your mom usually feed your friends this well?" he asked after a lull in the conversation.

"Yes, I get spoiled regularly by her cooking."

"It's great that you spend time hanging out with your mother. A lot of people lose sight of family these days. Letting petty crap break them apart. Some kids move clear across the country to get away from their parents. It's sad."

I wondered what it would be like to live across the country from Mom—me in Hollywood, her here in Westfield. Would we lose touch? Would our relationship survive the distance? Or would I finally blossom into who I was meant to be?

"I guess, but sometimes it's not healthy to be so close to family. At some point you have to cut the umbilical cord."

"Maybe for some people, but I'd give anything to have my dad back. Once they're gone, they're gone. If you ask me, nothing's more important than family."

I watched his features soften as nostalgia washed over him.

"I miss my dad too. Lots of memories here."

He returned to me then, as if shaken from sleep. "What was it like growing up on a farm with so much land? I grew up in the suburbs but I would have loved this … lots of room to get into trouble and get dirty."

"Ha! It had its perks, but when you're constantly mowing or pruning or weeding … and agriculture is so unpredictable. One season of bad weather can bankrupt a family. It's a stressful life, especially nowadays."

"I can imagine. I have a lot of respect for our farming communities. Tough people who don't get enough credit for what they do."

"Tell that to my mom and she'll love you forever. It's thankless work—she could use the encouragement. Consider yourself warned, she might try hiring you as a farmhand."

"If she feeds me like she did today, I might just accept the job."

My mother once told me that every relationship starts small. Over the years, I learned to look at the little things. So I observed. The smile. The teasing. Even the way he treated my mother. Any guy could bring flowers and charm a woman, but not every guy could win the heart of a parent. But Marc had. He'd lavishly praised her home cooking, declaring it superior to his own grandma's; his sincerity was obvious. Then he'd volunteered to help with the cleanup, not merely out of politeness, but in gratitude for her hospitality. Mom, bless her heart, didn't believe in automatic dishwashers and still did dishes the old-fashioned way. He'd picked up a dishrag and was about to dive into the sink of dirty dishes when she shooed him out of the kitchen, even popping the cloth at him playfully. Mom was now a fan of Marc's for life—unless he did something unforgivable, like breaking my heart.

Starting something with Marc while simultaneously chasing a screenwriting career might not be the best idea. In fact, it was a terrible idea. Someone was bound to get hurt, and that someone always seemed to be me. But how could I turn either opportunity down? Love or my dream? Which was more important? Which would make me happier? Either could come crumbling down at the slightest wrong touch. Marc could leave me for someone else. My career could end if no one liked my work. I could shy away from any risk to protect myself. Or I jump all in and take a chance at being skipping-over-the-moon happy.

Or find myself utterly, devastatingly, soul-crushingly broken.

Chapter 23
Allen

His secret was safe, but not for long. The police inquiries were mounting. The search for Susan making national news. And his need for Haley burning ... singeing a hole in his heart that urgently needed bandaging. To top it off, the moment Haley found out he was "watching her" she would probably never speak to him again. So he had to tread carefully, but the ice kept getting thinner.

Allen didn't know how she would feel when he confessed to secretly tailing her around town and researching her online. With just a few clicks, he discovered her mother's maiden name, her date of birth, her current residence. Then there were all the personal details he had unearthed through careful observation, like how she rarely followed a speed limit, her dependency on Mommy, even her new friend Marc—an undistinguished computer monkey, albeit a handsome one, he grudgingly admitted.

He'd need to break Haley's dependency on Mommy ... and put an end to Marc.

An easy task for someone willing to do just about anything.

He wondered if Haley would regard the fact that he kept four candid snapshots of her in his wallet as romantic ... or creepy. Women: they were so unpredictable. That's what he loved about them. And hated.

He settled back into the comfortable, if hideously upholstered Queen Anne wing chair, his eyes scanning the old-fashioned coffered ceiling as he formulated the words he would use when he told her everything.

The revelation would be expertly orchestrated, down to the vanilla-scented candles and crackling fire. There were several excellent wineries in town; he would procure a nice port and some cheeses from Johnson Estate Winery. Hell, he might even throw in strawberries and chocolate. The whole shebang.

Every last detail had to be perfect if he was going to win her over, gain her full and abiding trust. First he'd explain that he cared about her, that he wasn't in the habit of stalking young women. She had captivated him with her beauty and intelligence, he'd shyly confess, and thought about her constantly. But he mustn't come on too strong. He'd prey upon her sympathy, make her see him as a tragic figure. Sprinkle a few details about his past, about the stepdad who beat him when he dropped the instant mashed potatoes, the filthy apartments infested with scurrying roaches, the mother who left him crying in the street after he'd been pummeled black and blue by a neighborhood bully. Women loved to rescue a man, becoming the heroine, didn't they?

There was only one kink to iron out, a big one.

She'd demand answers about Susan's disappearance. So far, he had not been identified by the police as a person of interest at this point. Susan was a missing person, period. With no evidence that a crime had even been committed, he was off the hook. Would that be enough to assuage Haley? Well, there were other ways to placate her, if needed.

If only this damn sense of urgency wasn't rushing him. Allen hated to be rushed. But hiding out in Westfield was proving to be more difficult than he had imagined. He'd misjudged the town as a place where he could remain incognito; the troublemaker on the first day of the screenwriting class had dispelled that notion. The yokels were too polite to say anything to his face, but he'd felt their stares, overheard their whispers. Even sweet Mrs. Ellsworth, he suspected, had heard the gossip and was watching him with keen interest.

A knock at the door interrupted his thoughts.

"Come in!" he shouted.

Speak of the devil. Mrs. Ellsworth eased the door open and stood sheepishly in the opening. Her wide, periwinkle eyes roved around the room, as if expecting to see a corpse's feet sticking out from under the bed, or the proverbial skeleton in the closet.

"Good evening, Mr. Michaels," she said. "I was just wondering if you'd be interested in playing checkers again tonight … if you're not busy, that is."

Allen detected the strong note of curiosity in her voice and decided to have some fun. "Oh, I'm sorry, Mrs. Ellsworth, I do have plans this evening. Rather big plans."

Mrs. Ellsworth's eyes gleamed. "Oh?"

"Yes. You see, my next project is a horror film. The story's about a cuckolded man who murders his unfaithful wife. He gets away with it, but in his guilt, he finds himself irresistibly drawn to her grave. Visits it every night." He looked to Mrs. Ellsworth for a reaction.

"Every night?" she squeaked.

"The husband always goes at night. Until one night, he discovers the grave has been disturbed. He looks into the open hole. The coffin lid is ajar …"

Mrs. Ellsworth craned her gray head into the room, eyes bugging, pruny mouth puckered in a perfect O.

"… and then the husband notices footprints leading away from the grave. Just then, from out of nowhere— *whack!*" Allen clapped his hands. Mrs. Ellsworth gasped and practically jumped out of her support hose. "Well, I'm afraid I can't give any more of the plot away."

Mrs. Ellsworth lingered in the doorway, pale with fright and clutching the jamb. Allen bit his lip to keep from laughing.

"So tonight, Mrs. Ellsworth, I thought I'd pay a visit to one of Westfield's historic cemeteries. Soak up some ambience, as it were." Mrs. Ellsworth nodded vaguely. "You wouldn't have a shovel I could borrow, by any chance?" Allen shot her an impish smile.

"Oh, Mr. Michaels, you've been making sport of me, haven't you?" Mrs. Ellsworth cackled.

"You caught me, Mrs. Ellsworth. I'm sorry, I just couldn't resist. Lighthearted moments are rare for me these days." He added leadingly: "I suppose you've heard about my, er, troubles back in Hollywood."

"Well, yes, I have heard a few things, no details, you understand; it's no business of mine," she hemmed and hawed.

"I have to say staying in your wonderful establishment has helped ease my burden. I'm grateful for your hospitality. My only regret is that I shall be leaving in a few days."

"It's been a pleasure having you, Mr. Michaels," said Mrs. Ellsworth with genuine conviction. "You know, I never did believe all the malarkey I read—I mean, see—in those supermarket tabloids. Dreadful publications."

"That's very wise of you, Mrs. Ellsworth" He glanced at the baroque mantel clock on the antique highboy: 5:40. He rose and began to don his overcoat. "Well, I must be going. Better skedaddle to that cemetery before it gets dark."

Mrs. Ellsworth caught his jocular tone. "Oh, Mr. Michaels, you are a caution!" She paused, and decided to try to capitalize on their merry spirit. "Just where are you going tonight, Mr. Michaels, if you don't mind my asking?"

Allen put a finger to his lips. "Shush, Mrs. Ellsworth, shush. Now that would be telling."

He brushed by the old lady and, descending the creaking staircase, felt her eyes boring into the back of his head.

Chapter 24

I had a dream last night that still infects my brain. In it I had a choice to make. Two closed doors. I opened the one on the right and sunlight poured all over me, scented with a salty ocean breeze. It felt like California. I heard Allen Michaels calling my name and fans cheering—exhilarating.

I closed that door and opened the one on the left. Behind that door I saw Marc and two children—I can only assume they were mine since they kept calling me Mommy. A simple scene, no fanfare. Just love. I closed that door.

There I stood, staring at the two doors—two choices—knowing that I could only walk through one. Is that a sign of what's to come? Am I going to have to pick between love and my dream job? The thought terrifies me, because without love I have nothing, but without my writing I am nothing. How can I choose between two worlds, each perfect in its own way?

Puckering my lips with a swipe of lipstick, I finished the final touches of my makeup while singing along with Aretha Franklin. Yes, Aretha, tonight I really did feel like a natural woman.

Smoothing the sexiest black dress I owned, I realized it wasn't sexy at all as I stood before the mirror to get a view from all angles. Not lowcut enough. Not short enough. Too tight, and not in a good way. I had put on a few pounds since purchasing it, hoping my chunkiness didn't show through the silky fabric. Small silver hoops dangled from my ears, and a matching necklace adorned my neck.

Over the phone I had told Mom about my dinner date with Marc, asking advice on what to wear. Advice—from my mother. If that wasn't horrifying enough, she aimed the obligatory slew of questions at me as I dodged them as best as I could. *Is he your boyfriend? Have you talked about a future together? Does he want kids?* (Oh, how she would love a grandbaby.) I hadn't the heart to tell her I had no idea where the relationship was headed, so after a quick "I'll fill you in on the details later" I hung up and reminded myself to never ever seek dating advice from my mother.

With a twirl I checked myself out, hoping I wasn't overdressed. Was a dress too fancy for an at-home meal? Were jeans too informal? I finally settled on this because it was comfortable but cute, simple enough to be casual if I threw a sweater on top. Maybe the v-neck was a bit too conservative, but the spaghetti straps showed some skin, if that's what Marc was into. And what guy wasn't? While other girls promenaded with their asses hanging out of their miniskirts, the soft fabric fell at my knees, keeping my butt cheeks exactly where they belonged—covered.

My heart fluttered with nervous excitement no matter how much I told myself it wasn't a date *per se*, just a meal. A casual dinner of chicken Parmesan, roasted red potatoes, and homegrown green beans. I borrowed my mother's apple pie recipe for dessert. Nothing to brag to Rachael Ray about, but a home-cooked meal nonetheless, which Marc seemed thrilled about when I talked to him yesterday. A novice in the kitchen, I had fumbled through a cookbook that morning searching for a simple recipe I could manage. Anything chicken and nothing requiring heavy handling of knives. If I wasn't trying to impress

Marc, Thai takeout or subs fit any occasion, but for company I'd whip out the china and silverware.

As I belted out one last pitchy note that would make Simon Cowell cringe, the doorbell chimed. I glanced at my bedside clock—5:50. He was early, damn it. Running fingers through my hair that I'd spent the last half hour curling into long, loose tendrils, I clicked off the radio and rushed downstairs to the front door, tripping down the last two stairs before I caught myself on the railing. On the porch stoop I found Marc looking *GQ* good, with his hands behind his back.

"Hey," I said breathlessly. "You're early."

"Not too early, I hope." He pulled out a colorful wildflower bouquet and handed it to me. "I've always thought roses were a bad omen, so I got you these instead."

"They're gorgeous. And roses are cliché. These are perfect." I accepted the flowers and waved him inside. "Come in. You've got to be freezing."

"Nah, the frostbite's numbed me pretty good already."

The man looked good enough to eat. Black slacks, striped collared shirt that hugged arms that I wanted to hold me—I was pretty sure I was melting right then and there. His day-old stubble darkened his jawline, making me want to run my fingers against the sandpaper-rough skin. And the scent of leather from his jacket that clung to him ... God help me.

After hanging his coat in the closet, I ambled into the kitchen to put the flowers in a vase. I could feel his stare from the entry where he stood, and I may have slightly thrust out my ass—just a little in case he was watching— as I reached into the cabinet. It was childish, I know, but I wanted to leave an impression. Make him want me like I wanted him.

Returning to the dining room, I placed the flowers on the dining room table and remembered something.

"I have something for you too."

"For me?"

I ushered him into the living room where I'd prepared a spread of cheese and crackers on my grandmother's favorite serving platter, which Mom didn't know I'd pilfered. I figured the "hors d'oeuvres"—if you could call them that—would be filling enough in case dinner was inedible.

"Something little, to remember me by." I handed him a wrapped package, which he looked at questioningly.

"That's thoughtful. Thanks."

"Thank me after you open it. You might not like it."

He ran his fingers along the long, thin edge, tracing the package's outline, then tore off one edge and slid out a small picture frame. Captured inside the wooden border was a sunset, vibrant and beautiful.

Marc examined the image and smiled, his hazy reflection bouncing off the glass. He stood silent for longer than expected. I struggled to interpret his response.

"Do you like it?" I finally asked.

"It's beautiful." He looked up at me. "Thank you."

"It's a hobby of mine—taking pictures, I mean."

"Where did you take this picture? The setting looks familiar."

"Out back, in our woods. I hoped you would appreciate it … being a sunset enthusiast and all. Don't you dare confine it to a dark drawer."

"Not on your life. This is going on the wall in my bedroom. So it's the first thing I see every morning when I wake up."

I wish you could be the first thing I see every morning, I thought giddily.

The energy in the room drew us into effortless conversation about our jobs, my photography hobby, and his latest side project restoring a 1960 Chris-Craft Capri boat that he'd rescued from a farmer's barn. I sheepishly waved off Marc's compliments about my decorating skills, claiming I'd just thrown together some odds and ends from thrift stores and yard sales. It wasn't true, of course. I had fussed over every last detail from the color and texture of the throw blankets to the framed pictures on the walls—black-and-whites I had taken around town.

I yearned to show him how much I liked him. Something, anything to take the moment beyond friendship. I wanted to reach for his hand, touch his cheek, kiss his neck ...

And then, a flash of Jake blinded me.

Hot breath mingled together. Grunting, groaning. Bodies moving in unison. Our first—and only—time together.

Then his retreating form as he ran from me. As fast as he could. I would never see him alive after that.

That horrifying moment when I found him dangling from the rafter. Because of me. Because of what I'd done. A betrayal so unforgiveable, so horrible, that death was his only way out.

My muscles froze as I licked my dry lips and averted my gaze to my lap, as if the crease of my dress would chase the nightmare away. But there Jake was, face tinted blue, limp body lifelessly still, the air deathly solemn until my scream shook the silence away.

"You okay?" Marc asked, resting his hand on my shoulder.

I jumped at Marc's touch, suddenly realizing I wasn't in the barn, wasn't crumbling in a heap on the floor at the sight of my best friend, my first love, dead.

"I'm sorry. I should go check on the food."

I couldn't get away fast enough. Why was Jake haunting me now? Why couldn't my demons rest for one night? Why did my sin, my secret, constantly ruin any chance of happiness? Panic rose in my chest, suffocating me as I leaned over the kitchen sink splashing cool water on my face.

One, two, three, four, five ... I counted. "Please," I whispered, pleading to Jake somewhere beyond the grave, "please forgive me. Please free me from the guilt. I can't take it anymore." Water in an empty glass on the counter trembled, taunting me. I wanted to hurt something, someone. I snatched the cup and hurled it to the floor, heard it explode against the tile, watched the sparkling spray of glass shards. I couldn't move to clean it up; I couldn't do anything but stand there, eyes fixed on how the light played upon the pool of water. Angry tears spilled down my cheeks.

Footsteps behind me pulled me out of the cavernous pit. Turning away, I wiped away my tears with the back of my hand before facing him.

"Hey there. Everything okay? Need some help?"

"If you mean mental help, sure." There was no way he didn't know I had just been crying.

"My company's that bad, huh?" He offered a weak grin, though it didn't reach his pitying eyes. "It's just a cup. No big deal." He grabbed a towel off the countertop and began wiping the puddle up.

"I'm sorry I've ruined the evening. Just some bad memories hitting me hard. I don't know what's wrong with me today."

"Want to get it off your chest?" After tossing the sopping towel full of broken glass in the sink, he turned to me. Wrapping his arm around my shoulder, I felt a shift between us. For the first time since Jake, there it was: an awakening trust.

"Do you ever feel like a dark cloud is always following you?" His eyes searched me curiously, but I couldn't stop the flood of words. "I do. I feel like I lose everyone I love. My best friend Jake growing up, my dad ... and we're supposed to fill the void in our heart with new people, happy moments, but it's like every good thing slips through my fingers and I don't know why. Sometimes ... I feel cursed." It sounded silly hearing the words out loud. It had been years, but the wounds felt so fresh.

"What happened with your dad?" Marc asked.

"He passed away years ago ..." I swallowed the massive lump in my throat, growing from the swell of loss. "He's missed more than half of my life, and there are so many things I wish he could have been here for, so many things I never got to tell him. It's just ... still so hard sometimes. Why? Why can't I get over it?"

"I get it. I still miss my dad every day." His voice trembled as he said it. He understood me—for once, someone understood me.

Silence settled over the kitchen, wrapping two grieving people in its sympathetic balm. Only one who has felt the sting of death appreciates that moment to stuff the pain back down before it bubbles up.

"If you ever need to talk to someone," said Marc at length, softly, "I'm a good listener."

"I should be over it by now, right? I just feel so damn guilty. I can't push past it." *Stop*, I warned myself. *Please stop.* My jaw tightened as everything rapidly unwound like a loose seam, memory after memory pouring over me. I wanted to feel nothing but numbness, a small mercy on my soul.

"None of what's happened is your fault, Haley." Marc's voice drew me back from the netherworld. But he didn't know what he was talking about. He had no idea who I was, or what I'd done.

Or did he?

"You remind me of him—my dad."

"Really? You want to tell me about him?"

"He was the best person I knew." That simple string of words described my father perfectly. My eyes wandered, glazing over as I stared into empty space.

"I can only hope that I'm half the man that my father was," said Marc. "It seems like the whole concept of family has fallen by the wayside. Men being slaves to their jobs. Women juggling kids and jobs too. But no matter how much life demanded of him, my dad always made time for me."

There wasn't a sliver of personal space between us now. I'd broken down in front of him; any topic was now fair game.

"What about your mom?" I asked.

"She passed away when I was little. I don't remember much about her, and Dad never remarried, so it was just us two."

At least I had Courtney, though the age gap between us may as well have been an abyss. "You had no one else?"

"I did, but she left. It's a long story. Not one I want to get into." Marc's voice turned terse, angry. And suddenly I felt indignant for him. For me. A steaming, kettle-whistling anger.

"It's not fair. You losing both your parents. Me losing my dad and Jake. I get so pissed at how my family has had to live since Dad died. Have you ever experienced a Goodwill Christmas, Marc? Every Christmas or birthday, while other kids got new clothes or cool toys, my mom would take us to Goodwill where we'd pick out a used toy or worn-out clothes that never quite fit."

I remembered the first time I'd gone to a shoe store, amazed that they had more than one style in my size. I was ten. And my clothes came from garbage-bagged donations, all of which were decades out of style. I wore parachute pants years after they'd been replaced by bootcut styles, and my snotty classmates made sure to rub my nose in it.

"And having to watch Mom struggle to pay the monthly bills ... what kid deserves that? Ever since Dad died, it's been an exhausting uphill battle. How is that fair?"

My eyes welled with tears but I pressed on, unable to stop.

"Managing a vineyard was always a gamble, especially hiring out labor with no guarantee of how the harvest would fare. To make matters worse, we could never compete with the bigger vineyards. Then after Dad died, I'm supposed to pick up where he left off—as a kid, Marc. A kid. I didn't have a childhood after that. Sometimes I just want to know—why me?"

Those last words bounced off the kitchen cabinets. I busied my twitching hands by grabbing a paper towel and soaking up a remaining puddle on the counter. When I finished, I wiped the baseboard and floor until it disintegrated in my hand, a thrifty habit learned from Mom. Hardship taught us waste not, want not. The want not had always been hard for me.

"I promise you, Haley, you're stronger than you think. I know it's not easy, but you have to let go of whatever is eating you up inside. Or it will eventually rot you from within, turn you into something you don't recognize anymore." I sensed he wasn't talking to me, but to himself.

Marc Vincetti had secrets, just like me. Was chased by demons, just like me. Felt that rush of fury, just like me. We shared the same scars, like war buddies.

That's when I knew with certainty he had written me the letters. Had reached out to me from the shadows to pull me into the light. Was the one person who would save me. Finally I was ready to be saved.

I leaned my head against his shoulder, gazing up at him as he looked down at me with half-lidded eyes. It was there, tingling on my lips, the nervous anticipation of a first kiss. I closed my eyes, tilted my face up ...

The doorbell rang.

"Crap! Excuse me, Marc, I'd better see who it is."

I answered the door. There stood Allen Michaels in his thin overcoat, a cruel smirk on his face.

Chapter 25

"What are you doing here?" I whispered sternly, blocking him.

"I didn't realize you had company," he said, attempting to peer around me. "I'm sorry for popping in like this, but I was on my way home when I blew a tire. I managed to make it all the way to your house, though I'm sure my rims won't be thanking me for it."

"How'd you know where I live?" I asked.

Momentary confusion flashed upon his face. "I have all the student addresses in my briefcase. Mind if I use your phone? My cell phone's dead. I only need a moment."

It sounded all too coincidental, but sure enough, his black Mercedes sat at the curb, its hazard lights blinking furiously, front tire clearly deflated, noticeable even from this distance in the dark. Certainly he wouldn't puncture his own tire for an excuse to stop by ... certainly not. Only a psycho would do that. Oh God.

The options weren't really options. I could slam the door in his face and piss him off, ending any chance I had at making it in Hollywood. Or I could let him in, ruin my date with Marc, and resent Allen for the rest of the night. He could make it up to me later with a first-class plane ticket to LA.

"Sure, come in." As he brushed past, his coat flapped behind him as a bitter wind trailed him inside. No decent Westfield-winter-appropriate coat flapped. It should billow, puff, even suffocate, but never flap. "Why are you out at night in that thin coat? You'll freeze to death."

God help me, I sounded like my mother.

"I know. I just haven't gotten around to shopping for a decent coat. I won't be here much longer, though."

"You're leaving soon? What about the final class—and the screenplay competition?"

"It's still on the table. Just happening a little sooner, that's all."

"But *why*?" I insisted. "We paid for your expertise. You're screwing the whole class by bailing early."

A yawning moment later, he answered, "I got a job offer in LA that I can't refuse."

His vagueness irritated me. Apparently he was too good to bother to stick out his commitment to his students.

"I can't believe this—can't believe you'd do this to us."

"Can we talk about this?" he said, ready to stay a while as he hastily tore off his coat, like a rambunctious child on his first sleepover. He smiled, his teeth large and cheekbones high, pushing his smile too wide. Inhumanly wide. Jack Nicholson as the Joker sprang to mind.

I led him into the kitchen where the cordless phone hung from the wall. Marc introduced himself with a handshake, and the two men engaged in what at first blush seemed like idle chitchat. But beneath the surface there was definite tension; they were sizing each other up, and their meaningful glances at me suggested they'd each staked their claim for my affections—and were willing to fight for it. I can't say I minded; it was new territory for me, being fought over, being wanted. I felt desirable as the testosterone levels rose around me. *Me.*

I didn't realize then just how dangerous two rival men could be.

**

The dishes were done. The kitchen clean. The living room tidied up. But no matter how immaculate my house was, my life felt like such a mess.

I was in love.

I was in danger.

And I didn't realize how interwoven the two were.

Curling up against the arm of the sofa, I picked up a book and started reading. Anything to shift my brain off of Marc and Allen and the incessant strain of my heart and the screenplay project. Too many thoughts competed, splitting my skull in two.

Three pages into the book my eyelids grew heavy, and I didn't remember the book dropping into my lap as I slipped into an uneasy sleep ...

**

June 1996

"This was a mistake—a big one."

His body rolled off of mine, slippery with sweat, sex, and shame. As Jake hung his legs over the mattress, fumbling to pull his pants on, I crawled to the headboard, putting as much distance between us as the twin bed allowed. It wasn't nearly enough.

I couldn't remember how we got to my bedroom, when the first kiss happened, how our clothes ended up on the floor. The details blended into a hazy mixture of uninhibited touching and laughing. The empty bottle of vodka was to blame for that. As my stomach churned, I wasn't laughing anymore and vowed never to drink again.

"Where are you going?" My voice was timid—nothing like I usually was around my best friend. My only friend. And now ... my lover? No, this didn't feel like a lover.

We'd grown up together, climbed trees together, fished together, swam together. Had our little spats that didn't amount to much. Now all those years of friendship had been shattered in a mere moment. Well, more like five minutes. I had been watching the clock, counting down until he finished.

"I don't know. I can't go home like this. They'll know." He sounded as freaked out as I felt.

"Don't go. Let's watch a movie or something." I needed to go back to normal. Erase the last five minutes as if they hadn't happened.

Jake grimaced at me. "Seriously? Hale, how can you act like nothing just happened?"

"I'm not trying to pretend it didn't happen. I love you— you know that. I just don't want what we did to ruin our friendship."

His laugh was a sarcastic cackle.

"It's too late for that."

No, he couldn't take my virginity and then just walk away from me like I was dirty laundry. I wouldn't let him.

"So that's it—you're just going to stop being my best friend? Is that the kind of guy you are? Because that's not the Jake I know."

By now he had stood up and was pulling his shirt on over his head, his untamed hair poking up in a million directions like a little boy's. I'd never noticed his hair until now, or the way his arm muscles flexed as the shirt rolled down his bare chest.

"Hale, you don't know me at all."

Now it was my turn to laugh ironically. "We've been best friends for a decade. I think I know you pretty well."

"How's this for knowing me: I used you. I used you for sex."

"What the hell are you talking about?" Jake didn't use women, especially not me. Never me. It was part of the unspoken friendship code—you didn't use your best friend.

"You have no idea? In all our years together, you didn't figure it out?"

"Figure what out? You're talking gibberish."

He sighed like he was exhaling something so deep inside him that it hurt. "I had sex with you to see ... to make sure I was gay."

"Gay? You're not gay, Jake. You can't be gay. You just ... you know ... came." I whispered the last word like it was a secret.

"Yes, I'm pretty sure I am, especially now."

Now that hurt, a waspish, over and over again kind of sting. No, more like the tear of a gaping wound that could never be sewed back together.

"You fucking asshole." I'd never sworn like that before, but I meant it. I jumped up from the bed and bulldozed him through my bedroom door. "You took my virginity knowing you didn't even like me like that, just to determine if you're gay? You stole something precious to me, my first time! I hate you! You are such a prick. Get out, and don't ever talk to me again!"

I slammed the door behind him, sobbing loudly because I wanted him to hear my pain. I wanted him to see the damage he'd carelessly caused.

"Hale, I'm sorry." His voice sounded muffled against the door. I imagined him leaning on it from the other side. "Please, I need you right now. I'm a mess. I can't tell my family about this; they'll never accept me like this. You're all I have."

I pounded my fist against the door. "You should have thought about that before having sex with me, asshole. I mean it—go away! I never want to speak to you again."

And I never did.

**

I woke up with a killer cramp in my neck and a migraine blinding me. Dreams of Jake always left me battered. I deserved much worse.

Picking up my book that had fallen to the floor, I shuffled to the dining room to shut off the light. I'd almost forgotten about Marc's flowers, but there they were, so pure and bright. I leaned in to smell them, only now noticing the card tucked inside between the blooms.

I pulled it out, unfolding the paper.

How can I show you what you mean to me? Words can only express so much, and actions can only show so much, but how can a heart feel so much? It's enough passion to fill a lifetime together. You'll live forever in my thoughts, filling me with dreams of you and shared memories together. I hope you feel the same.

Yours forever

Perfect words in perfect script from the perfect man. It was all too much too soon, and yet not soon enough. I wanted to get lost in him, feel his heat near me. I couldn't explain what lured me so strongly, but could anyone really decipher love? Unexplainable, unfathomable, bottomless. But unconditional? That part I feared. That part wasn't guaranteed. And when I told him the truth, would he still feel the same about me?

There was no answer for me in the pitiless darkness. Until I told Marc everything, love was a lie.

Chapter 26
Allen

The cost of a tow truck was a small price to pay for getting what he wanted. But when things didn't go as planned, well, that's when Allen got angry.

After circling Haley's block a dozen times, his drive home that night gave him time to reflect. He wanted to be alone with his thoughts, untainted in the peaceful silence. Though overwhelmed with excitement at seeing Haley again, he had to admit that meeting Marc Vincetti was an unpleasant surprise.

Shaking his head, Allen couldn't imagine what Haley would want with such an *average* guy. Though Marc seemed friendly and likeable enough, there was nothing special about him. Besides, Allen brooded, all of Marc's cordial chatter was probably just a façade to make himself look good in front of Haley.

Allen read right through Marc, because men were predictable and selfish. Marc was no exception. Whatever skeletons Marc was hiding from Haley, Allen would unearth if necessary. This was no friendly competition; it was a matter of life or death.

How could Haley not see through Marc's charade? And even if she did fall for Marc's act, certainly she had to recognize that she could do better. Like him. Tonight only reaffirmed that. Her enchanting nature and Marc's dry personality were poles apart. She needed a creative counterpart like Allen to complete her. Allen was captivated as she emanated an energy and tenderness that so few people possessed. Haley was a rare jewel that he hoped to add to his crown.

Haley was the complete opposite of Susan. Luckily, he would never have to deal with that bitch ever again. Her nagging, her domineering personality, her demands—his soon-to-be ex drove him to do what he did. But Haley, on the other hand, was sweet and thoughtful and naïve. These traits were exactly what he wanted in a woman.

As he relived the evening detail by detail, he knew he wasn't going to get much sleep that night. Haley's infectious laugh would ricochet off the walls of his mind until the sun rose. He pictured her twisting her soft curls around her finger, attentive to his words. He'd never met a woman like her, certainly not in Hollywood where everyone was already "someone" and Allen was old news. Women didn't flock to him there. Not anymore. He'd lost his A-list status and rarely got a second glance from passersby these days; he was just another face in the crowd. Effervescent Haley would help him revive his celebrity. With her at his side, he'd never have to worry about feeling like a nobody ever again.

More determined than ever to keep her, Allen knew he needed a plan. But time was running short and he still had no assurance that she'd be following him to the West Coast.

"Stay the course," he told himself.

His Mercedes hit a pothole, jarring his focus back to the road with more holes than Blackburn, Lancashire. Thumping along the concrete chewed away by too much salt, he passed quaint houses with friendly picket fences and neglected tire swings swaying in the still, bitter cold air. It was nothing like Los Angeles where people overpaid for tiny apartments, inched along in traffic, and gunned it through the slums. And yet the so-called City of Angels—dirty, godforsaken—was his heartbeat.

He pulled up to the pitch-black B&B, where Mrs. Ellsworth slept and his single suitcase sat in a drab little room where no one waited for his return. Only then did he realize he was truly, utterly, desolately alone.

Who had he become? Allen Michaels—the man who'd clawed his way up from production assistant to mogul, who beat the shit out of his stepfather after dosing him with sleeping pills, who bested his cheating, conniving ex-wife at her own little game, who outran a police investigation—didn't lose.

"Fight for what you want," his father had told him before disappearing for the last time.

So Allen had taken the only piece of advice his father ever imparted, and decided he'd never give up without a fight, even if it meant a fight to the death. Susan could vouch for that ... if she wasn't "missing"; of course, he knew better. That was the only way to succeed in this business: become a force of nature. In his prime Allen Michaels had been a goddamn hurricane.

There was still a good chance that his plan would succeed flawlessly. Tomorrow she would get his letter, then she'd naturally accept the invitation to accompany him to LA, and a week later they would be riding off into the sunset together. She'd be unable to resist Allen's spell, happily leaving this shitty town and its shitty people in a cloud of dust. A perfect Hollywood ending. With Westfield in the rearview mirror, Marc would be history and Haley would be his.

On the other hand, there was a chance—a slim chance—that Haley would refuse his offer. Then what? No, he couldn't entertain that thought. It would be a life sentence for him, in a most literal way.

Every problem had a solution. He'd simply have to redirect Haley's focus back on him. Or maybe ... on Marc. On his dark side. On the secret Allen sensed Marc was hiding. It was there, Allen had seen glimpses of it during their conversation. It would take some creativity to dig deep enough, but Allen was a master screenwriter; he created stories, made damn sure there were no plot holes, brought them to life. Yes, that would be plan B. If Haley didn't join him on her own, he would use his own brand of magic to motivate her. One way or another, Haley Montgomery would be joining him in the City of Lost Angels.

Chapter 27

The mailbox was stuffed more than usual for a Saturday. At least three days' worth of ads, coupons, and bills were crammed into the spruce green metal box with a broken red flag that had at one point matched my green shutters. Time and weather had changed that, though.

I gathered up the mail before heading into the house. Several sheets of advertisements escaped my grasp and flittered to the wet slush below. Groaning, I bent down and collected everything, then treaded up the front walkway, feeling the icy mix seep through my shoes and socks to my toes.

I didn't care about the sopping wet mail.

Or my frozen feet.

Marc hadn't called since our dinner date and it bugged the shit out of me.

Pushing open the front door, a warm draft welcomed me inside. After tossing the sodden mail on the table, I noticed the blink of my answering machine. A dim red "1" winked at me.

"Hi ... *crackle* ... wanted to see ... *crackle* ... you'd want to ... *crackle* ... really need ... *crackle* ... talk..."

Then dead silence.

A man's voice, but unidentifiable otherwise. Most of Westfield had poor cell service, though most of the residents were Luddites who couldn't care less. Hell, I wouldn't have been surprised to find rotary phones in a majority of homes. Or two tin cans joined by a string.

As I contemplated whether to call Marc or Allen, I noticed a large Manila envelope peeking out from the pile of mail. I picked it up, finding my name and nothing else. No return address, no postage. I'd gotten used to these anonymous deliveries, but something seemed especially odd about this one.

I slit open the envelope with my fingernail and dumped the contents into my open palm. A letter, then a smaller, thick envelope. I read the letter first:

Dear Haley,

I want you to know how much I've enjoyed getting to know you as a fellow writer and as a friend. You are an amazing individual, among the most creatively brilliant that I know. That is why I am offering you a once-in-a-lifetime opportunity.

Perhaps it feels somewhat premature for me to make you this offer before you've completed the class, but it didn't take me long to see your potential. I have watched you grow as a screenwriter, and you have not only impressed me with your talent, you've also earned this more than any other student. As you know, I planned to select one individual from the class to present a screenplay to my colleagues. What better way to do this than to accompany me to a Hollywood premiere where you'll meet all the entertainment greats in one place? I can guarantee it's an experience you'll never forget.

Every aspect of your growth has proved time and again that you love what you do and are passionate about a future in this industry. That's what I was looking for all along.

Enclosed you will find an airline ticket to Los Angeles. My offer includes an invitation to a black-tie event that the most prominent writers, producers, and directors in Hollywood

153

will be attending. You belong among us, Haley. This will be your debut as my protégé. It will mark a Beginning for you, and a New Beginning for me. Together, we shall scale the heights.

Though I'm sure you would have preferred more time to weigh your options, the flight leaves this Sunday. If you choose to accept my invitation to join me in LA, I will look forward to being your mentor for years to come, and reveling in the success I've no doubt you will achieve. If you choose to remain in Westfield, I wish you every happiness.

I'm honored to have known you and worked with you, no matter how short the time.

Allen Michaels

I stood transfixed, reading and re-reading the letter. It was a screenwriter's lottery, and I had won the million-dollar prize. Whoopee!

Next I moved on to the smaller envelope, ripping it open like it was Christmas morning. A plane ticket was wedged inside along with a fancy invitation to a movie premiere for an indie film I had recently read about. I studied them, half expecting them to disappear or burst into flame. But they were real, by God. This was actually happening! Everything was coming together as I had once upon a time hoped it would.

I'd prayed for this day. Worked my ass off for this day. It had always been a forlorn hope; the unattainableness kept me motivated, made me keep my head on straight. Now within reach, I didn't know if I still wanted it. Hibernating until a script was complete, then pitching it to a bunch of penny-pinching suits. Dealing with all the sordid aspects of "Hollyweird." Associating with Allen

Michaels—that would mean living under a microscope. Was this what I had chased for so long?

The more I stared at that plane ticket, the more uneasy I felt. There was no guarantee how long I would be gone. I felt a nagging insecurity that I wasn't ready for this, that I wasn't cut out for that life. And the biggest dilemma of all: Marc. Would I get a second chance with Marc?

It was a rare problem that even Ben and Jerry's Cherry Garcia ice cream couldn't fix.

But there was something that could help—clear my mind, at least. I darted up the stairs to my office and threw open the lid to the window seat that stored a hodgepodge of junk that I didn't know what else to do with. Tucked in the corner, I grabbed the one thing that offered me calm during life's storms—my Canon EOS with an exchangeable 50mm 1:1.4 lens. Right where I had last put it.

Throwing the thin black leather strap over my shoulder, I skipped every other step on my way downstairs. Within five minutes I was mittened up and driving down Main Street, where two-foot-high piles of slush had been plowed to the curb. I passed through one set of lights, then the second, looking for the sharp left turn up ahead. I could drive this route blindfolded.

By the time I arrived and parked my car near the berm of the road, the sky had darkened to a midnight blue and the moon glowed brightly overhead, guiding my steps. I found my usual spot and pulled out the black leather camera case, buttery soft in my hands.

Sitting in my usual spot, I pulled the camera from the case. Normally I would have brought my tripod for an evening landscape shot, but I hoped my wide-angle fast lens would suffice tonight, with the aid of the celestial bodies above. After prying off the lens cover, I held the viewing lens up to my eye and found my target up ahead.

Even in its darkness, the distant glow of Erie, Pennsylvania, illuminated the horizon enough to reveal that picture perfect place where the sky met the earth. Land ended, heaven began.

Clicking once, twice, I felt the tension release with each shot. Adjusting the angle, I refocused, then snapped a few more. The whir of the shutter was the only sound in the tranquil air. The naked skeletons of the trees seemed to pose for me, like weary pilgrims lifting their long, bony fingers skyward in prayer, longing for springtime. My hot breath left a moonlight ghost upon the black canvas of the night.

After one roll of film, I reached for a second and found my case empty. Standing up from my crouched position, I crunched along the gravel path to my car. Maybe it was the chill of fresh air, maybe it was the consuming blackness, or maybe it was the *whir* of my camera, but I'd never felt so confident and so alive ... and so ready to make this decision.

Chapter 28

As the week passed, the talk of the town had been the weekend ICE Festival, a topic I usually avoided like the plague.

Do you have a date for the festival?

Bringing anyone special this year?

The ICE Festival is a great place to meet men!

Excuse me, but the ICE Festival was never a great place to meet men. For one thing, it was always colder than a witch's titty—not exactly ideal for kindling romance. For another, the John-Boy Walton kind of guys attracted to squeaky clean family fun weren't my type. The questions always received the same rote answers, year after year, and yet curious busybodies kept pushing me into an embarrassing conversation about my crap-ass love life. Of course, the offer of being set up with Mrs. Mason's nephew or Mrs. Murphey's son inevitably followed. What twenty-something woman wanted to be set up with a forty-something man who still lived with his mother? Not me, fuck you very much.

Even though I was single, I still had standards. Auditions closed.

This year, though, would be one for the books. For the first time ever, I had a date. Tonight. Me and Marc. Marc and me. I liked the sound of it rolling around in my mind.

I meandered around the perimeter of the ICE Festival grounds, snapping shots of bustling volunteers stringing up lights, setting up booths, and stacking wood for the bonfire. As the last of the crew dispersed, the winter sky was already darkening into twilight.

A sharp wind bit my cheeks. A perfectly cold night for cuddling into the crook of Marc's arm. Yes, it would be perfect. The smoky scent of a roaring bonfire and twinkling stars dotting the sky—I couldn't picture anything more romantic.

I shook off my slush-soaked boots before stepping into my car. Cranking up the defroster, I still had a couple of hours to spare before tonight's date. But one thing had to be taken care of first.

Tomorrow Allen would leave for LA without me, but he didn't know that yet. It was time to wrap that up and put a bow on it. Checking my cell phone, I had enough bars to make the call. He picked up on the first ring.

"Hello, this is Allen."

"Hi, Allen. It's Haley."

"I assume you're calling about tomorrow. Did you get my messages about what to pack?"

Ugh, he sounded so excited. I hated to drop the bomb on him like this, but it had to be done.

"That's what I'm calling about."

My stomach felt heavy, like I'd swallowed a bowling ball.

"This doesn't sound good. What's going on?" The anxiety in his voice threw me on the defensive.

Do it fast, like ripping off a Band-Aid, and maybe it wouldn't hurt so bad. Yeah, right. "I feel awful doing this, but I've thought about your offer and I've decided to stay here."

A long, tense silence, broken at last by his angry voice.

"Tell me this is a joke."

"No, no joke. I'm so sorry, Allen, but Los Angeles isn't my future. My future is here."

For a moment I thought he had hung up on me, then he said, "May I ask what changed your mind." It was more of a statement than a question. An accusation. Beneath the words he was calling me a flake.

What did it matter? It was my decision, period. But maybe I owed him at least an explanation.

"A lot of things. It's not the right time, and my mom needs me here." Lies, of course.

"Is it because of Marc Vincetti?"

"What?" Now he was being invasive and it was pissing me off.

"Just tell me the truth, Haley. You're staying back—or should I say *holding* yourself back—for a guy. A guy who doesn't love you."

How dare he! Speculating about my love life was way over the line.

"Allen, that's none of your business. And what would you know about how Marc feels, anyway?"

"Haley, I—"

"Shut up! You have no room to talk. You're in the middle of a divorce and your wife is missing—while you're clear across the country, apparently trying to get me—and who knows how many other young women—in the sack. You could give two shits about love."

"You're acting silly, Haley. And talking about something you know nothing about." The calm cool tone only riled me up more.

"Silly, huh? I didn't see it before, but you're an egotistical, manipulative liar, Allen, and to be honest, I don't believe that you have anything to offer me—or any girl who respects herself."

The moment the words hit the dead air I regretted it, but I was too flustered to take any of it back

"You've just made the biggest mistake of your life."

This was no point in arguing with him. My nerves rattled under my skin. Before I said anything else to make the situation worse, I hung up.

I waited for him to call me back with a retaliation, an apology, a peace treaty, as the space grew stuffy and hot with recirculated air. But my cell phone was silent. So that was that—bridge burned. I felt more uneasy than ever.

I couldn't waste emotions on Allen. I had tonight to think about. Marc, the ICE Festival, hopefully our first kiss. Push Allen out of my mind so I could invite Marc in.

Mental delete.

There. It never happened.

Then why did I still feel like that bowling ball was rolling around in my belly? There was only one cure for what ailed me.

**

Although it was dark by the time I got there, I tiptoed to my wooded haven. Normally I wouldn't have been so cautious, but something felt different this time. Like I was being watched. I shrugged off the ominous feeling and crouched into position and tugged my camera from its case.

It felt good to be alone in nature, viewing the frosty tree limbs glistening in the moonlight and the white-capped waves of Lake Erie through the eye of a camera lens. Though Mother Nature didn't answer my questions or solve my problems, she knew how to soothe my frayed nerves.

When I communed with nature, time lost all meaning. It was winter dark now, probably edging toward seven o'clock. I still had to go home and get ready for the ICE Festival. One last picture.

As I stood up and brought the camera to my eye, a twig snapped sharply behind me. I whirled around, scanning the ground for a small animal, but the blackness of the dense bushes hid anything that could be lurking.

I exhaled a nervous sigh and reached for my camera case. Time to go. Another crack split the silence and I strained to listen. Seeing no movement, I placed the camera in the case, when another twig snapped nearby. A rabbit, most likely, or a deer. Until I heard a pattern. The rhythmic sound of footsteps approaching as dry leaves crackled underfoot.

I spun around, eyes straining to pierce the gloom. The sound seemed heavier, larger than what I originally thought as my blood thrummed through my veins.

I turned, ready to run, when it spoke. Not words, but a low rumble.

"Go! Get! Shoo!" I finally screamed, hoping to scare whatever it was away.

I waited, listening. Again the growl of something angry. And possibly hungry.

It was then that I wondered if I was going to make it out of the forest alive.

Chapter 29
Marc

Marc simultaneously rapped on the door and rung the doorbell, hoping the combination would be effective, whereas just knocking had not. Still no one stirred.

"Where are you?" he shouted. The house was as quiet as a tomb.

He walked through snow-dusted mulch along the front of the house. Cupping his hands over his eyes, he peered into the living room window through the open blinds. Only a kitchen lamp was on, probably a lamp she always left on at night.

Heading down the pathway toward the detached garage, he peered inside for a sign of her car. Empty. Was he being unofficially blown off? It wouldn't have been the first time it'd happened.

Tired of waiting in the cold, he returned to his car, started it, and cranked up the heat. "Bleeding Love" by Leona Lewis played on the radio for the umpteenth time that day, another chart-topping love song for 2009. Maybe Leona was on to something, Marc wondered, as she sang about her heart being crippled by the vein that she kept closing, only to have it cut open by the one she loved. Another martyr for love.

The minutes dragged by. The dashboard clock showed that she was about fifteen minutes late, not late enough to call it a night.

No way was she wasn't getting out of their date without a face-to-face explanation. He'd demand that. He was a human being, damn it, with feelings. And he deserved respect. He would damn well get it, too.

Shifting the car in reverse, he rolled out of the driveway and headed into town where he could see her house from the corner convenience store. No, it wasn't stalking if they were supposed to meet. It wasn't creepy if he waited for her down the street. It was better than desperately sitting in front of her house, right?

Thirty minutes. He'd give her thirty more minutes. And if she screwed him over? Well, it would be the last time anyone fucked with Marc's heart.

Chapter 30

The growl grew into a predatory snarl. I blindly backed up. The animal stepped forward, matching my slow and steady pace step for step. I stumbled. *Shit!* The animal slunk into a patch of pale moonlight penetrating the pine needle canopy. Sharp white fangs glistened with slobber. Its hostile eyes feasted on me. The hackles of its thick dark coat stood on end. It crouched, ready to pounce.

Ripped to shreds by an unknown beast. Not the way I'd ever imagined cashing in my chips. Think, Haley, think. Dad had tried to teach me some survival skills. Was it bears that would eventually leave if you stood perfectly still? Or was that for mountain lions? Should I lie down and play dead? Sorry, Dad, I should have paid more attention.

One thing I did remember: Wolves traveled in packs. Where there was one, there would be more. Could I outrun it? Time to find out—*now!*

I took off, only once glancing back to see if the creature tailed me. So far, so good. By the time I reached my car, jumped inside, and slammed the door, I was exhausted and out of breath. Safe from the monster in the woods, at last. As for the monster that lived inside me, well, I could never escape that one.

I closed my eyes and leaned against the headrest while sucking in gulps of air. In my mind I pictured those gnashing fangs ripping me apart. The tears came, and my body shook with each powerful outburst. I let the fear boil over until my tear ducts ran dry.

After checking the door locks—not that the animal would know how to use a door handle, though we once had a dog that could open our refrigerator—I sunk into my seat. As my heart rate slowed to normal, I checked the time. Shit, shit, shit. I was late.

Was I *too* late?

Chapter 31
Marc

Marc saw her drive up to her house and dart inside. A few seconds later the house erupted into bright light. After waiting a respectable amount of time before leaving the convenience store parking lot, he inched slowly down the street.

He pulled in behind her car, got out, and stood for a moment under the front porch before knocking. A minute later he heard the click of her footsteps. As he hung back beneath the awning, a shiver of nervousness rushed him as he knocked. A minute later footsteps clicked closer. Then the front door swung open as he shuffled back. Best not to appear too eager.

"Hey, Marc!" Her body blocked the warm air from escaping. "You're late, mister."

"No"—he made a point of looking at his watch—"*you're* late. I was here earlier and you weren't home. I thought you might cancel on me." He forced a sly grin, appearing casual about it.

"Oh, God, I'm sorry about that. Long story. I'll tell you later. But we're here now, ready to party, right?"

He laughed, his gaze running up the length of her body. "You look good."

"Thanks. You too." She smiled, a smile he had come to figure out was genuine. "I just need to grab my coat and purse, then we can go."

She slipped back into the house, leaving the door slightly ajar, and he heard her rushing about inside. Shoving his hands deep in his pockets helped hide the nervous fiddling. Damn, he hadn't felt this anxious in years.

She had impressed him as having a fully functioning bullshit meter. He knew it would take more than the usual guy tricks—flattery, showering her with gifts, coming across as a hopeless romantic or rugged individualist—to get into her pants. But damn, he had to have her. He wanted her in his bed like he'd never, ever wanted another woman. He'd always heard that good girls went for bad guys; bad girls went for good guys. He decided to play it right down the middle with this girl.

When she returned, he cupped her hand. "You do really look amazing." His compliment left a sweet silence between them. They stood at the front door in quiet contentment.

"A woman never gets tired of hearing that." She smiled a flirty smile that a woman uses to reel a man in, but keeping him at arm's length. Everything inside him wanted to grab her waist and draw her closer for a kiss. Those soft pink lips were so tempting, so inviting, yet also so lethal to his ego, especially if she objected and pulled away.

There'd be time for that later.

A jolt of electricity shot through him as she brushed past him toward his truck.

It was a calm night—a perfect night for the festival. The sky was clear with endless stars dazzling in the blackness. The moon shone bright, illuminating the streets and casting pale light through bare tree branches. He couldn't imagine a more ideal night.

When they arrived at Lake Chautauqua, Marc parked close to the massive bonfire. The pleasant smell of wood smoke evoked boyhood memories of summer campouts in the Adirondacks with his dad. Bathed in the flames' orange glow, a throng of people stood huddling for warmth. Some revelers turned around in circles, as if they were on a rotisserie cooking evenly on both sides. Children toasting marshmallows, elderly couples holding hands, dads piggybacking kids, and knots of teens schmoozing and putting ice down each other's back represented the wholesome life found in Westfield.

Although Marc's thoughts were anything but wholesome.

"At the risk of sounding sappy, I've really been looking forward to tonight." Her voice carried like a whisper against the roaring of the fire.

"Me too. There's nothing quite like it."

She grabbed his hand, tugging him along. "How about we check out the ice castle?"

"I'd love to," he said, letting her lead. He was only too happy to show the world he was with this exquisite woman.

Her gloved hand felt small and delicate in his. She tugged him along, rather like an over-excited little girl towing a dawdling playmate, through the crowd until they arrived where the iced-over lake met the sandy beach. About twenty feet from the frozen shoreline, constructed on the beach, stood a large, glistening castle made purely of ice. Every color imaginable glowed behind the opaque blocks, giving the setting a dreamlike effect. Sculptures of angels blowing trumpets surrounded the castle, and ice benches were positioned for those who wanted to sit—and didn't mind a frostbitten ass.

The pair entered the castle to examine the detail up close. She found a private room and led him to a centerpiece erected in the middle. A fountain made of ice, the jets of water spouting forth frozen in distinctly phallic icicles. She removed the glove from her right hand and fondled one such shape with her fingertips.

"Oh, look," she said, "the heat from my hand is making the ice melt. Here, feel it ..."

She yanked off his glove and placed his hand beneath hers. She guided their hands over the icicle until their warmth caused a runnel of moisture to bead along the icy shaft, and to drip from its tip.

Marc swallowed hard. He wondered if she knew what she was doing. *Of course* she knew what she was doing!

It was all he could do to stop himself from kissing her right then and there. They stood in silence, his arms circled around her, her hand cradling his. She shifted a little, allowing her back to press firmly against his chest.

"Isn't this spectacular? That someone could craft such ornate work from blocks of ice?"

"Yeah, amazing," he answered mechanically, his mind on the bulge in his pants.

"Do you know how they sculpt this stuff?" She turned and looked up at him, her lips a tongue tip away.

Her question fell between the blanks in his head. All he wanted to do was kiss her.

"Earth to Marc?"

"Huh?" He blinked, shaking his brain awake. "Uh, the sculptors, they cut the blocks of ice out of the lake using chainsaws and logging tools. Then they use smaller chainsaws to carve the artistic details. Because some layers of the ice freeze translucent and other parts transparent, that gives the ice a striped effect when they stack them to make the castle walls."

"That's pretty neat. How do you know so much about it?"

He shrugged indifference. "My dad used to help out the sculptors back in the day. He taught me how to work with my hands."

"I bet you can do a lot of things with those hands." Her voice was thick with sexual desire, the only invitation he needed.

Tenderly lifting her hand to his cheek, he brushed it against his day-old stubble and intertwined their fingers. They were alone. The perfect moment. Keeping their fingers wrapped together, his arms tightened, turning her body to face his. As he leaned down to touch his lips to hers, a little girl, dodging another child in a game of tag, bumped into them, breaking the spell.

"Hey, you kids!" he said, annoyed. "Why don't you find someplace else to play?"

"You're not the boss of me!" returned the little girl. She stuck out her tongue and went squealing around the corner, her playmate in hot pursuit.

"Kids," she said, shaking her head. "Don't you just love 'em?"

"Right now, I kinda hate 'em. Maybe we can finish this thought later?" he asked, eyebrows wagging.

"If you play your cards right. Let's grab some food."

They found their way out of the ice castle and into the bustling crowds. Several food vendors lined the street serving a variety of ethnic foods ranging from hot sausage to halushki to deep-fried fish sandwiches popular among the Westfield natives. As they strolled down the line of temporary outdoor restaurants, each picked their favorite dish before heading to a private bench along the outskirts of the bonfire.

Marc watched as she ate her fish sandwich with extra tartar sauce. Her face in the flickering firelight was a bewitching study in light and shadow. Barely touching his hot sausage sandwich, he couldn't take his eyes off of her. When he did finally bite into the seasoned meat, he realized it probably wasn't the best meal to eat before initiating a first kiss.

He finished the sandwich and noticed her empty plate. He liked that about her, that she was confident in who she was, comfortable in her own skin.

"Great sandwich, but messy," he commented, displaying his greasy fingers.

"I can take care of that." She brought his hand to her lips and slowly sucked each digit clean, her eyes fastened on his, pupils huge with desire.

"There. Is that better?"

"Uh ... yeah. How about dessert?"

"Here? I didn't realize you were such an exhibitionist. Kinky."

"You're dirty."

"Maybe you should clean me up."

"God, you make it hard to be good."

"That's not all I can make hard." She glanced at his crotch and giggled. "Well, hello, Mr. Happy."

Embarrassed, Marc crossed his legs. "Damn, you're a tease. What am I going to do with you?"

"I'll think of something."

Crackling wood puffed hot ashes into the air, the warmth on his face and chest a sharp contrast to the crisp air against his back. He reached over and held her hand as they sat staring into the ravenous flames. He wanted to capture the contentment of this moment and bottle it, douse himself in it over and over.

As she leaned into him, he circled his arm around her and pulled her close, so close that he could hear the faint gasp of her breath. They sat in silence, feeling the curves of one another's arms circling around each other. She fit so completely in his embrace, like a missing piece of his puzzle.

When she lifted her chin toward his neck, she hesitated, waiting for him to meet her halfway. The sweet scent of her skin lingered; a tingling sensation shot up his back in nervous anticipation of the taste of her mouth.

Slowly Marc cupped her face, tipped her chin up, and dipped his mouth to hers. Closing his eyes, his tongue rolled over hers and her mouth welcomed his eagerly. The bustling crowd stood still, the quiet roar of the fire silenced, the cold air now hot and melty through his body. His hands traveled down her neck and settled on the small of her back. Their lips moved together, their tongues danced in unison.

He pulled away, and as their lips parted, she opened her eyes, meeting his. Tracing the curve of her jawline with his fingertip, he kissed her once more, this time on the tip of her pink nose. He rested his forehead against hers, all the while holding her gaze. He couldn't remember the last time he felt so alive, or wanted someone more.

Marc held her for several moments in silence. His mouth brushed against her ear as at last he spoke, so softly he could barely hear his own voice.

"I think I'm falling for you."

He searched her for a reaction.

"I might be falling for you too."

It took a second for her confession to hit home. There it was, out in the open, clinging to the cold darkness. There was no way she could take it back now. He had been planning for this moment, waiting for just the right time, and now everything was falling into place.

This perfect, beautiful night with its perfect, passionate kiss was all the confirmation he needed. She was his.

Let the game begin.

Chapter 32

Twilight had long since darkened into dusk, and the evening winds picked up as the night grew late.

My quick trip to the porta potty ended up turning into a half-hour gab session with Mrs. Ellsworth about a mysterious man renting one of her rooms.

"He's a quirky one, he is," she had reiterated for the umpteenth time in her quavery voice. "Coming and going at all hours of the night, talking to himself. Why, one night he was even going to the cemetery, if you can believe it!" She clucked her tongue. "Thank the Lord he's leaving tomorrow."

Eventually the conversation about-faced to me—my job, my mother, and we couldn't forget my love life, a topic that everyone couldn't help but probe.

"Seeing anyone special, honey?"

Growing restless while Marc waited, I couldn't tell her about him—not yet. News spread fast in this town, and I wasn't sure if he'd be cool with it going public just yet.

On my way to find Marc, a sweet-toothed craving lured me to the concession stand where I vacillated between a chocolate fudge brownie sundae and cinnamon-sugar toasted almonds. I ended up getting both. It was a night to celebrate, after all. Might as well go all in.

Another twenty minutes later, carrying both desserts and two spoons for us to share, I surveyed the festival grounds for my boyfriend. Was it too soon to call Marc that? I didn't know, but I liked the sound of it, even if I only voiced it in my head.

I expected him to be somewhere around the bonfire, since nearly everyone huddled close to escape the bitter wind, but the darkness concealed any sign of him. There were only a few stragglers wandering beyond the fire's toasty yellow glow. I finally found him off to one side sitting on an Amish-made bench with his legs extended casually. I paused before approaching, taking in the image. The wind tossed his thick chestnut hair, and his cheeks were ruddy from the intense heat. His handsome face was pensive as he stared into the inescapable magnetism of the flames. God, he looked good enough to eat.

As I headed his way, a woman approached him from the opposite direction and sat down. She leaned against him, and they laughed together like old friends. Okay, I could be fine with harmless flirting, but when her hand rested on his knee, my jealousy kicked into overdrive.

I hated her immediately. Her skinny cheerleader body, flawless skin, bottle-blond hair, whore lips that had probably kissed countless other men. She was beautiful and sexy. Everything I wasn't. I was prepared to cuss her out. Storming my way toward them, I stopped when Marc looked up at me. My eyes pleaded with him; he dully gazed back. He smiled then, a cruel smirk, like he knew exactly what he was doing.

The other woman. I didn't know if I was her, or if the other girl was, but one of us got played by the master player.

After giving my heart to him, this was his game? To string me along, make me fall in love, then squash me like a bug beneath his boot. Why go through all the bother? Had I done something to him? All his letters, his honeyed words, now felt so empty and meaningless. Like a spiteful cosmic joke, and our love was the punch line. Curiosity egged me closer, though everything inside me screamed to turn away.

I decided not to give him the satisfaction of making a scene. I didn't know where I was running, but I had to leave. Go anywhere but here. He had seemed so perfect for me, but in a single day he both created and crushed my whole world. How could he do this, be so heartless? And the timing. Damn it, I gave up Los Angeles for him. To dump his shit on me now, after it was too late to change my course, was more than unfair; it was vindictive. How was I going to fix this mess I'd made of my life?

And then something inside me broke. I heard the *snap*, felt the pinch. I was pretty sure it was my heart. Allen had been right all along.

I ran until it burned. Blindly hurtling into the pitch-black night, tears stinging my eyes. I slowed my pace and looked back, half expecting him to chase me down professing apologies. But he didn't follow. Long-buried feelings for Jake bubbled to the surface. The pain felt just as raw as it did as a sixteen-year-old girl stumbling on her dead best friend.

I wanted to make Marc suffer like I was suffering. Hurt him like I hurt.

Stopping to rub out a cramp in my aching legs, I stepped into a puddle of slush that soaked through my shoes into my socks. I burst into loud, angry sobs, and I didn't care if the world heard my breakdown. I needed someone to hear, to see me. See me, please.

Once upon a time Marc had seen me. Cared for me. Might have grown to love me. And now, here I was, invisible. I wanted to escape, but to where? I had nowhere to go, stuck in hell. Westfield was a reminder of suffering and loss—my father, Jake, now Marc. Maybe leaving Westfield behind could be the ultimate revenge. Could I go through with it? Anything was better than this.

Without thinking, I pulled out my cell phone and dialed. Voice mail picked up, and while the message instructed me to leave a name and phone number and he'd contact me at his earliest convenience, I choked down the tears and steadied my voice.

Beep.

"Hi, Allen. This is Haley. Look, you were right about Marc. He doesn't care about me and I just want to move on. If you'll still consider taking me with you to Los Angeles, I'd like to go with you. Call me back and let me know. And ... uh ... I'm really sorry."

If Allen found it in his heart to forgive me, I could give Marc a big "fuck you" while I moved on and he suffocated in his small-town life with his small-town girl and small-town job. I was destined for bigger and better things than Marc could ever give me. At least, this is what I had to keep telling myself.

A moment later my phone beeped. A text. I rarely got them, considering my phone plan charged extra for them.

I got your message. Of course you can come. As for Marc, I'll take care of him for you. - Allen

I wasn't sure what to make of that last line, but I was too pissed to care. Marc ... LA ... Marc ... LA ... until I realized ... checkmate. There was no decision to make. I had already lost the game I didn't know I was playing.

Chapter 33
Marc

Marc was too tired to notice the dozen messages left on his answering machine Saturday night when he got home well after the bar closed. Too drunk to see the large, unmarked package on his front stoop. Too drained to do anything but fall into bed fully clothed and fully unaware of the whirlwind going on around him.

Dawn appeared, towing a gray Sunday morning behind it. As Marc nursed a hangover with a cup of coffee—black, like his soul felt—the blinking "12" on his answering machine stopped him dead in his tracks.

When he pressed play, the sound of heavy breathing sobered him up faster than the strongest brew ever could.

Message after message, each the same. Who the hell would leave such creepy messages for him—and why? Clearly he had done something to piss someone off. And that's when it hit him. It was so terribly obvious.

She had figured it out, figured *him* out.

Maybe he had gotten a little carried away, but this was overkill. He massaged his throbbing temples. *Think, dammit, think!* This wasn't just a game; along the way he had fallen for her for real. She needed to know that before this got out of control. Or maybe it was already out of control.

He was too sick to think. One too many drinks last night. As he headed to the kitchen for a refill, he heard a door squeak upstairs. Was someone inside the house?

Stealthily he climbed the stairs, avoiding the creaky ones. The view to his bedroom was blocked by the thick oak railing that ran up to the landing.

He stopped again and listened. A sound was coming from his bathroom. Slipping into his bedroom, he grabbed his Glock .40, holding it in the Weaver stance his dad had taught him, and rounded the corner toward the bathroom. Just as he was about to kick open the door, the heat vent whirred and a burst of hot air nudged the door. The door squeaked again. Was it just the vent he'd heard? His elbow nudged the door open, and sure enough, empty. He quickly checked the remaining rooms—all empty.

He was alone.

All alone.

Where the hell was Sheba? With the hangover, he hadn't missed Sheba's slobbery morning kisses. When he called her name and didn't hear the clink of her nails on the floor, he tried to remember last night. Had he let her out and forgotten to let her back in? It was all a haze of fumbling keys, tripping feet, and falling into bed. The poor dog must have spent all night outside in the cold. He hoped she'd forgive him after he shared some eggs with her for breakfast.

A cold gust of wind slapped him across his bare chest when he opened the back door.

"Sheba! C'mon, girl! Time for breakfast!"

He strained his ears for the sound of her dog tags jingling as she ran for the house. Nothing. Dead silence.

"Sheba, it's time to eat!"

Sheba was a little more stubborn than most dogs. If she was upset, Marc knew it. Life on the street had hardened her some.

Marc stepped into his boots, shrugged on a coat, and headed outside. The wind off the lake felt extra bitter this morning. Gingerly avoiding the minefield of icy patches, he made his way around the front of the house.

"C'mon, Sheba!" He willed the wind to carry the call to her, but still no bounding furball in sight. Something was wrong. Dread filled him.

His stride turned into a jog, which quickened into a run down the gravel driveway.

"Sheba! Where are you, girl?"

Then he spotted something. A shadowy lump, thick and soft looking, lying near the end of his driveway, much too close to the road. His heart started racing as panic set in. When he reached the end of the driveway, he found Sheba lying on her side, eyes closed; the tip of her purple tongue stuck out of her mouth. He sank to his knees beside her. His fingers probed for a heartbeat on her left side just behind the foreleg. He couldn't find it. He pressed his ear against her chest, but he couldn't tell if she was breathing or not. He spoke softly to her.

"Sheba, girl, what happened to you?" He looked up and down the street, uttering silent curses at whatever heartless coward had hit her and kept going.

When he picked her up, her body was limp yet warm.

She might still be alive. Holding her to his chest, he felt the pressure of oncoming tears. There was no time for worry; he needed to get to her the emergency vet. He'd deal with whoever did this once Sheba was okay.

This time he wouldn't hold back.

**

No car had struck Sheba. The culprit was antifreeze, the vet had told him. A common animal killer. Sweet, and lethal. The vet said Sheba could have licked antifreeze off the ground from a leaking vehicle. It took less than three ounces, he said, to poison a medium-sized dog. Sheba was lucky, though; she hadn't ingested enough to kill her. After administering antidotes, including activated charcoal, Sheba would be kept in intensive care to prevent kidney failure. The prognosis was good for a full recovery, and Marc had his fingers crossed.

Sheba was family to Marc, his baby girl. Someone had to pay for hurting his family.

As he rolled up his driveway to the house, he would never view this stretch the same way again. When he walked down the driveway to pick up the mail, he'd remember sprinting up, carrying his beloved dog. It would be a horror he'd never forget. And yet a part of him didn't want to forget. He wanted to get even.

Somehow he knew this was no accident. Someone did it to make a statement. To tell him they were watching, waiting. It was the same warning the mysterious telephone caller was sending—only now it almost cost him his dog. What if he was next?

As he stepped onto the front porch, he noticed for the first time a brown unmarked box, drawing him with a magnetic force. His first instinct was to toss it in the garbage without opening it. But what if it shed light on the identity of person behind all this sick shit? He couldn't risk not finding out.

Once inside the house, he dropped the box onto the dining room table. His heart slammed into his ribcage and his hands shook with rage as he grabbed a pair of scissors and sliced through the duct tape holding it closed. At this point he fully expected to find a bloody body part inside. Nothing would surprise him.

Except for this.

Chapter 34

"You must stay drunk on writing so reality cannot destroy you." Ray Bradbury was so right; that philosophy is the only thing that's keeping me alive right now.

I caught Marc last night with another woman. Or am I the other woman? God only knows what's happening.

Allen was right. How could Allen have known? As if he scripted my future before it happened. I don't know who to hate more. Marc for hurting me. Allen for being right. Or me for being so vulnerable and stupid.

I know I need to leave before I do something I'll regret. Maybe it's too late for that.

Beep. "Haley, it's Mom. Please call me as soon as you get this. I have something urgent—"

Skip.

"Haley, honey, please call me. It's Mom again. I need to speak with you immed—"

Skip.

"Haley, this is Shelly from work. Sorry to call you on the weekend, but we've been worried about you. Where have you been?"

Skip.

"It's Mom again. You can't go to Los Angeles with Allen—"

Skip.

I wasn't in the mood for Mom's theatrics; I had somewhere to be, after all. On a plane heading for my destiny. I'd catch up with Mom, Shelly, my boss once I got to LA. After a long conversation with Allen late into the night—full of tears and apologies and consoling words—he had agreed to take me back as his protégé. I'd burn bridges today—bridges to my job, to Westfield, to Marc. And I didn't give a shit. Let them burn.

My suitcases sat by the living room entryway, zipped and ready to go. Pacing the living room, I examined the luggage with uncertainty, hoping that the throbbing in my skull would stop. With only three hours of sleep and rattled emotions and nursing a broken soul—because that's what Marc had become to me, part of my soul—exhausted and tense didn't begin to describe how shitty and confused I felt. I had spent much of the night furiously packing, then unpacking, then packing again until my heavy eyelids refused to stay open a moment longer. Even after slipping into bed, my sleep was as restless as my spirit. Marc invaded my dreams—his fingertips on my face, his lips meeting mine, his arms around me warding off the chilly night air. Just as it was getting good, I felt a knife plunge into my chest. It was *her*—whoever his new fling was, stabbing me over and over. I awoke with a scream and felt frantically for the wound on my body. No blood, but the hole in my heart was still there.

Did he ever really love me? What about his notes? Where do I go from here?

The slut was clearly someone he knew. What previous life of his did she belong to, and why was she coming back now, popping out of the woodwork just when things were going so well for me? As much as I wanted to spit in Marc's face, I still loved him. Maybe that made me a glutton for punishment, but my heart wanted what it wanted … and lately it wanted what wasn't good for me. I glanced up at the clock on the mantel; it ticked away the minutes to an inevitable good-bye that I resisted all morning.

I wanted a reason to change my mind about California. I found none.

I used to see myself growing old with Marc, picture-perfect in my imagination. Now I saw nothing but cold darkness where my future should have been. I was tempted to call Marc, but there was too much to say and not enough guts to say it. What could I say that would change anything anyway? He wanted to protect his secrets at the expense of my heart.

The plane ticket in my hand challenged me to make a decision. Holding it up, my fingers trembled, ready to tear it in half. Fleeting memories of Marc's letters and our time together pressed in on me, but the obstacles between us were too wide and deep. This paper held my last chance at prosperity and fame. How could I shred that?

Taking one last look around me, the house was in perfect order, as it always was. I would miss it, along with a few flashes of my life here.

A horn honked outside my house—the cab I called to take me to the airport. A second honk, longer and more impatient, followed the first, rushing my thoughts. It was time to make a decision. The toughest decision of my life.

I reached into my pocket where I carried Marc's first letter. There was all the evidence I ever needed—his profession of love. Proof that he had loved me at one point. I held it up and read it once more, tore it in half, then again and again until the pieces fluttered to the ground. I made a point of trampling them as I ran to meet the waiting cab.

**

I arrived at the Erie International Airport lugging my entire future behind me in a pair of worn suitcases. I pushed my way through the mass of people and into the monstrous lobby area. Overhead signs seemed to point in a hundred different directions, intercom announcements adding to the chaos. Crowds shuffled around me, jostling one another like bumper cars.

I looked for a sign leading me to the luggage check-in. By the time I checked my suitcases and proceeded through security, I only had ten minutes until my flight's departure time. I didn't even know my gate number. A check-in girl had written it on the ticket, but I couldn't tell if it was the letter C or a G. Relieved to come across a flight itinerary screen scrolling through the flight details, I found my flight number and gate. Eight minutes until departure. Shit.

By the time I sprinted to my gate, I joined a slowly moving single file line of passengers heading into the terminal. Searching for Allen, I spotted him near the front of the line.

Sweaty from running, I wiped my brow dry and caught my breath. So this was what my new life would be like—always catching up. Places to go, people to meet, deadlines to plan for. Allen had told me the job required extensive travel, and at first it sounded thrilling. The hustle and bustle of adventuring all over the world would definitely be a change from the slow-paced life I was bored with. But right now I had second thoughts; it all sounded so stressful and exhausting.

The line moved up as passengers began boarding, Allen at the head.

"Good morning," a lady in a navy blazer greeted me.

"Good morning," I replied. But it didn't feel good. It felt wrong.

As I handed my ticket to the attendant, I realized this wasn't at all what I wanted. Living out of a suitcase, hailing cabs, massive crowds—that just wasn't me. With no one to share it with, what was the point? If I traveled somewhere, I wanted it to be with him. If I wrote something, I wanted to share it with him. Wherever I was, whatever I did, I wanted him to be at my side. Right now, standing in line to board a plane took me further from my heart's desire. I knew what I wanted, and it wasn't the bright lights of Hollywood.

It was a certain future versus an uncertain love, but I was willing to gamble that Marc and I could talk it through, figure it out. Together. Leaving my checked luggage to head to LA without me, I left the flustered attendant still holding the ticket and ran, my high-heeled boots clicking toward the exit.

"Haley!" shouted a voice, barely reaching me above the hubbub.

I stopped, glanced back to see Allen frantically waving. He was making his way through the crowd toward me.

"Where are you going?" he yelled.

"To win Marc back!"

"You're making a huge mistake!"

Now he was only a few yards away. People had begun to stare at us. I didn't give a damn. I felt like making a scene. A big, dramatic farewell scene. Just like in the movies. When he was close enough that I didn't have to yell, I let him have it with both barrels.

"No, you're wrong—I *almost* made a huge mistake. You might write and talk real pretty about love, Allen, but you don't understand it. You don't *feel* it. It's alien to you. All you care about is yourself. I see that now. I belong in my quaint little town with Marc. Yeah, I know you think he's ordinary. Maybe he is. But he's genuine, a real person, not some phony-baloney Hollywood egomaniac. So you can take your fame and fortune and your big premiere and shove them up your ass!"

Allen stood gawking at me, gobsmacked. A little group of onlookers broke into spontaneous applause. So that was what it felt like, to be the center of attention. No wonder actors craved it, but this small taste was plenty for me.

I soaked up that good vibe for a moment and then got the hell out of there. I had made my heart a promise, and I aimed to keep it.

Chapter 35

By the fourth time my cell phone rang on my way home, I asked the cabbie to turn down the radio—what kind of cab driver blasted reggae, anyway?—and picked up my cell phone.

"Hello?" I was agitated and showed it.

"Did you see the news today?" Mom was almost hysterical.

"No, Mom, I'm on my way home from the airport right now. I haven't checked the news."

I heard a big sigh of relief. "So you're not on the plane then?"

"No, I'm not going."

"You're not with that teacher of yours?"

"No, I'm by myself right now."

"Thank God you're not on that plane, Haley! I've been trying to get hold of you all day. I was watching the news and you wouldn't believe what I saw. They've been covering this story for the past couple days."

I groaned as she clearly relished dragging this out. Mom was a news junkie—CNN, Fox, CNBC, she watched them all—which I guess was exciting when you had nothing else to get excited about. When Myron Cope—the long-time voice of the Pittsburgh Steelers—died last year, you would've thought Mom lost her best friend. She mourned his passing for months. So her stampede of random news facts was nothing unusual.

"Go ahead. Tell me, Mom."

"Allen Michaels—he's all over the news."

"What?" I must not have heard her right.

"His wife, ex-wife or whatever she is—they found her body last night."

He had mentioned things not going well with her, but murder? No, I hadn't seen that coming. It took a minute for me to find my voice. "Are you serious?"

"I wish I wasn't. She had several stab wounds in her abdomen and he must have dumped her in the woods and tried to cover her body up with brush. Some hiker found a partially decomposed body and they think it's her."

"Do they think he did it?"

"Evidence points to him. They can't find the murder weapon, though. The police are looking for him now. He disappeared from his Los Angeles home a few weeks ago, but they weren't able to trace him here. They had questioned him when she first went missing, but there was nothing to imply foul play. Until now."

No body, no crime. I'd watched enough *CSI: Miami* to know that.

"Any idea why he would have killed her?"

"The media's saying they had a pretty ugly separation and she filed for divorce, giving him motive to kill her. He's worth a fortune and her demands would have left him pretty bad off after the divorce."

"I ... I can't believe this. He seemed so ... well, I wouldn't say normal—nobody from Hollywood is—but not a killer."

"People aren't always what they seem, I guess. You should know that more than anybody." She was referring to Jake. A truth that I still couldn't stomach. "Allen's gone, right?"

"I saw him leave this morning."

"You watched him physically get on that plane?"

"Well, no, but ..."

"What? Sweet Mother of Jesus! So he could still be around? Haley, you've got to hide!"

"Get a grip, Mom! I'm sure he's gone. He was boarding when I got there." I didn't tell her that he ran after me, or that I had told him off.

"You should alert the police anyway. They should know to expect him at the Los Angeles airport."

"I will."

"I want him out of our town. Oh, and the police might want to question you about him and his whereabouts, so be prepared."

"Why me?"

"Well, you were the last one to see him. And you know where he's heading. Make sure you call them, okay? It's not safe having him running free."

"Okay, I'll take care of it." Talking to the police was the last thing I wanted to do.

"Call me if you need anything, honey. I'm just glad you're okay. I don't know what I would have done if—"

"Mom, it's okay," I interrupted, not wanting to explore worst-case scenarios. Losing Marc, following a wanted killer to the other side of the country ... I had already endured enough worst-case scenarios today to last a lifetime.

"I know, but I just couldn't bear to lose you."

I couldn't listen to another word. My brain was on overdrive, and I hadn't even had my coffee yet. I needed food, a nap, and then I'd deal with this.

"Mom, everything is okay. I'll call you later. But right now I need to take care of something."

She thought I meant calling the police, but that could wait. I had loose ends to tie up first.

Chapter 36
Marc

It wasn't a body part. But what Marc found inside the cardboard box was just as disconcerting.

Marc's stomach felt like it was digesting rocks as he read the threatening note strategically placed atop a thick sheaf of papers:

Stay away from her. If you don't, I hope you're ready to die for her, because you'll be next.

Marc couldn't help noticing the heartless motherfucker apparently behind Sheba's poisoning had strangely elegant handwriting. What kind of person hurt an animal? A jelly-legged coward who hid behind anonymous letters. Marc was in shock. But after a breath, anger replaced the alarm. Slamming the note on the table, he pulled the box toward him, wondering how many more threats he'd find. At least fifty pieces of paper, he guessed, as he gauged the thickness of the heap.

As he reached in to return the original letter back to the box, he discovered an image on the back. The threat had been written on the back of a candid photograph of him and Sheba sitting on his back porch. A black marker scribbled out Sheba's face. So he was right. Sheba's poisoning was no accident.

And he was next.

This was it. The test his loss-filled life had spent years preparing him for. Either cower or fight back. He'd always cowered—there was no other option. When his mother died he was too little to fight for her. When his father got sick, he stood by, holding his hand as death ravaged him. When Julie broke his heart not once, but twice, he helplessly watched her go, first as a boy, later as a man. Everything was a series of meaningless moments amounting to little more than a lesson that joy would always slip through his fingers like grains of sand. There was no point fighting for what he wanted; he'd lose it in the end regardless.

Accustomed to death, Marc had always been acutely aware of his mortality; he had done nothing of consequence with his life. Yet as he faced the very real possibility of its ending at the hands of this deranged psychopath, his personal accounting amounted to little. He'd helped out a person or two, but what did that matter in the grand scheme of things? He'd die and the world would continue to spin, missing not a beat without him. The sad reality of his existence felt worse than the fear of dying.

And now his life was threatened without a chance to rectify his transgressions—particularly his latest one. His act of revenge on the woman he ended up falling head over heels for. He'd spent so much time obsessed with figuring out how to hurt her that he hadn't seen the hurricane brewing around him. Maybe he deserved this shitstorm. Yes, he decided. Justice was due.

Stay away from her, the note said.

Either it was a jealous ex-boyfriend or someone who simply wanted to make his life a living hell. But without more information, there was no way to stop whoever it was. Or was there? He couldn't take this lying down, whether he deserved it or not.

As determination settled in, he wondered if the cops would take this seriously. An animal poisoned with antifreeze was an animal cruelty case, but he had no proof it hadn't been an accident. But that incident, coupled with the threatening note—surely that was enough to warrant an investigation. And he hadn't even looked at the rest of those papers. He didn't like to admit that he was afraid to. After reading the threat, there was no telling what kind of sick shit they contained.

Out of the corner of his eye, the answering machine blinked new messages he never got around to listening to earlier that morning. He pressed Play.

The breathing was soft, unnaturally rhythmic. Like puffs of forced air. Maybe he could trace back the last number that called. Pressing *69, he hoped the caller hadn't masked his number. Following a piercing beep, a digital message told him the number was blocked.

"Figures," Marc mumbled.

There was no choice but to involve the police, as trivial as it would sound. The threat was real, unignorable. Perhaps they could trace the number or analyze the box of letters and find out if there was any way to start narrowing down his stalker's identity.

**

Officer Rice had come and gone, taking Marc's statement and filing a police report. He had handed over the letters, notes, and pictures after spending hours leafing through the discomforting artifacts of someone's obsession. Some were nonsensical, others eerie, all of them disturbing:

I'm your number one fan.

I do wish we could chat longer, but I'm having an old friend for dinner.

I tried to taste the life of a simple man. It didn't work out.

This one very simple idea that changed everything. That our world wasn't real ... that in order to get back home we had to kill ourselves.

At first they seemed innocuous enough. Mostly random thoughts. Until it registered what some of the notes were. Movie quotes. Not just any movies, horror flicks. *Misery. The Silence of the Lambs. Se7en. Inception.* What were they trying to say? All Marc could read between the lines was that the sender was crazy.

The officer labeled it a case of animal cruelty and communications harassment—but they'd need more if they were going to find and stop the motherfucker.

"Can you check for fingerprints?" Marc asked.

"Sure," Officer Rice nodded, "but unless the person is already in the system, it won't help us find out who he is."

"So what the hell am I supposed to do in the meantime?"

"Until your life is directly threatened, or there's someone who witnessed this box getting dropped off ..." Officer Rice gestured to the thick woods creating a wall of privacy for whoever did this to do so undetected. "You can see there's not much we can do. No witnesses. You have no known enemies—that you're aware of. We'll run fingerprints, but that's as far as we can go right now. But if anything else happens, let us know," Officer Rice told Marc as he left.

What was the point if it'd only be a slap on the wrist? Because that's all that communications harassment or animal cruelty would get the sick bastard, if caught. A damn slap on the wrist.

Their hands were tied until a dead body showed up, and by then it'd be too late as it most likely would be his own. Apparently it'd be up to Marc to protect himself.

He retreated outside to his back porch for fresh air to clear his head. Agonizing over the minutiae wasn't helping him see the big picture. There was a reason he was targeted. What the hell was it? He was tired of trying to force an answer. It wasn't up to him anymore. It was beyond him now.

Numb with worry, he clung to the spectacular view that offered momentary comfort. A nimbus circled the sun as it slowly sank into Lake Erie, painting the sky and whitecaps a sherbety orange. It reminded him of something. What, he couldn't quite place. All he knew was, he'd never get tired of the spot, his personal oasis. He just wondered how much longer he had to enjoy it.

With so much stress pulling him down, sinking him into depression, he headed back into the house. The back door slammed shut behind him as he stopped in the living room. The picture on the wall—the one Haley had given him during their dinner together when Allen Michaels had stopped by. His memory wandered to that night. Allen had been kind of an odd duck, but he suspected everybody from California was either a fruit, a flake, or a nut. More to the point, that night he could tell Allen had more than a professorial interest in Haley. And if anyone would veil threats with movie quotes, it would be Allen.

Marc hadn't thought much about it at the time, but now the pieces started to fit together. The old bastard had the hots for Haley, and Marc stood in his way. A clear-cut case of jealousy. He should have realized it before.

Allen was old—no match for Marc physically. Hence going after his dog instead. But hadn't he left for Los

Angeles already? At least that's what he had said. Creating an alibi, maybe?

He pulled the frame off the hook on the wall and examined it, compelled to look closely at the picture. He unhinged the back flaps that secured the cardboard backing and pulled it off. A personal note was written on the back of the picture:

May our friendship be as beautiful as a Lake Erie sunset.
– Forever Yours, Haley (2009)

He turned it back over, replaced the backing, and hung it back up.

As he paced the kitchen rummaging through the pantry—though he wasn't hungry—he grew antsy. It was too quiet. The kind of stillness that makes room for thoughts, worries, paranoias. He felt eyes watching him, but none of the windows had blinds—he'd take care of that later. He'd never needed them before now, because who would be traipsing around his wooded private property stalking him anyway?

But apparently someone had been.

Leaning against the kitchen sink, he gazed outside as darkness fell. Words flittered across the glass pane: *Stay away from her.* Only one *her* mattered.

Suddenly there it was, a face from the long-buried past.

"Holy shit."

He knew exactly who was behind the threats.

Chapter 37

The moon hung low and huge, a glowing ball almost touching the horizon. It was getting late and she was anxious to see Marc. Not an excited anxious, but a worried anxious. After listening to his voice mail, she heard urgency and fear. He hadn't said much more than that he needed to see her as soon as possible, and to be careful. What did that even mean? By the time she called him back, his cell phone was turned off and his landline busy. Something wasn't right.

She sped down the highway, cornfields and vineyards sliding by outside the window, passing slower traffic with the urgency of a NASCAR driver. She glanced in her rearview mirror, her foot like lead on the gas pedal, when she noticed that the same headlights had been behind her for the past few miles.

Thinking little of it, she continued, but subconsciously gripping her steering wheel tighter with each passing minute. Knowing several back roads that could get her to Marc's faster, she pulled off at the next exit. Headlights followed. Strange. It was an unpaved country road, rough as a washboard, that only local residents used. But at this time of night it could have been anyone behind her, she decided, tossing the thought aside.

Searching for her next turn in the deepening night, she decided to detour down some even more obscure roads that cut through the dormant cornfields and vineyards to shave a couple minutes off her time. Expecting the tailing headlights to have been long gone by now, she glanced up. Still, two yellow beams pursued her. Only about a mile until she'd be in town; they'd probably turn off on Main Street. Her pursuer seemed to keep a safe distance behind her, but always within view.

When Main Street came and went, and the same headlights threatened her from a little closer behind, she tested her pursuer even more. Slowing down at the first green light she came to, she cruised up to it until it turned yellow, then darted through just as it turned red. Sure enough, her pursuer stayed on her tail.

"What the fuck—?"

Panic set in. Did this have something to do with Marc's warning? Eyes on the road, she dug her fingers into her purse for her cell phone, found it, and flipped it open. The battery light blinked. Damn it! As she flipped it open the screen went dark. She tossed the piece of shit on the seat. She was on her own.

A sudden jolt rattled her as she lurched forward, a muted crunch of plastic. If she turned around to look, she might lose control. She floored the pedal to add some distance, but it wasn't enough. The car hugged her bumper, inching closer by the second.

She was back in the boondocks now, alone, being chased by some psycho, the yellow-white beams from hell blinding her as her rearview mirror bounced the light directly into her eyes.

She glanced down at her gas gauge; the arrow hovered on empty. A dead cell phone battery *and* a near-empty gas tank. Could things get any worse? The night was growing late, and she needed to get somewhere public.

A sharp bend up ahead offered the only chance of losing her pursuer. It'd slow whoever it was down, giving her time to slip into the side road that went by Corby Hancock's cornfield. She hit the curve doing 50 and skidded into the next turn. She glanced in the rearview:

the coast was clear. Just as she hoped, the distance between the cars had been enough; she'd made the turn undetected.

But she wasn't taking any chances.

Pug Jenson's dying gas station, barely open these days, loomed up ahead. It was closed for the night, but at least the floodlights were on, and Pug's rusted-out old hulk of a wrecker—which she thought looked unnervingly like the Creeper's vehicle in *Jeepers Creepers*—sat alongside the single pump island, looking scary as hell. These signs of life, she prayed, would make her pursuer think twice about stopping. She pulled behind the cinder block building and shut off her lights. No one would spot her car in the gloom, and from this vantage point she had a view of the road and the pump island.

Her hands trembled, but as the minutes passed, her sweaty palms began to relax their grip on the steering wheel. *God help me!* A dark sedan pulled up to the pump island and sat idling. A figure emerged, wearing a wool cap and a long coat. A tall man, pear-shaped. He reached into the car and tapped the horn twice. He looked to his left and to his right, and then took a long piss against the pump. As he pulled away, she couldn't suppress her giggling.

Over the next fifteen minutes just one car whizzed by the gas station. Her pursuer had likely given up on the chase, but that didn't mean he was done with her.

Chapter 38

I pulled onto my idyllic residential street lined with old-fashioned streetlights and quaint happy homes. All of them blind to the horrors that darkened the street just outside their closed doors.

They had no idea what monsters lurked in the dark. But I did.

Mentally and emotionally drained, I wanted nothing more than to go to bed and forget the day ever happened. I parked in my driveway, seeing my dark, empty house with new clarity, with a saddened realization that I was alone. I was too exhausted to call the police about Allen's flight to Los Angeles; if I knew my mother, she had likely beat me to it. All the drama would have to wait until morning. Sleep was what I needed. Lots of sleep.

I stumbled inside, too numb to take off my shoes or my coat or to lock the door behind me. Wandering through the darkness, I found the sofa and fell into the worn cushions. I managed to shed my coat while grappling for a throw blanket before falling into a fitful sleep.

**

Jake isn't home, and there's only one other place he would be when his mom tells me on the phone that he had ridden his bike to my place over an hour ago. I sprint down to the barn, knowing I'll find him at our usual hangout. I'm eager to talk. Apologize, mostly. I had been angry at him. Angry at him for letting me make love to him when he didn't love me back. Angry that he used me. Angry that he lied. I should never have yelled at him, though. Never have threatened to tell his secret.

I run to the barn ready to say all of these things, to give him a million sorrys, as many as it takes for him to forgive me. As many hugs as it takes to fix things between us.

When I get to the barn it's eerily quiet. I know something's wrong. I hear a strange creaking sound I can't place. As I round the first horse stall, there he is. Jake. Hanging from a rafter that creaks under the weight of his swaying body.

I run to him shrieking "No no no, please, Jake, no," clawing to pull him down. But his body is already cold to the touch. As I crumble to the floor littered with hay and clumps of dry dirt, I find a letter. From Jake.

As I lift the paper, I find myself no longer in the barn next to Jake's dangling body, but now in my bedroom, curled up in the corner of my bed, weeping as I read words from the boy whose future is covered by the dust of moments never lived:

Haley,

I'm sorry. I'm sorry I hurt you. Sorry you had to see me like this. But I can't live a lie anymore. And I can't come out of the shadows. That's where I've been hiding for the past two years, unable to be real. I first realized who I truly was two years ago. I wish I could have told you then, but I was afraid.

I never meant to use you. I've always loved you, you know that, right? What we shared was genuine, but I have feelings inside that I can't explain. I try to explain—to myself, to people that demand to know why I'm so goddamn weird—but the words never come out right.

I'm gay.

Wow, that was easier than I thought. And God, it feels good to get it off my chest. I'm gay and my family will never accept me like this. We both know what it's like to be a misfit because of who we are—or who we aren't. But at least you have your Mom and sister who love you for you, and you have me. I have no one on my side, not even you. My own family is disgusted by me. Maybe I am an abomination, but aren't we all? My father drinks. My mother gossips. And I like men. Am I really so unlovable because of this?

Rather than endure their judgment and hatred, it's easier to disappear. To end whatever is messed up in my head that makes me this way.

I almost told you once, about a year ago. We were passing notes in math class, and I wrote it down. Then tore it up it in shame. I'll miss our notes to each other. I kept them in a box all these years, reading them when I needed a laugh or a smile.

I know I let you down, but it's easier than trying to survive a life I don't fit into. Maybe if people showed more love than hate I'd be alive right now. Hell, a lot of people would. But people thrive on hate. They love that taste of self-righteousness.

If you ever miss me, I left the box of notes for you in the hayloft. I hope they'll keep you company when I can't.

Goodbye, Haley. You'll live forever in my heart.

Jake

**

Morning followed a night of regretful tears, and I awoke with a twinge in my neck and a throb in my skull. I had propped my head at an awkward angle on the arm of the sofa, leaving me with achy regret for sleeping on the couch. My eyes felt sore from crying. I could feel they were bloodshot.

Lack of sleep was catching up to me as I sniffled. A cold, most likely. I wondered if medicine would clear my sinuses. Too bad there wasn't a magic pill for exorcising one's demons.

Pushing off the quilt that I had cocooned around me, I hobbled to the table where I had left some of my favorite letters from Marc. I had planned to use the memorabilia in a scrapbook for him one day, for a birthday or an anniversary we'd never celebrate together. Even if I did forgive him for screwing me over, how could I know he'd never do it again? Yet I clung passionately to a glimmer of hope that maybe, just maybe, we could still have our happily ever after.

I flipped through my heartfelt poems, the tender prose, my scribbled journal entries predicting our future together ... words from my silly, stupid heart. If our love for one another was so pure, so deep, so fucking wide, how could Marc replace me with someone else—and so quickly? One minute we were in love, the next he was flirting with someone else.

I will win him back. I must *win him back,* a familiar voice avowed from the depths of my despair. It was the voice that had given me comfort while going through the trauma of losing my father. The same voice that helped me cope after Jake took his life. Rising again from the ashes, now it became the voice that confirmed that Marc was the one for me. This was the only voice I trusted nowadays.

He's not worth it, a second voice countered.

I just need to fight harder, the first voice bristled.

But I was so tired of fighting. My entire life felt like one perpetual battle.

Then I heard a third voice—a soft whisper, gentle as a summer breeze.

Let him go. Just let it all go.

The calm took me by surprise. It made so much sense—just let him go. Move on. Let it heal, the hole that first opened fifteen years ago and had been festering ever since. The answer was right there in front of me: just let go.

Just let go? That would be the easiest thing to do. But could I just let Marc leave me like Daddy left me? Like Jake left me? Maybe this time I can control it. Maybe this time I can have what I want. I deserve to be happy, don't I?

And still the babel of voices raged:

I must win him back!

He's not worth it!

Just let go!

I deserve to be happy!

"Stop it!"

I hadn't meant to scream out loud. But it felt good. Damn good. I still felt confused, but at least the voices were silent now.

I frantically rifled through the pile of papers, looking for answers, solace, I didn't know exactly what. All I knew was that I wanted the pain to stop.

A photo of Marc smiling. Damn, he looked fine! I pressed the photo to my chest. A goodbye—that's what I needed. My gaze found the fireplace. There was enough kindling to start a fire. On the mantel I found a match, lit it, placing the red flaming tip against the crumpled corners of the picture. The flame took. Tossing it into the stone cavity, I grabbed the stack of papers, knelt by the hearth, and one by one fed them into the yellow flames until every last letter had turned to a powdery gray dust.

"Well, I guess this is it," I muttered through swelling tears. "It's over now. I'm giving up."

Everything I had grown to love was ashes now. Memories lost to the flames. No more Los Angeles. No more Oscar-winning screenplays. No more Marc. In my efforts to hold onto it all, I'd lost it all.

Pain sliced through my head. All I wanted was to be numb, to feel nothing. No ache, no sorrow, no joy, no pleasure.

There was only one way to achieve that freedom.

Chapter 39
Marc

It had been more than a decade ago since Marc was last here at Papa Giovanni's Ristorante with Julie Carter. Their first real date, he remembered. Two teenagers, crazy in love—and lust, that night. Amid the fuzzy details of what they ate and what they talked about, one thing did still live in vivid Technicolor: how beautiful Julie looked that evening.

Tonight she didn't look ravishing. Tonight his nerves weren't tingling with teenage anticipation. Tonight wasn't a night to celebrate. Tonight was about survival.

Holding Julie's hand, Marc stepped through the fancy arched entryway that led into the dimly lit lobby. A gust of wind tagged along, whooshing past him into the waiting area. Hidden on the outskirts of town, Marc had once considered the restaurant his and Julie's little secret. Since their last date here, new ticky-tacky home sites had popped up, growing the clientele.

Tonight, there wasn't an empty table in the place. On each table was a votive candle and a single rose in an elegant bud vase. From hidden speakers came Luciano Pavarotti's incomparable tenor voice singing "'O Sole Mio." The mood was achingly romantic, and the delicious food was an irresistible aphrodisiac. Couples sat staring into each other's eyes, fantasizing about the passionate sex that would cap a perfect evening.

Marc nodded toward the bar, and Julie followed. A penguin-suited waiter passed by, carrying a straw-wrapped bottle of Chianti. He smiled and bid them *buonasera.*

The décor hadn't changed a bit—warm neutral colors and vivid countryside murals depicting the owner's Sicilian origins. Marc saw the same cracks in the ceiling, the result of the building settling. The menu handed to him by the bartender offered the same authentic Italian cuisine he remembered.

This particular restaurant held a special significance for the couple: they'd come here on their first official date as teenagers. Of course, back then twenty dollars a plate was steep for a kid who worked part-time after school as a gas station attendant. But Marc had insisted on bringing Julie here to impress her. She had jumped at the chance, as he knew she would, and in an unexpected act of charity had ordered the cheapest entrée on the menu.

As Marc's memory ventured back to that era where big bows and puffy sleeves were all the rage, he had no difficulty remembering what she wore on that date. A lipstick red dress—always her best color, especially being a blonde with a rosy complexion.

The bartender cleared away the mess of half-finished drinks and soggy napkins from the bar top.

"What can I get you?" he asked distractedly.

Marc wanted to get trashed, and quickly. He'd already emptied half a six-pack at home. "Three fingers of Macallan, neat. And an order of calamari."

He ignored Julie's glare of disapproval. She hadn't earned the right to judge him yet.

The bartender turned to Julie. "And you, ma'am?"

"A dry martini and bruschetta. Oh, and an order of the stuffed mushrooms. Thanks."

The bartender returned shortly with their drinks. Marc immediately picked his up and downed it in one gulp.

"Okay, mind telling me why you wanted to come here, of all places?" Julie demanded snottily. Some things never changed.

"I wanted to come someplace familiar, comforting. I can't be at home right now. I'm a fucking man afraid to be in my own house. How pathetic is that?"

Julie rested her hand on his. "Babe, it's not pathetic. Someone tried to kill your dog. You're clearly being targeted for some reason."

As the bartender delivered another, Marc sipped it this time as his nerves settled.

"I know who did it."

"What? You do? Why didn't you tell the police?"

"Because I wasn't sure before, but I'm sure now."

Her eyebrows rose in a question mark. "And?"

"Your ex. He's trying to break us up."

"No, that's ridiculous. We split up on good terms. Besides, there's no way he'd hurt your dog. Or any dog."

"Then explain this, Julie." He handed her the note.

"*Stay away from her*," she read aloud. "I don't know what this means, but it's not my ex. It's not even his handwriting."

"Then who, Jule—who wouldn't want me with you? It's not like it's public knowledge. No one knows we're dating. He's the only one that makes sense."

Her sigh was leaden. "Okay, I have something to tell you, but please don't be pissed. Can you promise that?"

Rolling his eyes, he lifted his scotch like he was saluting the pain. "Lay more shit on me. Let's just deepen the cuts." He turned to her. "Just tell me."

"Greg and I didn't mutually break up. He broke up with me ... for another woman. That's how I know it's not him, because he was very much done with me."

"Oh, I see. Someone gets a taste of her own medicine." The words snaked out in a slow slur. The alcohol was finally doing its job. He embraced the numbing sensation that made him feel like telling the whole world to go fuck itself.

"Don't be so cruel." The wounded look on her face told him he'd cut her deep.

The stool tilted under him, the room shifted crookedly.

"Hey, you alright? You're not looking too good." Julie hopped off her stool to his side, holding him upright. "And I'm sorry I lied about Greg before, but I didn't think it was relevant. I wanted to be with you regardless. I realized I had made a mistake leaving you like I did."

Ha. What poetic timing to discover her heart's deepest desire after being dumped. How fucking romantic. "Should I feel honored? That you picked me because you got kicked to the curb like you did to me? Should I get on my knees in gratitude that I made the cut?"

He stumbled off the stool onto the floor in a mock groveling kneel.

"Knock it off and get up. You're drunk."

"No fucking way. Really? You can tell? I didn't think it was obvious."

The bartender sat the bruschetta appetizer in front of them. "He bothering you, miss?"

"No, I'm fine," Julie assured him, adding wryly, "My date's just practicing his proposal. Needs work, huh?"

The bartender smiled. He moved away, eyeing Marc warily.

Marc climbed back up on the stool, laying his hand on hers.

"I'm sorry I'm being an asshole. I'm just upset is all. This whole thing has got me all twisted up inside."

Julie rested her head on his shoulder. "I suppose I deserved it. Let's just enjoy our food."

The stuffed mushrooms were no ordinary stuffed mushrooms, monstrous in size, filled with crabmeat, cheese, and herbs that delivered a sweet kick to the taste buds. Upon picking one up, Marc envisioned a flashback to their first date.

"You remember ordering these on our first date?" he murmured. Nostalgia mixed with alcohol had calmed him somewhat.

"Of course. That's why I ordered them. I've never stopped loving you, you know. I was a bitch back then, but I was also really young. Young people make stupid mistakes. I just hope you can forgive me."

"Just back then?" he ribbed.

She replied with a playful elbow jab.

As his teeth sank into the buttery vegetable's flesh, he turned to her.

"You're my vice, Jule. I'll always keep forgiving you, no matter how much I want to get revenge for how you broke me."

"Revenge? What are you talking about?"

"I have a little secret of my own. Ever since I heard you were back in Westfield and single, I've been planning this—planning to woo you then screw you."

Her eyebrow lifted. "Are you serious?"

"Why do you think I said yes to dating you again? It wasn't because I was feeling all warm and fuzzy. I wanted to hurt you like you hurt me—twice, in case you've forgotten. Somehow I keep falling for you over and over, no matter how much damage you do."

Julie sat in a contemplative silence so unlike her. She always had a retort or a joke or remark for everything. Not this time.

"I ... I'm so sorry, Marc. I wish I could show you how sorry I truly am."

He waved her off. "Ah, you'll get a chance, I'm sure. For starters, how about don't do it again? I can't worry about the scales that balance out fairness and justice anymore. It's too fucking exhausting. I want to be with you, it's that simple for me."

"It's that simple for me too," she muttered into his cheek as she kissed him.

"So you forgive me?" Marc asked, his forehead pressed against hers, eyes locked on hers.

"Of course. Do you forgive me?"

"I always have, always will."

It seeped in slowly at first, then rushed over him. *Freedom.* Freedom from worrying about getting even with her. Freedom from bitterness or vengeance. Freedom from the fear of losing her all over again.

Losing her would kill him ... if someone else didn't kill him first.

**

Marc forgot his fear; alcohol will do that to you. After soaking up Papa Giovanni's vibe, they were both as horny as hell. Julie had driven home; Marc was in no condition. They stumbled through his front door, hands grabbing, arms pulling, bodies undressing. With his mouth pressed against Julie's, his "Let's head upstairs" was muffled by her probing tongue and excited giggles.

Their coats landed on the stairs as he tugged her up the stairwell behind him, their steps rushed and eager. They made their way to his bedroom, pausing every few steps to kiss and grind their bodies together.

Their kisses resumed as they stepped onto the landing, working their way toward his bedroom with passionate pauses to make out. It'd been so long since

Marc had her in his arms, and he couldn't wait another moment.

In the bedroom's doorway Julie stopped, pulled away, gasped. Marc's eyebrows lifted with curiosity, then fell as her startled expression became a scowl. He turned to look in the same direction. Haley Montgomery sat calmly on his bed, hands folded on her lap, legs crossed.

"What the—? How did you get in here?"

"The better question is what you're doing here with ... whoever this skanky whore is."

Julie was livid. "What the hell, Marc? Are you gonna let this fat bitch talk to me like that?"

"Yes, Marc," said Haley evenly. "Are you going to let me talk that way to your skanky whore?"

Marc swayed a little. His tongue felt swollen and cottony. "Get the hell out, Haley. Get. Out."

"I'm sorry, Marc, I'm not going anywhere."

"Okay, you asked for it."

He lurched toward the bed, grabbing for her. That's when he saw it. The glint of cold steel resting next to her thigh.

Chapter 40

After waiting almost an hour for Marc to come home, busying myself with a self-tour and an exploration through his personal effects, I was beginning to feel impatient. I had originally just wanted to talk things through. Figure it out together. Ask the hard questions I needed answers to. Why break up with me for someone else, without even telling me? Why drag me through the humiliation of it all? Why encourage me to sacrifice my career for him, just so he could play games with me? Did I ever really mean anything to him?

I was the best thing he'd ever find—I knew this. *Knew* it, because no one would ever treat him as good as I would. Ever.

I would never cheat on him, betray him, or hurt him. Because love didn't commit those sins, and I loved him. I loved him with such a ferocity that I would do anything—*anything*—to keep him. And I had. I showed up, in the middle of the night, ready to win him back. Ready to bleed my heart on the floor for him.

When he never came home, I grew restless. Angry. Then worried. Had Allen come for him in a fit of jealousy? A strange car sat in the driveway—not Marc's, but not Allen's. If Allen had turned his rental in at the airport, maybe he'd picked up a new one. The later it got, the more convinced I was that Allen had something to do with Marc's absence. That's when I found the steak knife in the kitchen, in case Allen came for me next.

These were the thoughts that niggled at me while I waited. All that worry for Marc. While he was out on a damn date with that bitch I saw him with at the ICE Festival.

Yes, I had already pieced it together. I wasn't as dumb as I looked.

Now here we all were, this cozy little trio.

"I'm *so* sorry I spoiled your little fuck session, Marc," I said. "God, I can smell your breath from here. Really tied one on, huh? I doubt if you can even get your pitiful little dick up, you bastard." I turned to her. "I'm Haley, Marc's girlfriend, in case he didn't tell you. I apologize for calling you a skanky whore. It's just that I couldn't think of anything nastier. That's a joke. It's okay to laugh." No reaction. "*Laugh*, dammit!"

She managed a nervous titter.

"I can't keep calling you skanky whore, I suppose. Your name—what is it?"

"Julie."

"Julie what? You have a last name, don't you?"

"Julie Carter."

I heaved a sigh of recognition. So *this* was the girl who had destroyed Marc not once, but twice. He had mentioned her before, but I had no idea this was *the* girl that got away. Well, she wouldn't get away this time.

Picking up the knife next to me, I stood, stepped toward them, the blade pressed against my leg. Their bodies shifted back in unison. Marc grabbed Julie's arm and pulled her behind him. Gallant son of a bitch. He looked at me, lips trembling.

"Why ... why do you have a knife, Haley?"

He no longer swayed or slurred his words; being scared shitless had sobered him up fast. He was afraid. Of me. I found this mildly humorous. Turning the knife over in my hand, I shrugged.

"I don't know. Maybe to protect myself … from you."

"Can you put it down before someone gets hurt?"

I heard the patronizing calm in his request. Calm me like a fussy child. Silence me, send me away. This asshole didn't even notice my pain.

"I'm really trying to understand what happened, Marc. You led me on, proclaimed your love for me, then just bashed what we had over the head with a club … all for the same girl who did the exact same thing to you? I don't get it. I thought we had something more. Something deeper."

"We … we do …" he stuttered.

"Was I just a pawn for you to get back at her?"

"No!"

"I don't believe you."

I took another step forward, bringing the knife up to chest level. Marc shuffled back, Julie still protectively behind him. I advanced slowly, inching them toward the stairs.

"Be honest, Marc. Did you even love me?"

"Of course, Haley, I love you. Please put the knife down so we can talk." Liar. Love didn't do what he did. We both knew this.

Stretching the knife toward him, my hand trembled. I didn't know why I aimed the point at him, readied the blade to cut him like he cut me. I had no intention of physically harming him; I didn't even know why I gripped it so steadfastly.

I had always thought I couldn't break any more than I already had, but Marc managed to find the last surviving piece before he crushed it.

He must have seen me soften, because he added "Let's sit down and talk."

"You know, I'm tired of talking. It's not like I can trust anything you'd say. You're a selfish asshole who tromps all over vulnerable women. Well, I have news for you. I'm done being your damn puppet."

We were at the top of the stairs now. I shoved Marc, pushing him back into Julie. She fell back onto the first step, grabbing the railing with one hand and reaching for Marc with the other. The tips of their fingers touched briefly. Her stockinged foot teetered, slipped. She plunged backwards, somersaulting *thump-thump-thump* down the stairs, pinballing off the railing and wall all the way. When her head struck the hardwood at the bottom there was a loud, sickening snap. Marc and I stood at the top staring with open-mouthed horror at her gruesomely contorted body.

No one moved for a shocked moment, then all hell broke loose. We rushed down the stairs, Marc to kneel beside her, me at a safe distance from them both. He cradled her head in his arms.

"Julie, open your eyes. Julie!" he begged through tears. Without looking up at me, he ordered, "Call 9-1-1!"

But I couldn't move. My feet felt rooted where I stood.

"Fuckin' call 9-1-1, Haley!" he yelled, this time turning around.

Blood bloomed on his shirt from where a gash on Julie's head rested. I thought I saw a shallow breath, and then she shuddered a final goodbye.

"No! Julie, come back. Please hang on!"

Laying her skull gently on the floor, he rose and lurched toward me, jaw clenched and veins popping with rage. "You did this! You killed her!"

"No, it was an accident! I never meant to hurt anyone, Marc—it was all a big bluff!" But he was blind with fury. Suddenly I feared for my life.

As he got within arm's reach, I swung the knife out, hoping not to make contact. I didn't want to hurt him; I only wanted him to back away. But the point hit his stomach, sunk in, and as I pulled back, a wound wetly gaped at me. He glanced down, eyes wide with shock. He grabbed his abdomen and fell to his knees.

"Oh my God! Marc! Are you okay?"

"Please, Haley ..." He coughed, hawking up a bloody ball of phlegm. Cupping his chin, I forced him to look at me.

"You can't tell anyone I was here. You understand that? If you say I was here, I'll tell them you pushed Julie. Do you hear me?"

He nodded. But I needed more.

"I'll blame you for everything—my word against yours. So it's our secret, right?"

"Yes," he said breathlessly.

"Okay, so we both promise not to tell anyone about Julie. Agreed?"

"I prom—"

The sentence dropped with him to the floor in a dull *thump*. The blood was seeping into his shirt faster, widening across his chest. The knife fell from my fingers, my senses lost in the horror of watching him bleed out.

I pressed my fingers to his neck, found a pulse, and exhaled. The blood—so much blood for such a shallow cut. The blade had barely touched him, I thought. I found a towel in the bathroom and wrapped it around his midsection, tying a knot to keep it tight. As I got up, I slipped in the blood and fell in a sprawl. Clambering to my feet, I saw the blood dripping from my forearms.

Blood has a different feel than water—thicker, clingier, viscid—and I became keenly aware of this as it soaked my clothes and skin. By now my body was acting on autopilot and I wasn't in control. The urge to vomit pulsed my stomach, and I ran for the front door and heaved over the front porch railing. Coming back inside, my brain rummaged through a million scenarios—all of which ended with me in prison for murder.

But I wasn't a murderer. Not yet. Marc was still alive. I'd make sure he lived. Julie, on the other hand, wasn't so lucky. But it was an accident, one that no one would believe. I had the means, motive, and opportunity for murder—that's all the cops would see. The only solution was to get rid of her body. It was a horrible, unnatural thought—*getting rid of a body.* But what choice did I have? If I hid it well enough, Marc and I could still have our future together. We'd make a pact—neither of us tell the cops about Julie, neither of us go to jail. Because if I went down, he was going down with me. This was all his fault, after all.

Dispose of her body, dump her car, leave no trace that she had been here. It was simple math. The most logical conclusion.

I headed for the garage, found a shovel, then wandered into the woods, searching for the perfect burial site. Lucky for me he had countless acres to choose from. When I found just the right spot, easy for digging, I trudged back to the house to fetch Julie's corpse.

Although she was twig thin, a boobless kind of skinny that reminded me of a tween boy, she was damn heavy to carry by myself. Somehow I managed to drag her around fallen trees, gnarled stumps, and jutting exposed roots to the spot where she'd rest for eternity. Maybe I'd even plant flowers for her, I thought mordantly.

With Julie's body on one side of me and the shovel on the other, I grabbed the handle, aimed it for the wet earth, pushed my weight into the spade, and dug. Blood and mud smeared across the front of my shirt in a blot of rusty red, and my jeans clung stickily to my thigh. I welcomed the patter of light rain tapping the leaves above, if only to wash away the guilt that stuck to my skin like tar.

217

Wiping the drizzle of raindrops mixed with sweat from my forehead, I rested a moment, caught my breath, leaning against the shovel handle with blistered palms. I hadn't thought to bring work gloves. I hadn't expected to be burying a body, after all.

Another, then another, moving earth bit by bit, shovelful by shovelful. I might as well have been hauling cement at the rate I was going, but it had to be done. Tonight. Fear drove my limp arms, my achy wrists, my blistered hands to keep digging. This deep black hole would bury the nightmare once and for all. One unmarked grave—that's all I needed in order to put the past behind me.

To hide what Marc and I had done. To wake up from this whole nightmare.

But was it ever really behind me? Because even as I dug, I felt my choices wrap their fingers around my neck, squeezing me, choking me, killing me. Sucking in a panicked patch of air, I could barely breathe. As much as I wanted this to be the end of the suffering, a cold reality chilled me to the bone: it was only the beginning.

Julie Carter was now a missing person. The cops would come looking. If anything tied her to Marc, he'd point the finger at me. I knew better than to assume he'd take the noble high road. After all the manipulations, empty promises, and lies, he'd throw me under the bus the first chance he got. But permanently silencing him wasn't an option. I still loved him, no matter how black his heart was.

Dawn was nearly here. I was running out of time.

Standing in the hole, it appeared big enough, wide enough, even if I had to bend her to fit. I pulled myself up out of the hole, the ache of hours of digging shocking my muscles with sudden frailty. And I was only halfway done—I still had to bury Julie's body.

218

Then I grabbed the shovel and hid my very last secret.

Chapter 41

It wouldn't hurt. Just one slice across—not too deep—and it'd be over. Like a paper cut. A very deep paper cut.

I knew better than to cut lengthwise. That would kill me, and that wasn't my intention. At least not today. No, today I just needed to show Marc how serious I was about our future together.

One cut. One swift movement across pink flesh. In a moment of desperation it sounded so easy, so quick. But as my hand hovered above my wrist with measured pressure, the cool stainless steel kissed me with its jagged teeth. My courage waned as my hand trembled with each heartbeat that pulsed beneath the knife's serrated edge. Only a thin layer of cells wrapped my precious lifeblood like cellophane.

No doubts, no hesitating. One slice and this part would be over soon enough.

I cringed as the blade slid into my skin, moving right to left, catching on the thin tendon about halfway across. My mind blocked out the pain, focusing all thoughts on his face—the only face that mattered to me now: Marc's.

But the demons pushed through.

Julie's gray skin, shiny with death. Her blood sinking into the tiny gaps in the wood floor. The sickly-sweet scent of mud and leaves scraping under the shovel blade. Her arms and legs flopping into the hole. The sound of sirens after I called 9-1-1 from Marc's home phone before running frantically to my car.

We had made a pact, Marc and me. Tell no one about Julie. Take the secret to the grave.

And if Marc told? Right now I was creating my insurance plan. Maybe he attacked me and that's how I got these cuts. Or maybe he drove me to kill myself because of his cruelty. I could come up with something to discredit him—no, to *destroy* him—if he reneged on our agreement.

Under the force of my steadied hand, I sliced the blade across and out, watching blood ooze from the cut, then build momentum as it trickled down my palm the way rain collected on a windowpane. The puddled droplets eventually dotted the quilt around me, the crimson chaotically adding to the kaleidoscope of colors.

I needed to make the phone call while I still had the strength and ability to dial. I fumbled to open my cell phone, then concentrated on pressing each of the memorized numbers. The line rang. Voice mail picked up, just as I expected.

"I kept my promise," I said. Marc would hear the message and understand. I'd never tell ... even unto death.

As my eyelids drifted lazily closed, I remembered a promise I had made to Daddy. *Find freedom from the pain.* But there was no freedom except in pain. Cycles of history attested to this truth as soldiers laid down their lives in the pursuit of freedom—freedom from tyranny, from slavery, from religious persecution. And the biggest sacrifice of all, Jesus Christ on the cross saving all of mankind. Bloodshed was the only means to freedom. And it was the only solution to my lover's battle.

Yes, Daddy, I kept my promise to you too.

**

Whether it was due to my throbbing headache or the loss of blood, I had blacked out and woke up God-knows-how-long later. The droplets no longer coursed down my wrist, rather they gelled to my body, working to seal the wound. Yet the wound of my heart was still gaping.

Pulling my shirtsleeve down over the cut, I realized I could never bleed out the sadness, the bitterness, the monster inside me. Perhaps suffering wasn't enough to cure me. Cleansing required exfoliation, and scrubbing took work. It was raw and harsh, but even that could not eliminate all traces of the past. The scars would always remain. But I didn't know if I could live with the scars anymore. There were too many now. Life without Marc was a life not worth living.

This time I'd cut my other wrist the right way. Down the street, not across the road.

I lifted the knife. It felt oddly heavy.

My hand dropped back to my side.

Try again.

But still my arm lay limp.

Maybe it was hauling a body through the woods. Or hours of digging. Or more hours of burying. Whatever the reason, with every ounce of strength now fully sapped, I couldn't make the next cut—the last cut. I hated myself for being so weak. I was too pathetic to kill myself correctly.

Absorbed in my self-loathing, I closed my eyes and entered my own world where nothing could hurt me. I shut out the spinning living room and the deafening silence. Mentally tuned out from my surroundings, I ignored the knock at the door, the booming voice outside, the squealing doorknob that turned with ease. I barely heard the door creak open, then approaching footsteps.

"Marc?" I whispered.

No answer. I was dimly aware of a shadow shifting across the room.

A panorama of images swept through my dazed mind: Marc's smile, each heartfelt note, Julie's dead eyes, Jake's hanging body, my father's frail hands, the heap of burned bloodstained clothes, the ashes of letters that had once been my connection to Marc. Poof! In a cloud of smoke I had destroyed our relationship and any evidence I was at his house last night. It was time to finish what I set out to do.

With a microburst of energy I willed myself back from my trance, pushing myself up on the sofa by my elbows. That's when I saw the figure looming underneath the living room archway.

"Haley Montgomery ..." he said.

But it wasn't Marc. And it wasn't Allen.

The stranger stepped toward me. I eyed the fireplace poker on the hearth, but he would easily overpower me, even with my weapon. Now another man stood beside him. As they stepped into the light I caught the glint of their badges. I jumped up, tried to run. A steel grip seized my arm.

"Haley Montgomery, you are under arrest for the murder of Julie Carter," the police officer said. "You have the right to remain silent ..."

His partner spun me around by the shoulders and cuffed my wrists behind my back. The cold metal clamped my skin, its grip painfully tight. I felt blood drip down my hand, and I decided it was time to make Marc bleed too.

Chapter 42

"Do you know why you're here, Ms. Montgomery?" The plainclothes detective took a sip of his black coffee and offered me a condescending smile. A uniformed officer stood next to the door.

The interrogation room wasn't anything like what I'd pictured in my television-inspired imagination. There were no cement block walls or a naked light bulb hanging from the ceiling over a folding table and metal chair. Instead, the drywall was painted a light gray to complement the heavy-duty blue carpet. The room smelled like lemon-scented Lysol furniture polish, not stale coffee and doughnuts. Waffle lighting flickered every so often, exacerbating my exploding headache.

I clenched my arms against my chest, shyly meeting the cold stare of the middle-aged man sitting across from me.

"Comfortable, Haley?" he asked.

Comfortable? As if. All I could think was: what the hell did Marc tell them? "Not exactly. But thanks for taking off the cuffs."

"Just a formality, you understand. Ready to talk now?"

I thought for a moment about the dangling question: Why *was* I here? A question of my own: What the hell did Marc tell them?

"You said this was about someone named Julie Carter, but I don't know anyone by that name."

"So you weren't at Marc Vincetti's house last night?"

I chewed on my bottom lip, a nervous habit. It was better than biting my nails, which my mother had criticized out of me during my teen years. "No, Detective …"

"Patella," he answered sharply.

"Detective Patella, I wasn't at Marc's last night." No one but Marc could verify one way or another. Let the battle of he said/she said begin.

"All right, let's start from the beginning. How do you know Marc Vincetti?"

"He's my boyfriend," I answered. I didn't bother to amend it to the past tense. No point giving myself a motive for taking Julie out of the picture.

"And how did you two meet?"

"Does it matter?"

"Just answer the question, please."

I recalled Marc showing up at my door that very first day, with his coltish grin. "Marc helped me with my computer." I didn't elaborate, keenly aware that he was taking mental notes. "Why is that important?"

"I don't want this to take any longer than necessary, so if you just answer the questions, you can get out of here quicker."

"Okay." He was getting the backstory. Piecing the puzzle together.

"So how long have you and Marc been"—he cleared his throat—"dating?" The word held a pungent sarcasm.

"Why did you say it like that?"

"Just answer the question, please."

"Since February."

"Hmm. Can you tell me a little about your, uh, relationship?"

This was my chance to paint the picture. Broad strokes, but with enough nuance to make me look innocent. "We love each other. Not that we don't have

225

rocky times, but that's normal. Sometimes Marc gets angry, hits me." I lifted my wrist and pulled up my sleeve, showing him the fresh scab. "But he's always sorry afterwards and treats me good otherwise. We even talked about getting married and having a family."

He glanced behind him at the officer standing by the door. "Do you two go out on dates often?"

"When we have time. We both work and are busy people."

"So you're still working? You didn't stop showing up for work a couple weeks ago?"

How did he know about that? It felt like the temperature rose 10 degrees. "Yes, I did take a leave of absence because I was supposed to take part in a screenwriting mentorship in Los Angeles, but it ended up getting cancelled. Is that a crime?"

"Apparently you didn't notify your boss of your leave of absence."

"I must have forgotten to tell him."

"I'm just curious as to what you've been doing with all your free time."

"I told you. Working on my screenplays." None of this had to do with Julie's murder. And why was it so damn hot in here? "Look, I have a right to know why you dragged me in here."

Detective Patella leaned back in his chair and laced his fingers behind his squarish head. It was all I could do not to stare at the pit stains, like yellowish moats, in his button-down shirt, which was at least a size too small. His unfashionably wide tide seemed to be choking him like a noose, making his face flush and his porcine eyes water. Observing how his belly spilled like a sack of potatoes over the waist of his khakis, I noticed something I'd rather not have seen. Detective Patella obviously wore boxers, not briefs. And he hung to the right. Gross.

226

"Haley, are you and Marc fighting right now? Did something happen that upset you?"

"No," I lied. "Why?"

"Because people hurt one another sometimes. Even those they love. It's perfectly natural to want to hurt back."

"Is Marc hurt?" I already knew he was.

"Marc suffered an injury. Stabbed. Do you know anything about that?"

I hoped my manufactured shock was convincing. "What? Marc's hurt?"

"He says you stabbed him after you shoved his girlfriend down the stairs."

The bastard sold me down the river. I knew it!

"You can be honest with me. You won't get in trouble if you were defending yourself."

If only he knew what really happened—that it all actually was a tragic, deadly accident. But no one would believe it. A man got stabbed and a woman died, then I buried the body. An accidental death, a cover-up—telling the truth didn't bode well for me no matter how eloquent I was. Lies would be my only saving grace. Marc would have to be the sacrificial lamb.

"We have reason to believe that a woman was murdered at Marc's house then buried somewhere close by. Your elusiveness gives the impression that you are covering for him."

"No, I'm not covering anything," I insisted. Then acting as if I thought better of it, I added with a sigh, "Marc has a temper. And sometimes it gets out of control. But I don't know about anyone named Julie or what happened to her. I can't imagine him actually *killing* someone, but I also can't imagine him cheating on me, which apparently he was doing."

"Haley, a woman died and he's claiming you did it in a fit of jealous rage. Give me something to prove your innocence."

"How do I do that if I wasn't even there?" I yelped. Maybe Detective Patella would swallow a truth-lie cocktail. "I was at home. I've never heard of or met Julie. I don't know what else to tell you other than that he's lying. Do you really think I could overpower two other people—one being a man twice my size and weight?!"

Although I was yelling, he was unfazed.

"Did you make several phone calls to Marc on Saturday night? And don't lie, because we can check phone records."

I didn't remember calling him, but I also drank a bottle of wine after I got home. Chasing away the blues and all that. In fact, I had felt that bottle of red the next morning with worst migraine ever. "I might have. Why?"

"Someone—I'm thinking you—left quite a few blank messages on his machine. I got a chance to hear them. Pretty creepy, if you ask me. What I want to know is why."

I couldn't say pocket dialing, since my flip phone couldn't do that. I could never afford the touchscreen model that had just come out this year.

"During our date at the ICE Festival, I saw him with another woman and got upset, so I left. After a bottle of wine, I might have called him, but I don't remember doing it."

"So you went to the ICE Festival together?"

"Yes, sir."

"Did he pick you up?"

"Of course, he's a gentleman."

"And when you left, what did you do?"

"I went for a drive to clear my head. I was hurt and angry; I needed to think."

"But if he picked you up, how did you get your car?"

A simple question, and yet I didn't know the answer. The details were veiled in mist in my head. I couldn't clear the fog. The detective, slovenly though he was, was no fool; he picked up on this. How had I gotten home? I couldn't remember, but I could never confess this.

His smug expression irked me. Sitting there watching me from his high horse, his scrutiny making me shift uncomfortably in my seat. The plastic squeaked beneath me.

Detective Patella reached for a cream-colored folder sitting on the table and flipped it open. He spun the folder around and slid it toward me.

"Do you know what these are?"

I stared in surprise at the familiar stack of documents. "Yes. They're my notes from Marc."

Question was, how did he get them?

"So he wrote you these?" He tapped a stubby index finger on the top page.

Of course he wrote them. Isn't that what I just said? "Yes. Did you go through my things?"

He grunted. "You don't remember dropping these off at Marc's house early yesterday morning?"

"What? I never dropped those off."

He flipped through the stack and plucked out a love letter and laid it in front of me. "Pretty passionate stuff."

Embarrassed and enraged, I reflexively turned the page over. "Why do you have those? They're my personal business! Besides, what do my letters have to do with anything?"

"When we brought you in this morning, we found charred scraps of some letters. Why were you burning them? Was it because of Julie?"

"Fine, yes, I wanted to get rid of them after I saw him with her! Haven't you ever suffered a broken heart, Detective?"

"Yes, I have. But I don't kill over it."

"I'm telling you, I didn't kill her. Did Marc cheat on me? Yes. But do I still love him and want to be with him? Yes again. How does burning his love letters make me a murderer?"

"Because Marc also received a death threat in the same handwriting. Your handwriting."

The accusation was absurd! I would never write threatening letters to the man I loved. He was supposed to be my future husband. I had planned to have his children, for goodness sake. Still, my palms were clammy with nervous sweat.

"My handwriting? But I didn't write those."

"I want you to take a look at something." He pulled out a photograph and turned it around for me to look at. It was the picture I gave Marc when we had dinner together. "Do you recognize this picture?"

"Yes, I gave that to Marc."

"So then you admit that this note on the back is your handwriting." He flipped the photo over.

"Yes, that's mine."

"Now take a look at this—" He pulled another piece of paper from the folder, this time a letter:

Stay away from her. If you don't, I hope you're ready to die for her, because you'll be next.

"Do you notice anything familiar about this letter and the note on the back of the picture you gave Marc?"

I studied them both, not sure what I was supposed to be looking for.

"I don't see anything familiar."

"Haley, look at the Y in your name and the Y in the note. You use a very specific swirl on your Y's—completely unique to your handwriting."

230

"No, someone could have copied me."

"Haley ... c'mon. I have some experience in handwriting analysis, and in my opinion, you wrote both of these. A handwriting expert could confirm my suspicion."

I shook my head. "No, that can't be right. Marc does the same thing with his Y."

I pointed to one of his love letters where the Y curled up in the same way. But he went right on, ignoring my logic.

"Right now, based solely on the threats, I can charge you with communication harassment. But it's not looking good for you now that Marc's saying you poisoned his dog, killed Julie, and stabbed him. You did threaten his life, after all." He waved the paper in my face. "It all points to you."

This couldn't be true. He was lying, trying to get me to confess to something I didn't do. They needed someone to blame. I was the perfect patsy. But how could I get him to believe my innocence?

I felt a darkness touch me on the shoulder, *tap-tap-tapping*. A dark companion I couldn't outrun. He didn't offer soothing words. He showed up to destroy me.

Look at what you've done, you worthless piece of garbage! the voice taunted.

Why was it torturing me? Why me?

You are a liar and a killer and a psychopath.

But I wasn't, was I? I needed to know the truth. I reached out to the middle of the table where the detective had piled his evidence against me and pulled a letter closer. I skimmed over the handwriting while the overhead waffled lighting blinked.

Leafing through each one, I read one after the other. The Y's—the curly loops at the end—those were mine. Was the detective right? Certainly I didn't write letters to myself. That was ... freaking crazy!

As crazy as being in love with a man who had courted me just to make his ex jealous. And I had dreamed of a future with this man. Becoming his wife. Having his children. God, how self-deluded I'd been!

I stared blankly into the detective's accusing eyes. The truth hovered between us, that I was crazy, that Marc never wrote a damn word, that I loved a man who didn't give a shit about me ... that I killed a woman who didn't deserve to die.

Chapter 43
Marc

The metal door sprung open and slammed shut behind Detective Patella. Marc looked up, eyes swollen with tears.

The detective joined him around the circular faux wood table, taking a seat next to a policeman who scooted over to make room. Dropping a folder in the center of the table, the detective grunted as he pulled his chair in, the metal legs screeching across the tile like chalk on a chalkboard. The corner interrogation room, stuffy and too small for three large men, was directly adjacent to where Haley now waited. It took every ounce of Marc's strength not to walk over there and deal with that bitch once and for all. The pinch of the stitches in his bandaged abdomen reminded him he was in no condition for confrontation. Besides, the cops would be on him like stink on shit before he could make a move.

Marc shifted his gaze from his hands to the nameplate pinned to the policeman's chest. "Officer Rice, was there anything else you needed to know?"

"No," he answered, then passed the tablet to the detective. "I think we have our timeline."

"Fill me in," Detective Patella urged.

"Well, comparing Haley's statement to Marc's, and judging by the number of letters, we know that Haley has been stalking him for a while now. We have Marc's first encounter with Haley when he fixed her computer. At the time, Marc had just started seeing Julie Carter." Officer

Rice paused and glanced up at Marc. "That's when things got weird."

At the time, Marc had never noticed it. Willing his brain back to each interaction with her, his brow creased as he reeled in each memory. She had been curiously attentive. Even the way she looked at him, as if watching his every move, examining him. Those big green eyes probing him, masterminding how she could win him, or ruin him.

"How so?" the detective asked.

"The night of the ICE Festival was when the shit really hit the fan," Marc interrupted. "I had gone with Julie, had a nice night. But that night after I dropped Julie off, I got home and my dog went missing. I found her almost dead at the end of my driveway the next morning. That was also the night of all the messages and the death threat. Later Julie shows up at my house crying because she was being tailed by someone. I thought it was her ex-boyfriend, but I'm sure now that it was Haley."

The vibration of Marc's leg quickened as his shoe tapped a beat on the tile. In a way, Marc was responsible for Julie's death. The irony of it all was that he had initially set out to hurt her, break her heart a little like she'd done to him. But never kill her. If he had never been nice to Haley, Julie would still be here, cuddling with him on the couch talking about how many kids they wanted someday. That white picket fence fantasy would never come to pass.

And it was all Haley Montgomery's fault.

Marc wasn't a praying man. But today, this moment, he prayed that crazy bitch would get what she deserved.

Chapter 44
Marc

Marc was finally on his way home from the police station after a grueling day of questioning and a warning not to leave town. Exhausted and traumatized, he drove in silence, letting everything sink in. At least they knew the truth.

Haley Montgomery. Who would have guessed? Seemed like such a sweet, normal girl. It seemed ... preposterous. He almost felt bad for her, living in a make-believe world. After he recognized the handwriting on the back of the picture, it all made sense. That was why the scenery in the photograph seemed so familiar. It was the view he looked at every single day from his back porch. The unique tree with two trunks sprouting from a single root structure. How hadn't he realized that was a silhouette of his tree in the picture? She had been lurking around his house, taking pictures while stalking him.

The thought sent a shiver up his spine. Seeing his cell phone on the passenger seat, he wondered how many missed work calls he had. Turning it on, it chimed to life, showing one message. His hand shook as he speed-dialed his voice mail.

"You have one new message. Press 1 to listen to your message."

His trembling finger jabbed the 1.

"I kept my promise."

That was it. The whole message. Not recognizing the voice at first, he pressed repeat, listening carefully.

"I kept my promise."

The voice belonged to Haley. She must have called before the cops brought her in. Not only was he stuck in a nightmare with her, but now her cryptic message was tattooed on his brain. What did she mean? She kept her promise? What promise? He wondered if it was it another threat, a clue to something terrible about to happen. He had to stop the thoughts before he went nuts too.

He drove in a daze, and when at last he blinked himself back to earth, he realized he wasn't anywhere near his house. He was on Haley's street, crawling up to her address. Had he actually subconsciously planned to stop by her house? He shook the insane thought away.

As he sped off, an overwhelming urge sent him into a U-turn back in the direction of her house, with "I kept my promise" replaying in his mind. Her house was completely dark. He had expected that. She was in jail, so of course no one would be home.

Marc pulled his F-150 into the driveway and shut off the engine. He sat staring through the window at nothing in particular but feeling compelled to stay. After a while he opened his door and got out. Without thought or reason, his legs carried him to the front door of Haley's house—a place he knew he shouldn't be.

Internal sirens couldn't stop him now. This was beyond his control. Breaking and entering held no weight today. Something told him he'd find the answer to this crazy goddamned mystery inside.

I kept my promise.

Marc numbly approached the front porch and reached for the door handle. Click. It was unlocked and swiftly swung open. Déjà vu swept over him. This whole experience seemed so familiar, as if he'd seen it before—a solitary man standing in an empty doorway. Probably a horror film showing the scene right before the guy got brutally bludgeoned by the waiting killer.

A smell of burned paper wafted from the fireplace. He stood in the dim hallway staring in. He stepped inside and patted his hand along the wall until he found the hall light and flicked it on. He peeked around the living room. Nothing unusual. Kitchen, pretty much the same as he remembered.

Circling back to the entryway through the dining room, he paused at the foot of the stairs leading up to the bedroom and office. It was stupidity incarnate to do what he was thinking of doing. But he wasn't in control anymore. He had to know what was up there, the secrets she had hidden. There had to be some clue as to what made someone so seemingly normal in fact insane.

At the second-floor landing, he creaked open the office door where he first helped Haley with her computer. It felt like eons ago, but it had only been a matter of weeks. Upon looking inside, everything appeared the same. Except a little more cluttered. Papers mostly. He recognized a tablet of pink heart-shaped paper—the same paper on which were written several of the notes enclosed in the box he had received. He walked to the desk and found half a dozen notes on the desk. He read the one on top:

I am so sorry for my betrayal. I never meant to hurt you. You are my everything. I promise you, we will be together forever. I assure you that my heart belongs to you alone, and together we can get rid of Julie so that you'll never have to worry about her again.

His eyes widened at the threat lurking between the lines. Then another:

My angel, we will be united as one. You are my perfect match. Without you, life is death.

The letter ended there. He scanned further down to the bottom, a heart crudely sketched in the corner.

"What the hell?" The sound of his own voice startled him. He crumbled the note, slamming it onto the desk, then backed away. This wasn't any girlish infatuation. No, this was deep. This was psychotic.

A journal was flipped open next to the stack of notes. He leaned over it, reading the cursive script, wondering what further insanity lurked in the corners of her mind:

Help me, please. Last night I woke up with that choking sensation again, like two taloned hands were wrapped around my neck, strangling the life out of me. Do I feel this way because Marc—my reason for living—has been stripped from me? I remember this very same feeling when my father died. Then again when Jake killed himself. It's frighteningly familiar. I don't want to suffocate anymore. I worry that I feel too much, that something's wrong with me.

Tonight I write secret thoughts, hoping that by writing I will bring Marc back to me. It's been so long since Marc and I have seen each other or spoken to each other, but in my dreams we meet every night. In my dreams we've shared so much. It's so real that sometimes I'm not sure what's real and what's not anymore. But I do know this: love is real, and I love Marc. And his letters to me testify to his love. That is the only thread I can cling to in order to keep my faith alive that we're meant to be.

He's my life, and without him I have to no reason to live. Maybe when I'm gone he'll feel the same about me.

The door creaked behind him, scaring him from the depths of Haley's journal. He wasn't alone. Sensing a strong evil presence, Marc rushed out of the room. The heat kicked on, nudging the door another inch.

"Damn it," he cursed under his breath. Man, was he jumpy. He hated her for destroying his life, for making him afraid of a damn breeze. He was vulnerable because of her, and there was no way to erase what she'd done to him. She'd made him weak. He despised her for that.

When he turned toward the staircase, the open bedroom door invited him in. Though his gut warned him to get out of the house, his curiosity prevailed. He stepped over the threshold, and the floorboards moaned a warning that he ignored.

A girl's room. Decorated in soft floral patterns and pink and beige hues. The closet door immediately caught his attention. Taped to it was a picture—the same one Haley had given him. Weird. Steeling himself, he flung open the door. The air went out of him, like somebody had sucker punched him in the stomach.

Inside were hundreds, if not thousands, of pictures— scattered all over the floor, taped to the walls, stuck to the ceiling, and lined along the back of the door. Pictures of him. Marc sitting on his couch at home. Marc in his car. Marc with a cut-out picture of Haley pasted next to him.

He stumbled back a couple of steps. A fucking closet shrine dedicated solely to him. There was no doubt now: Haley Montgomery was certifiably nuts. She had been stalking him all along, taking pictures, watching him, forging letters from him. And if the police let her go, who knows what would happen next.

Chapter 45

The pressure had been building all morning. After what seemed like endless hours of waiting, and watching as heads bobbed back and forth on the other side of the tiny rectangular window, I thought my skull would explode. Detective Patella returned to the interrogation room, his piercing glare announcing my fate. But I wouldn't go without a fight.

"It wasn't murder," I blurted.

"Sure." The detective humphed, then ran his hands through his buzz cut of salt-and-pepper hair. I heard the arrogance, felt the derision, as if I was a common criminal or troublemaking child.

I couldn't hold it all in any longer. I had to tell the whole story—the truth.

"I swear, it was an accident. I would never hurt Julie or Marc on purpose. I was there that night, but all I did was push Marc, and he stumbled into Julie. That's how she fell down the stairs."

"Then you covered it up. That's a crime, you know."

"I was scared. Marc was so angry, and he came at me. That's how he ended up stabbed. I only buried her because I didn't think anyone would believe it was an accident. I was trying to protect Marc."

"Haley." There a note of compassion in his voice this time. "You do realize you and Marc never dated, right? That it was all in your head."

The sobering words felt like a knife to my heart. Was I delusional about everything? I had truly believed Marc loved me. And I loved him with all my heart. We were going to get married and have children together someday. Was it all a figment of my imagination? And if so, what other lies was I living? Was Allen even real? It made me question everything—my own existence.

I shook my head. He was wrong. He was trying to manipulate me. A police tactic to get me to confess. I couldn't contain the tsunami of tears. But Detective Patella, cold and callous, barreled through my sobs.

"You've been playing make-believe with him since you met. He was nice enough to befriend you, but instead of taking his friendship for what it was, you blew it up into some made-up love affair. Then when he and Julie started dating, you couldn't stand it. Here she comes, his old high school sweetheart, sweeping him off his feet, stealing him from you. But he was never yours, Haley. The night you saw them together at the ICE Festival, you couldn't take it. So you lashed out. You thought that by threatening him you could make him leave her. Poisoning his dog, that was low. And of course, your revenge wouldn't be complete without killing Julie."

The detective threw a nod at the blue-uniformed officer standing by the door.

"Poisoning his dog? No, I love animals."

An image popped into my head. The vicious wolf in the woods near his house when I was taking pictures, the one that had nearly attacked me—that I was afraid would hurt Marc. Oh shit. That wasn't a wolf. It was his dog. It had probably acted territorially, protecting its turf.

How could I explain that I thought I was protecting Marc from a savage beast? They'd never believe me.

"We found an open bottle of antifreeze in your garage."

I scoffed. "Everyone has a bottle of antifreeze in their garage."

"It doesn't matter. What matters is that accident or not, you're responsible for Julie Carter's death. Cop a crazy plea if you want, you're under arrest."

"You may look at me like I'm the psycho, but what I felt was real. I did what I had to in order to protect Marc. I can't lose someone else I love. I already lost Jake, my father, and I couldn't lose Marc. *I couldn't lose Marc!*"

No one moved. No one spoke. I realized I had been raving. I looked down at my lap in embarrassment and shame, feeling the cops' eyes boring into the pathetic little psycho that was Haley Montgomery.

After a few minutes I looked up. Sure enough, Patella was staring at me with something like pity. And maybe a little fear.

"What ... what do you think they'll do with me?" I asked.

"That's not up to me to decide, Haley. Maybe ... maybe the judge will recommend that you just need ... help."

Help. I knew what that was a euphemism for.

Whatever happened, they'd take away my freedom.

So be it.

Freedom without someone to enjoy it with was worthless anyway.

Chapter 46
Marc

June 2009

The television was a blank screen in Marc's living room, the fireplace cold and empty. Sheba lay across from him on his makeshift bed—the living room sofa with a pile of pillows and blankets in the middle. Marc glanced down at her with droopy eyes as she rested her chin on his lap. He could feel the dark rings circling his eyes from weeks of sleepless nights. Julie's absence from what should have been her spot next to him in bed was a constant reminder of her death, making it impossible to fall asleep without booze or Benadryl. That's when he moved to the couch.

Haley's trial was held at the Westfield Village Justice Court on Elm Street. Although she was convicted of involuntary manslaughter and tampering with evidence, with a mandatory sentence of three years to Dunkirk Mental Hygiene Clinic, he couldn't get her out of his head. He often relived the trial in his recurring nightmare, except the ruling was terrifyingly different: Haley was released, with her specter looming in his entryway. Each time he woke up screaming and lathered in sweat.

He was forever scarred. Sometimes, at night, when he walked past his window, he'd catch a glimpse of her face—those unblinking eyes, green as a black cat's, peering into his house, watching her next victim. A moment later he'd realize it was his own reflection. When driving, he'd think he saw headlights following him, until the car behind him would eventually disappear into the night. The shrine of pictures, the threat letters, the breathing voice mail—every moment burned into his memory, and he doubted it would ever go away.

Marc was a mess. It took all his strength to meet Sheba's pitying stare, as if she understood. It was strange to him that his former self—a physically strong and emotionally healthy, independent man—could be reduced to a severely depressed invalid.

Kindly Mrs. Ellsworth, who was Westfield's unofficial doting grandmother to anyone in need, visited often. He couldn't appreciate her home-cooked meals, since he'd lost his appetite for food, and her constant gossiping nearly drove him to jump out a window—which he sometimes thought wasn't the worst idea, considering how shitty things were. Mrs. Ellsworth fed Sheba and took the dog out to do her business, performed light housekeeping, and offered to do Marc's laundry. There wasn't much of it. The shirt on Marc's back had been worn and slept in for three days now—and smelled like it, too. He knew it was bad if he got sick from his own stench. He hadn't taken a shower since his last change of clothes, and his face hadn't felt a razor for over a week.

Though wallowing in his own filthy misery was comfortable for now, Marc knew he had to eventually join the human race again. Get back to work before his business went down the crapper. In the pit of his empty stomach he knew he couldn't survive long under the emotional strain. But Haley was gone now, so there was no need to worry, right? In the meantime, he and Jack Daniels would keep each other company.

Chapter 47

I had never liked how I looked in white—pale and ghostly—yet I would be stuck wearing it for the next three years, at least. A white linen gown was the standard attire for the mental institution the courts had committed me to. It was this or jail. At least here I was allowed to write. And even pee in private.

"What are you thinking about, Haley?"

Dr. Rosin, my psychiatrist, had been nice from day one, always smiling at me as he sat in his chair across from mine, his butt squeaking against the leather every time he shifted, which seemed to be a lot. The office where we met was impersonal and cold, except for the leather chairs—his a deep brown, mine red. Other than those, not a drop of color in the whole room. They could at least have had a print of *The Scream* on the wall. You can't get more colorful—or more appropriate, for a nuthouse—than that. The artist, Edvard Munch, once commented on the meaning of his most famous work: "I heard a huge endless scream course through nature." Well, hell, that pretty much described my whole life.

Over the past few weeks I couldn't help but feel insulted that Dr. Rosin expected me to trust him completely and confide in him fully simply because he had a PhD behind his name. Trust was earned, not handed out freely. Didn't they teach that at psychiatry school?

But that's not what I was thinking about right now.

I was wondering if any of this would help. If the treatments and meds and counseling and lectures would actually fix my warped brain.

They wanted me to recover, whatever that meant. And I wanted to recover, whatever that meant. But it seemed near impossible. "Recovery" wasn't a magic word where a pill a day would keep the crazy away. No, it ran a lot deeper than a few loose screws in my head. They wanted me to mentally regurgitate everything that had happened, including my mother's testimony against me, Julie's death, Marc breaking my heart, and my own crazy belief that he'd in fact broken my heart.

Oh yes, the good doctor had asked me a question. And I aimed to answer it.

"I'm thinking about how to get better. I want to get better," I finally replied.

"Do you really?"

"Of course." Part of me wanted to make the delusions go away. I wanted to be normal. How could I have blindly lived in a fantasy for so long?

The other part of me preferred fantasy to reality.

"Getting better is going to take some work, Haley. Are you willing to work at it?"

"Yes."

"Then I'm going to need for you to open up to me more. Trust me."

Trust. That five-letter word again.

"I'll try."

"Okay. Can you tell me what you were thinking when you wrote your letters, Haley?"

"I wasn't really thinking anything. I don't even remember writing the letters most of the time."

"So you blacked out during those moments?"

I nodded.

"Do you remember anything before or after you wrote the letters?"

"Sometimes, I guess. I'll remember being at my desk, then everything goes black—like I'm doing things in the dark, but I don't really see what I'm doing. It's like I become a different person when I'm writing, and my mind just tells me what to write and I write it. My heart tells me what to feel and I feel it. My brain tells me what to believe and I believe it. So when I'm writing, the words take on their own life and I follow. And afterward I'd always get a headache. I don't know why."

Dr. Rosin nodded, then wrote something down. I wondered what he wrote. I suspected it was bad.

"Your mother shared with me that this started a long time ago. Is that true?"

Correction: Mom shared with the *public court* that it started a long time ago. It was one of the more tragic moments in my life—hearing my own mother tell the judge about what happened after Jake's suicide. How young, innocent, sixteen-year-old Haley found Jake's body and hadn't taken it so well and started writing herself letters from Jake as if he'd been alive. Mom had let it go, assuming it was a coping mechanism to deal with what I saw. No kid should witness death like that, especially so young. Jake's lifeless form dangling from a beam in our barn, my dad's bungee cord wrapped around his neck, his eyes vacantly staring into space. Bruises where the rope squeezed the life from him. It must have taken a long time for him to die that way.

What Mom didn't know was that his suicide came on the tail of losing our virginity together. Then finding out he was gay. I gave him my body and he killed himself the next day. Finding his body only ensured the psychological break was deep.

I shouldn't have been there. In the barn. I didn't know Jake had been depressed after our fight, but when his mom called asking if he was with me, I had a feeling where to find him. Our hang-out. Our secret place where sometimes he'd smoke pot while I watched. And sure enough, he was there. Dead.

No matter how many times I tried to banish the memory, it stuck to me like superglue. It wouldn't leave. And that's when all this started.

That's when I pretended Jake was alive. It made me feel better. Simple as that.

It started with journal entries about the pain, then a letter from Jake. Someone had mentioned that writing a letter to someone who has hurt you could help you heal. So why not write a reply from Jake? By God, it worked! Then another reply.

Eventually Mom found one.

Gabrielle never told anyone about my letters. It was our dark little secret—sweeping her daughter's descent into madness under the rug—a secret that had been chasing me down since then. A secret that imprisoned Gabrielle as I got worse. Not that I had any clue. I was blissfully ignorant. And that secret finally caught up with both of us.

"Yes, I was sixteen. It was my version of self-therapy, I guess."

"But it didn't fix the problem, did it?"

"No. But it offered temporary relief. For those moments as I wrote the letters I felt like Jake was back in my life and everything was alright again."

"So why Marc? You had no previous history with him. Why did you decide to target Marc?"

Target. That meant Marc was a victim, and I was a ... I shivered at the conclusion of that sentence.

It was a question even I didn't know the answer to. Then I remembered his warm touch, his soulful eyes. Familiar. He felt familiar. He felt ... safe. That's why he was chosen.

"I suppose it was because he reminded me of my dad," I said as I thought it out. His hands, his genuine kindness. Yes, he was a lot like Dad. "And I just really wanted to love someone. Be in love. Be loved back. I don't know why him, except that something about him intrigued me from the first time I met him. He was so sweet to me, and flirted with me. It could have been a glance or the way he said something. I wish I could psychoanalyze myself, but I don't always understand what I'm doing. And it terrifies me." I paused. It was the truth. I scared myself. And yet I was stuck with myself, always.

"Why does that scare you?" the doctor probed.

"Because I don't even know what's real and what's not. If you woke up and found out that everything you thought to be true wasn't, how would you feel? Could you ever trust yourself again? I can't trust myself, so how can I ever trust another? That inevitably leads to a very lonely life, Dr. Rosin."

The doctor looked thoughtful a moment, though he said nothing.

"Doctor, I want Marc to have his happily ever after. But let me ask you this: When will I get mine? Especially with a mental illness like this?"

And just as I expected, the doctor had no answer.

While I was delusional about the substance of my reality, I knew full well the implications of my mental illness. My *insanity* was also my *sanity*. My obsession with love gave me hope, even if it was false. I was in love with love. But if that hope was taken from me, I'd have nothing to fall back on when facing the harsh reality of loss, death, pain. In the world of mental illness, the voices offer

249

comfort, silencing pain's screams. Would waking from the safe world I had created lead to a culture shock far worse than false hope?

After a long pause, the doctor finally said what we both had been thinking: "It boils down to this. Life is a series of ups and downs. You can't have the ups without the downs. So first you have to accept that, Haley."

It sounded so elementary, but it was true. Yet why did it seem like I had more than my fair share of the downs but no ups? Where were my ups? I had to create them, for God's sake!

I nibbled on my lower lip as the doctor continued, keeping the debate to myself.

"Secondly, Haley, you can choose not to act on your impulses. You can't always control the thoughts, but you can control many of the actions. Make a conscious effort to live within reality—by enduring the pains we all must suffer and embracing the joys that come. If you cling to a delusion that only accepts the joys, but never actually obtains love, you'll never live out the real experience, which I assure you is much better. Ultimately, Haley, you are your own worst enemy, but also your own best advocate. You have the power to choose happiness in whatever circumstance you're in, or you can choose to be miserable. You can either build yourself up or tear yourself down. Your fantasy is your prison, Haley. Reality is your freedom. Which do you want the most, Haley?"

The matrix of life. Reality or fantasy? Which was better?

Was it really so bad to live in a fantasy world? Everyone did it in some form or another; mine was just a little more blatant. As long as I was chained to my imagination, reality would cease to exist. And reality sucked pretty damn bad.

"But what about when I'm not in control of my brain? What then?"

"You're in control of the medicine to help your brain, right?"

"Yes."

"Then take it, religiously. That's the first step and the hardest one."

Reality or fantasy. I had two choices. But only one of them was comfortable, easy, and allowed me to be myself.

Chapter 48

Marc

Marc felt empty inside with nothing but a bottle of Jack to fill him. There was no need for a glass.

When the doorbell rang, he considered letting whoever it was stand on the stoop until they gave up and left. Until he thought of Mrs. Ellsworth. No matter how deep the abyss he hid in, he couldn't upset Mrs. Ellsworth. Thoughtful old ladies like her deserved better than a closed-door rebuke. Especially since she'd been looking out for him since Haley's sentencing ... and Julie's death.

Julie's death always came as an afterthought. His brain hadn't yet wrapped itself around that truth. Denial. Shock. Whatever it was, he didn't want that reality. Maybe Haley hadn't been so crazy after all. Real life sucked.

The doorbell chimed again, forcing him off the sofa. When he opened the front door, a warm summer breeze wafted over him, the sun reaching him through trees full with green life. It took a long moment for him to recognize the woman standing in front of him.

"Gabrielle Montgomery." Her name tasted sour on his tongue. The woman who birthed the hellspawn that had killed Julie. The last time he'd seen her was at the trial, and he could live without ever seeing her again. "What are you doing here?"

"I know I shouldn't be here, but I had to talk to you." She spat out her words in a mad rush as the door closed in her face. "Wait! Please wait."

The door opened a little. Marc stood firmly in the doorway. "Speak your peace," he said coldly, "then get the hell out of here."

"I feel terrible about what Haley did to you. But I wanted to express my deepest regrets over what happened and apologize that I hadn't seen what was going on sooner. I know it's not worth much now, but I know what it's like to lose a loved one and I just ... I just needed to say I'm sorry."

Marc's neck heated with an emotion he didn't understand. Pity? Empathy? Whatever it was, he felt moved and stepped aside.

"Would you like to come in?"

"Thank you, but I don't want to impose." She paused, glanced behind her like she was nervous, then continued. "I was devastated when I found out Haley had ... well, you know. But the sad part is, I wasn't surprised. Haley, as you know, had mental issues. It's not an excuse, I know, but she's had a ... hard life, to say the least. She lost her father at a very young age, then her only friend killed himself. She's the one who found him, poor kid ... but I guess you already know that from the hearing."

Gabrielle looked down and spoke into her hands, which fidgeted with the dainty cross around her neck.

"And I wasn't always the most attentive mother. Shortly after Frank got sick, I nearly lost everything. My poor husband dedicated his life to it ... I could never tell him we were on the verge of going into foreclosure. To this day I wish I wouldn't have kept that from him. You never want there to be unspoken secrets left on the deathbed; those secrets will rattle in your brain for years to come. There he was fighting for his life while I tried to run the vineyard by myself while raising two girls—but it was all too much. I failed in so many ways. I failed Haley, and now I failed you and Julie. I hope you can forgive me."

When Gabrielle looked up, Marc saw the tears in her eyes, and blinked away his own. He felt sorry for this woman. She had lost her husband and now her daughter, for all practical purposes, and somehow blamed herself for it.

"There's nothing to forgive you for. You didn't do anything wrong."

"But I knew, Marc. I knew when I first saw how excited Haley got about you that something wasn't right. She was so in love with you, and so soon. Too soon. I should have talked to you. If only I had talked to you maybe none of this would have happened. Julie might still be alive. I regret it every day."

Marc lost it. All the pent-up pain and regret and fear came gushing out in a gut-wrenching howl ... of relief.

Gabrielle pulled his brawny body into a bony hug that reminded him of his mother. She was tiny and frail, and yet somehow he felt small in her embrace.

"It's okay, honey," she whispered against his wet cheek.

It was the first time since Julie's death that he felt like it would, in fact, be okay. Maybe not today. Maybe not tomorrow. Maybe not this year. But someday, he'd begin to heal.

He knew the first step to making that happen.

Chapter 49

One year later ...

Guilty by reason of insanity.

Five words I would never forget as they bounced around in my skull for a year now. I had never been quite sure what I was guilty of—loving too much, I guess—but the insanity part tore at my soul. I had never felt quite so broken as I did when they judged me as insane the day of my sentencing. My court-appointed attorney assured me it was a good thing. But then again, he wasn't being labeled as *insane*.

After a year of force-feeding me cures for my insanity, here I was, at what I hoped to be the end of the line: Dr. Rosin's personal office.

"You seem to be improving quite well during your stay here, Haley."

I found his word choice ironic, as if I had been staying in a five-star hotel by choice. Let's be honest—I was imprisoned here, and if being brainwashed was an indication of improvement, then consider me healed.

By now I knew the right things to say, the right things to do, the way to act and pretend away the crazy. A win-win. Dr. Rosin's ego would inflate with pride at his success, and I would get the hell out of here.

After months of these sessions, I had grown accustomed to knowing what Dr. Rosin needed to hear, and today was a big one. The most important one. I could tell it was important because we met in his personal office this time, the room full of color and books and personal touches.

Must be big news.

The white-smocked Dr. Rosin sat with his hands folded across a large mahogany desk, peering over bifocals perched precariously near the tip of his Roman nose. I wondered how he kept them perched in place. A bookcase dominated the wall behind him, showcasing neatly lined leather-bound books from the floor to the ceiling. Judging from the titles, the volumes were all medical or psychology-related. Dr. Rosin's professionally-framed diplomas lined another wall, each bearing the university's gold stamp of approval. Well, la-di-da!

I wasn't impressed. This man had been dictating my fate since the beginning, and it was almost comical how he told me what to think, as if he actually understood how my brain worked. It bugged me. He couldn't relate, but he pretended to. He was just like me. Pretending his own reality. The blind leading the blind.

He apparently had a weakness for celebrity gossip rags. The latest issue of *US Weekly* sat crookedly on the desk corner closest to me. The headline shouted in bold red letters:

ALLEN MICHAELS: Did the Mogul Murder His Wife?

And below, smaller but just as sensational:

Kidnapping. Drugging. Torture. Stabbing. The sordid story of the legendary producer's fall from grace as his murder trial continues.

The picture of a cuffed Allen, head bent low in shame, with a month's worth of untamed beard, looked nothing like I remembered him.

Oh yes. Dr. Rosin had commented on how well I was doing.

"I feel like I've taken some big strides, Doctor."

"Do you know why you're here today?"

I shrugged and smiled like a meek child. "Good news, I hope?"

Dr. Rosin's beady brown eyes searched mine. He smiled smugly, as if he could no longer see the demons that dwelled within, for he had vanquished them. Then he leaned forward and flipped through a few pages of my chart, running his finger along some of his indecipherable doctorly scribble.

"You've been continuing to meet your therapy expectations and we're looking to release you early."

A lot earlier than I expected. The judge had sentenced me to three years for manslaughter and for attempting to cover up the crime. My attorney was convinced I'd get out early if I "worked hard," as he'd put it. Worked hard at not being myself is what he meant. I wondered just how easy it was for anyone else to suddenly cease to exist, taking on a new personality. If it meant getting out of this loony bin, I would do it, though. And clearly I succeeded. I'd performed like the perfect circus monkey, doing tricks on command. And now I would get my reward.

I suppose I should be grateful it was this and not jail. The judge been lenient because I hadn't pushed Julie. Had I never buried her ... well, I would have gone home instead of here.

My surprise must have registered on my face as Dr. Rosin added, "Do you think that you are ready for that step?"

Sitting in the cold plastic chair with nothing on but a paper-thin hospital gown for a shirt, drawstring-free sweatpants, underwear, and slippers, I had been waiting for this day since the moment the cops had delivered me, in handcuffs, as if I were a raving lunatic. People are always saying how time flies. Not when you're stuck in a mental hospital, pal. Each day was an endless exercise in tedium, thick and sluggish, until it melded into the next day, and the day after that, and the day after ...

Yes, doctor, I was ready.

"I feel like I have a handle on my illness," I stated confidently and clearly. I had learned that using "feeling" words made him happy, and to always recognize my *illness*. "And as long as I take my meds and take care of myself, I definitely feel like I'm ready to go back into the world again."

He smiled. I had said the right thing. "It's good to hear that you've come to terms with your disorder. Now, as you know, we've had some difficultly diagnosing you. Mostly because not a lot has been documented about erotomania. But it seems that several environmental issues have contributed to this illness, like your father's passing, Jake's suicide, and your lack of good, healthy relationships. You've spent your whole life trying to fill the void of those lost relationships, Haley, but not in a healthy way."

He waited for the circus monkey's response. Might as well flatter the old boy.

"You're absolutely right, Dr. Rosin. And I never would have recognized the truth ... without your incredible insight and expertise."

"That's kind of you to say. You've admitted that Marc reminded you a lot of your dad, which is probably why you were so captivated by him. But based on my observations, you've been able to understand how your mind functions and you now have much better control over your erotomania. You seem to understand how to differentiate between healthy and unhealthy relationships, and I understand you are prepared to continue therapy after you're released. Is that correct?"

The room felt hot. It often did when he psychoanalyzed me, dragging Daddy and Jake into it. I felt the sweat beginning to bead on my brow, nudging its way through my skin. The interview wasn't over yet, and I knew I needed to wow him.

"Yes, I'm looking forward to meeting with my therapist twice a week and he'll help me stay on an even keel."

"Excellent. What do you think you need to work on with your therapist when you meet?"

"A lot of things, I guess," I answered innocently. Yes, doctor, I was so eager to learn more about my failures. "I want to try to make real friendships and stay socially active. But I know that right now I am not ready for a romantic relationship."

He nodded approval, so I continued.

"I mainly want to focus on me for now. And I'll need to continue to identify any false beliefs, trying to see things for what they really are. I've decided to stay away from screenplay writing for a while until I can learn to cope with real life better. I used movies as my fantasy, my escape into another life. You helped me to see that, Dr. Rosin. I think if I make those changes and have my support system—my mom and therapy—I can live a normal life."

His glowing smile told me all I needed to know. "I'm impressed that you have made that connection on your own and are willing to make sacrifices in order to help yourself. That shows true maturity." Dr. Rosin thumbed through a few more sheets that I assumed documented my brainwashing—I mean *progress*. "It is evident that you are making wonderful strides in your personal growth, so ..."

His voice trailed off as he closed the file, looked up, and examined me. I knew what he saw sitting pitifully before him: a messed-up patient, not a person. His open hands rested palms down on the yellow folder as he ruminated, his mouth opening and closing like a fish's. He jabbed his wire-rimmed bifocals up to the bridge of his hooked nose, cleared his throat, and leaned back in his regal chair, striking a thoughtful pose. My God, the bastard was milking this dramatic moment for all it was worth.

"It all sounds like a good plan, Haley. There's just one last thing I'd like you to do."

"Yes, Doctor?"

"I'd like for you to summarize your experience here over the past few months. Tell me, what did you learn, how do you think you've improved, what would you change about your treatment here?"

It was a loaded question, yet I knew the correct answer. My scripted answers in therapy sessions had prepared me for this moment. But I took my time anyway, just to make sure he knew I had thought it over.

"Well, I know that I've had difficulty in the past discerning fantasy from reality. I was deluded into thinking that Marc loved me, and that we had a relationship that didn't exist. I made up letters to myself, pretending they were from him, because I felt like something was missing in my life. I felt that by having Marc, I could feel whole again. I thought he would make up for things that were missing from my life, like my dad."

I had the doctor's full attention, so I shaped his perception of me like soft clay.

"I allowed myself to live in my own make-believe dreamworld where false relationships became real—in my head. But you've helped me see that I can't control other people or their feelings toward me. I can't control the unfortunate events that happen to me, like my dad's death. I can only control myself, my imagination, and my feelings. My treatments have helped me to overcome any unhealthy or irrational thoughts. I can honestly say that the world is different to me now. I see things as they really are."

Dr. Rosin beamed with pride. "Well, I think that you've answered all my questions. Remember to continue to focus on what you've learned during your time here, and I wish you all the best. I will be signing your release today, and I assume you have somewhere to go once you leave?"

"Yes, I'll be staying with my mother in Westfield. That will give me time to get back on my feet, find a job, get my life back together. And she'll be able to supervise me and keep an eye on me if I need help or anything."

"Wonderful. Well, then, I guess this is it. We'll miss having you here. You were a delight to work with. Your release papers should be ready by this afternoon. And we'll have a nurse drop off all your personal things at your room. Good luck out there."

He rose and extended his hand, and I returned his warm handshake.

"Thank you, Doctor," I said as gratefully as I could manage.

What I was really grateful about was getting the hell out of this bughouse.

I let myself out through the heavy wooden door and nearly skipped all the way to my room. The hallway was empty and sterile, with only the occasional groan or psychotic episode echoing from a room on my floor. When I entered my cell—at least that's what it felt like—my room looked different. It was no longer "home," as it had been for the past several months. It was just another colorless room on a strip of about fifty matching ones. It didn't belong to me, and I didn't belong to it.

Today represented a huge step toward freedom, and there was one last thing I had to do before it would be complete. When I had first been admitted, the staff had stripped me of any writing implements for fear that I'd use them to do harm to myself. Apparently crazy people did that sometimes; I later witnessed a girl on my floor's unsuccessful attempt to hang herself with her own sheets. But I wasn't crazy. I had been in love. And when my treatments verified that I wasn't suicidal, they started giving me perks, like pens and paper.

Four months in, my therapist encouraged me to creatively communicate my feelings through writing. Of course, writing was my first love , so I immediately jumped on board with the exercise. Each day I turned over my journals to my psychiatrist, yet there was one little secret I kept to myself, well-hidden and for my eyes only. I could never let them find it.

I went over to my beside table and pulled the drawer completely off of its track. On the drawer's underside was a letter-size envelope (saved from one of Mom's "care packages") that fit snugly within the drawer's frame. I'd further secured the parcel with four strips of masking tape from a roll I'd stolen from a supply closet.

Inside the envelope was a handwritten collection of all the thoughts and feelings I experienced since meeting Marc—my own form of self-therapy. I chronicled the events that happened, and the ones that only existed in my mind; it was the only way I could sort through the memories with—and without—Marc. Though my therapists tried to erase that entire block of time, it would always remain a part of me that would never die.

In those rare moments when the ward was quiet, usually in the dead of night, I would close my eyes and see him, breathe him, love him. I had planned the ending to our story together for the past several months, our happily ever after.

It was time to finish the story. I walked softly to the door, peering around the doorframe, seeing the hallway was completely vacant. I'd have enough time before the nurse came with my clothes that had been confiscated upon arrival.

I turned off the light switch and dug an untrimmed index fingernail into the flat-head screw that held the plate on. The screw was loose enough to work out quickly. I pulled off the plate. Hidden in the electrical box was a hoard of pills—at least a month's worth. I stuffed the pills into my bra and quickly replaced the switch plate. No point leaving evidence behind that I hadn't been taking my meds in case anyone ever looked inside.

Guessing I'd have about an hour to myself, I made myself as comfortable as possible on the mortuary slab the nuthouse sadists claimed was a bed.

I slid a thin batch of paper out onto my bed. A screenplay I had started but never finished:

```
FADE IN:

INT. PAPA GIOVANNI'S RISTORANTE
    It is late evening. HALEY MONTGOMERY sits at
a booth watching MARC and JULIE from afar.

    HALEY:  (talking   to   self)   Tonight's   our
night, Marc. Tonight we'll finally be together
at last. I will spend my life making you happy.
I promise. I just hope you understand why I
have to do this for us to be together. (she
inhales deeply)

CUT TO:

MARC AT THE BAR WITH JULIE

    Haley discreetly strolls through the dimly
lit restaurant to the bar in the corner, where
the BARTENDER is wiping the counter. MARC and
JULIE are sitting across at the bar. Soft music
is playing in the background.
```

MARC: (looking at bartender) Another scotch, please.

JULIE: And a dry martini for me, thanks.

BARTENDER: I'll be right back with that for you.

MARC: Thanks.

The bartender leaves and Marc and Julie sit in silence listening to the music.

The bartender makes the drinks and sets them aside to help another customer. Haley discreetly pulls a plastic bag from her pocket. She looks to make sure no one is watching, then dumps the bag's contents—the powder from ground-up pills—into the drink and stirs it with a swizzle stick until it dissolves.

HALEY: You'll be sleeping well tonight—and forever. Enjoy your last night on earth, Marc. I'll be joining you soon.

The bartender sets the drinks in front of Marc and Julie.

BARTENDER: Can I get you anything else?

MARC: No thanks, I'm good. (holding glass up in a toast) Here's to new beginnings. (he toasts to Julie, then drinks it in one gulp)

From a shadowy corner Haley is watching, then smiles.

HALEY: (to herself) And final endings.

DISSOLVE OUT

Yes, I had followed Marc and Julie the night of Julie's death. Yes, I had almost tried to poison them. The plan was stupid—so Romeo and Juliet. I hadn't succeeded, thank God. It was a lot harder to sneak drugs into someone's drink when they would recognize you.

I should have known it then—that something was wrong with me. Contemplating drugging someone—what kind of lunatic does that? I held the remnants of that old fantasy in my hands and tore it in half, then in half again. I wasn't that girl anymore. I wasn't that fantasy.

I felt relieved shredding up the old me.

"Haley, are you ready to go?" Nurse Edith's voice startled me. I whipped my head up and shoved the papers under my leg.

The nurse carried a clear plastic bag and dumped the contents beside where I sat. A sweater, jeans, tennis shoes, and a matching ring and necklace tumbled out onto the bed.

"Does this look like everything?"

"Yep, looks about right," I answered.

I wondered what it would feel like wearing my old clothes again. I'd dropped at least a dress size, and no wonder—the hospital food looked, smelled, and tasted like crap. The new, improved, svelte Haley Montgomery, courtesy of a mandatory stay in a county funny farm. I guess I should be happy for small favors.

"Go ahead and get dressed then. The front desk has already arranged transportation for you—your mom. Should be here shortly. Any questions?"

"No, none that I can think of. But thank you for everything you've done for me."

Smiling warmly, Nurse Edith opened her arms in invitation. I hugged her because I really would miss her. Unlike some of the other nurses, who tended to be rigid and vindictive, even cruel, Nurse Edith was the sweet and kind embodiment of the Nightingale Pledge.

"You are so sweet, Haley. I know you'll be just fine out there."

"Yeah, I think so too."

"Just remember—one day at a time," she said as she let go and walked to the door. As the pad of her Crocs dwindled in the distance, I grabbed the jeans and reached into the back pocket to see if it was still there. I felt the crinkled paper, surprised but delighted. I pulled it out and unfolded it.

I had brought it with me when I first got taken into custody. Marc's handsome face looked back at me. It was one of my favorite pictures because usually his gaze looked past the camera. Rarely could I get a direct frontal shot. But this particular picture captured everything I had loved so much about him—from the sparkle in his eyes to his devil-may-care smile. I turned the photo over.

Always and forever.

"What do I do now?" My voice faltered as I pocketed the picture.

I couldn't lie to myself any longer. I needed my happily ever after.

Chapter 50

As I dropped my bag to the floor to wish a final farewell to Suzie at the front desk, the sweet black receptionist with a flair for red lipstick and dangly jewelry dropped an envelope on the counter.

"This 'un's addressed to you, sweetheart," Suzie said. I'd always found her Southern drawl maternal, like a mother hen herding her brood to her breast.

"Something from my mom or my sister, I suppose," I said without enthusiasm. They were the only ones that had written me during my stay.

"Naw, honey, it ain't from either one of them. I recognize their handwritin' by now. Ain't got no return address. Maybe it's from a secret admirer."

"Ha ha, Suzie," I said good-humoredly, picking up the envelope.

"Your mama should be here any minute."

"Thanks, Suzie. I appreciate everyt—"

"Honey, I hate long goodbyes. I know you cain't wait to get your ass out of here. Now, shoo!" She grinned from ear to ear as she flicked her heavily beringed hand at me.

With a wave good-bye, I grabbed my belongings and headed for a chair in the empty lobby, anxious to examine the envelope. A momentary fear that I had sent it to myself gnawed at me, until the Westfield postmark washed it away. I hurriedly tore open the envelope. Inside was a plain piece of paper, folded into thirds. I unfolded it and avidly read the handwritten letter:

Dear Haley:

I hope this letter doesn't come too late, but I've had plenty of time to think about what I wanted to say to you if given the opportunity, so here goes. I found a letter most appropriate, since it was always your preferred method of communication, ha ha. (Too soon?)

First of all, it's me, Marc. The one whose life you destroyed. I've been so angry at you for the past several months that I wanted nothing but suffering for you, like you made me suffer. I've hated you for so long that I feel a strange emptiness inside me now that I've decided to let that anger go. I can't hold on to it anymore. It's eaten enough of my soul.

So I came to the only logical conclusion. To forgive you for what you've done. For stalking me. For haunting my nightmares. For your part in Julie's death. For stabbing me. For hurting my dog. For causing my paranoia over who might be watching me at any given moment. For making me face a real, raw, tangible fear for the first time. You awakened me to the horrors of life that I never knew existed before, and I almost couldn't find my way out of the shadows.

But here I am, out on the other side. I made it through, back into the light. My grudge was only holding me in the darkness, so I'm setting us both free now, Haley.

Everyone needs forgiveness. Everyone has struggles. Maybe we're all "mental" in one way or another ... some of us just hide it better than others. But we all seek the same thing: love. An unconditional love that accepts us, frailties and all. That's why you picked me, isn't it? You wanted love.

It's a need we're born with. You're not crazy for wanting it; you just went about it all the wrong way. I see that now.

I found out you're being released soon, and my first instinct was to protect myself from you. Frankly, Haley, I've been terrified of you ever since that fateful day when Julie died. I even had nightmares that you would escape and try to kill me. But it's exhausting being on guard. I'm done with living in fear. With forgiveness I'm giving us both another chance—you a chance to show you care enough about me to let me move on, me a chance to one day trust another human being.

In this envelope you'll find a dried rose, probably a crushed mess by the time it reaches you. This rose was my parting gift to Julie back when we were teens and she left me the first time. Now I'm giving it to you, hoping you'll accept it as a parting gift as you walk away for the last time. Like this dried up rose, feelings can fade over time, even feelings of bitterness.

I hope you find the love you're after—love for yourself above all else.

Sincerely,

Marc

As I laid the open letter on my lap, a teardrop fell, rolled down my cheek, splattered on the paper.

Tucked in the bottom of the envelope was the dried rose, still intact, to my surprise. I picked it up, a thorn pricking my fingertip.

Accept it. That little niggling voice I hated so much was speaking. I wanted to shut it out, but for once it sounded like it had something worthwhile to say.

"I screwed up too bad," I said to the empty room.

It's never too late to start over.

Marc offered to let it all go. No more nightmares. No more blackouts. No more searching for a love that didn't exist. There was a promise right in front of me—a promise to start over. Accept it, or reject it. That was the choice.

Again came a soft whisper. *Accept it.*

Maybe my happily ever after wasn't with Marc, but with myself. Maybe I could learn to love myself. Maybe that could be enough.

I reached into my back pocket for the picture of Marc. I examined it carefully. In truth, it was just a face of a man, a man I hardly knew. A man who didn't love me. Was this really what I had been fighting for?

I gazed at Marc's face, blurry through my tears. With fierce resolution I tore the photo in half, then in half again and again until it was a pile of unrecognizable shreds.

Once and for all I surrendered the make-believe world for the real one—one that I could and would survive on my own two feet. I didn't need a false love, because I had something real—me. Live and in stereo and in the flesh.

Maybe I was a little batshit crazy, but as I wiped the tears on my sleeve, I decided to give myself a chance. A chance to love myself like no one else ever could or would. And it would be enough.

Epilogue

The familiar crunch of rock beneath the tires welcomed me home as Mom turned into our long gravel driveway. I'd spent the drive home catching up on all the latest Westfield gossip—Blake Hendricks finally proposed to Brenda Channing (it only took him a decade!), Katrina Hodgins was pregnant after four years of trying, and Jeannie Coswell got her tongue pierced to complement her latest tattoo rebellion.

WHAM 1180's news radio compensated for any lack of conversational fodder, though with me drilling Mom about everyone and everything, there was rarely a dull moment. Beneath the easy conversation however, I sensed she wasn't telling me something. I could read her like no one else. I suppose our shared secrets connected us in a way that didn't require words.

Mom grew silent as she slowed her approach. I relished a moment of nostalgia as the house crept into view. My home. Where I belonged. Where I would pick up the pieces of my old life and rebuild. That was my focus now; love and Hollywood could wait.

As we rounded the last curve, a man stood at the foot of the porch. At first I thought it was Marc and my heart caught a snag. But he was much older, hair peppered with gray, with a bit of a paunch in his gray t-shirt. A shotgun was draped over his shoulder.

"Mom, do you know this man?"

She parked the car and turned to me. "I've been wanting to tell you for a while, but I wasn't sure it was the right time."

"Tell me what?"

"Do you remember that man you saw in the woods—we thought he might have been a hunter?"

I did remember, but it seemed like a million years ago. One night there had been a light in the woods, and I'd briefly seen a man in a plaid shirt or coat and a knit cap. I hadn't thought he was a hunter, though; I thought he might have been Marc or Allen, but Mom convinced herself it was a hunter who had wandered onto our property.

"Yes, I remember chasing him."

She laughed. "We joke about that still. You scared the bejeesus out of him that night."

"Huh? What are you talking about, Mom?"

"His name is Aaron. He's the new neighbor. And my boyfriend."

Mom waited for my response. I was too shocked to speak. She went on.

"We've been dating, and he's been helping me out around here."

Until now, I hadn't noticed the fresh coat of paint on the siding, the new front door, the porch swing now a happy shade of green. As I scanned the vibrant blossoms lining the driveway, I smiled at her.

"Does he make you happy?"

"Happier than I've been since your father passed away."

"Then I'm glad for you. You deserve good things, Mom."

She touched my cheek. "You do too, honey. Come on, I'll introduce you."

As I reached to shut off the radio while Mom unlocked her door, a familiar name caught my ear.

"The trial continues in the Susan Michaels murder case," the news bulletin announced.

I turned the volume knob up.

"Sorry, Mom, but I gotta hear this," I said.

The report continued: "Mr. Michaels is currently in jail awaiting what promises to be a sensational trial on charges of his wife's abduction and kidnapping. More details after this commercial."

"Oh my goodness," I muttered. While I was hidden away from the world, it felt like it had rolled out of control.

"I hope that awful Allen Michaels gets what he deserves," Mom said as I flipped off the radio. "I know he was friendly to you, Haley, but I wouldn't trust him as far as I could throw him. I heard he was actually trying to get a book deal to cash in on all this ... Hollywood wickedness. Can you believe it?"

Yes, I could believe it. In the time-honored Hollywood tradition, Allen continued to circle even the most sordid opportunity like a vulture. I was glad I hadn't sold my soul to the devil after all. Maybe I was still redeemable.

I opened my door and headed toward my mother's new boyfriend, her new life and mine. "Let's not worry about the past. We've got a new future to look forward to."

Then we walked, our fingers intertwined, through the sun-dappled trees toward a new beginning. And I felt whole.

**

What happened to Allen Michaels' wife, Susan? Who was *really* behind her murder? Find out in the companion short story *A Fatal Affair,* available at all your favorite retailers.

A husband in love with his wife. A wife willing to do anything to escape him. An affair turned deadly.

From *USA Today* best-selling author Pamela Crane comes a domestic noir short story about a deadly obsession.

The pregnancy test he found in the garbage confirmed it: Fatherhood at last. But when his wife announces her desire for divorce—and a majority of their assets—Hollywood icon Allen Michaels loses not only his wife, but his sanity. As Allen reveals the gory secrets of his mysterious past, with love leaving him battered and broke, **how far is too far** to avenge the promise of "til death do us part"?

Unleash Allen's hidden demons in this darkly riveting novella as he takes justice into his own demented hands...

A FATAL AFFAIR

Author's Note

Erotomania (i-rō-tə-mā-nē-ə); *noun*: a psychological disorder marked by the delusional belief that one is the object of another person's love or sexual desire.

Once upon a time, in a land not so far away, in a time I wish I could forget, I met a real-life erotomaniac. In fact, I became his obsession. I had been nice to the wrong person and lived—barely—to regret it.

One never would have guessed he was anything but normal, despite a few eccentricities. For several months after a terrible ordeal involving nights of terror, followed by police intervention, a job change, as well as a relocation, I struggled to forget it, let it go. During the course of the police investigation it came out that he had been seeking help for a mental illness called erotomania, where one severely reads into the words and behaviors of the object of affection, often attributing meaning that isn't there. In most cases it's innocent; in other cases it can be deadly.

Even after he disappeared, the trauma persisted to haunt me. There was only one way to relinquish the pain of the memory. Writing this story, you ask? That was part of it, but the biggest part of it was to forgive him.

Forgive the person who singlehandedly shattered my ability to trust anyone? It sounded almost as crazy as he was.

I struggled with that concept of forgiveness—how could I forgive someone who tried to utterly destroy me? I'm talking text threats of gutting me and holding my heart in

275

his hands, candid-pictures-of-me-in-the-mail crazy. I couldn't live with the paranoia anymore, yet I was too afraid to live without it. What if I trusted another monster again?

Religion talks about loving one's enemies, but certainly that did not apply to deranged stalker psychopaths. Then I dug a little deeper and found myself at a dead end: Every human being is only one step away from committing heinous evil. We all walk a fine line between thinking and doing. One weak moment can make room for an act you'll never forget and always regret.

After realizing the frail state of humanity, I suddenly saw a reflection of myself that changed my entire worldview. How could I *not* forgive the person who wronged me, for in turn I would be condemning my very own self for those I've wronged in my lifetime. And that day, upon the realization of my own inherent monster, I decided to forgive. Reconcile, no. That was not an option. But forgive, yes. Let it go, yes. Sleep at night, eat regularly, and let my distrust go—yes, yes, yes. Forgiveness is a freeing thought and a freeing reality. It freed me to see that erotomaniac as a person.

Maybe there's a loveable villain inside all of us.

Acknowledgements

When someone offers to help me, I don't decline it. As a writer-editor-mother-wife-farmer-zookeeper-multi-tasker, I'll take whatever support I can get. I'm fortunate enough to have an amazing support team.

My husband is always at the top of my praise list. I wouldn't have become a writer without his encouragement, and I wouldn't have the time to write if he didn't watch the kids for me weekend after weekend, evening after evening. He's my everything. Thank you, honey, for pushing me to keep going.

Second on the list is always you, my amazing fans. If you didn't buy my books, I couldn't afford to invest so much time into this dream. You're who I do this all for!

Of course I could never forget to include my family and friends—you have served so faithfully as my beta readers, my editors, and my support group. It's been an incredible journey that I wouldn't have wanted to venture on without you.

Thank you to my editor Kevin Cook at Proofed to Perfection, the best among the best, for helping me bring my thoughts to life and prepping my stories for the public.

To the littlest fans I have, my amazing children: Talia, Kainen, Kiara, and Ariana. You make me laugh, cry, tear my hair out, feel like a kid again, and give me greater life purpose. Thank you for being the greatest gifts of all.

A Final Word...

If you enjoyed *The Admirer's Secret,* you might enjoy one of my other books. Feel free to browse my other titles at www.pamelacrane.com. Find an error in one of my books? I'd love to fix it, since even the best editors miss things (they're only human). Please email me at pamela@pamelacrane.com.

Want to support me as an author? I'd be honored if you'd review the book. If you're kind enough to write a review, email me at pamela@pamelacrane.com and I'll thank you personally with a free gift!

If you'd like to be notified of my upcoming releases or enter my giveaways, join my mailing list at www.pamelacrane.com for chances to win free prizes and pre-release offers.

PAMELA CRANE is a USA TODAY best-selling author and professional juggler. Not the type of juggler who can toss flaming torches in the air, but a juggler of four kids, a writing addiction, and a horse rescuer. She lives on the edge (her Arabian horse can tell you all about their wild adventures while trying to train him!) and she writes on the edge...where her sanity resides. Her thrillers unravel flawed women who aren't always pretty. In fact, her characters are rarely pretty, which makes them interesting...and perfect for doing crazy things worth writing about. When she's not cleaning horse stalls or changing diapers, she's psychoanalyzing others.

Discover more of Pamela Crane's
books at
www.pamelacrane.com

Printed in Great Britain
by Amazon